# Give Me Your Answer

# Give Me Your Answer

## K.D. Miller

The Porcupine's Quill

CANADIAN CATALOGUING IN PUBLICATION DATA

Miller, K. D. (Kathleen Daisy), 1951 –
Give me your answer

ISBN 0-88984-208-6

I. Title.

PS8576.I5392G58 1999      C813'.54      C99-931708-3
PR9199.3.M54G58 1999

Published by The Porcupine's Quill,
68 Main Street, Erin, Ontario NOB 1TO.
Readied for the press by John Metcalf; copy edited by Doris Cowan.
Typeset in Ehrhardt, printed on Zephyr Antique laid,
and bound at The Porcupine's Quill Inc.

This is a work of fiction. Any resemblance of characters to persons,
living or dead, is purely coincidental.

Represented in Canada by the Literary Press Group.
Trade orders are available from General Distribution Services.

We acknowledge the support of the Ontario Arts Council,
and the Canada Council for the Arts for our publishing program.
The financial support of the Government of Canada
through the Book Publishing Industry Development Program
is also gratefully acknowledged.

1   2   3   4   ·   01   00   99

For all my families

♦ ♦ ♦

I am grateful to The Porcupine's Quill and *The New Quarterly* for recommending *Give Me Your Answer* for grants from the Ontario Arts Council.

Many thanks to writers Mary Borsky, Melinda Burns, Merike Lugus and Andrew Leith Macrae for providing helpful feedback on the stories as they grew. Thanks too to artist Gabrielle de Monmoulin, for an eerily apt cover photograph.

I am indebted to three remarkable couples: Richard Outram and Barbara Howard, for helping me keep my whale honest; Rob Miller and Leah Wallace, for their unstinting technical and moral support; and Tim and Elke Inkster, for making such beautiful things of books.

Finally, I wish to thank my editor and good friend, John Metcalf, who always says, 'I could be wrong,' but never is.

# Table of Contents

# Sunrise Till Dark

ONE SIDE OF AUNT ELLA'S FACE was purple. One arm and one leg were, too. The purple skin looked rougher than the rest, and I wondered if it would feel hot if I touched it.

She and her brother, Uncle George, who was not purple anywhere, sipped their soup exactly together. I watched them. First they raised their spoons to their lips, then they took the same shivery sip, then they lowered their spoons back down to their bowls. As if they'd practised.

I didn't think they really were my father's aunt and uncle. He called them just plain Ella and George, and he was too big to have aunts and uncles. I thought they were too old to be each other's brother and sister, too.

They didn't act anything like Ted and me. Uncle George hadn't drawn a skull and crossbones with black crayon on white paper and hung it in his bedroom doorway to keep Aunt Ella out. And she never sneaked into his room, waited there till she heard him coming, then ducked past him, screeching.

'Are you guys married?' I asked them once when we were visiting. The second the words were out in the air where I couldn't pull them back in, I knew I had made another mistake. Even though everybody laughed. Because my brother started to smile that slow smile of his.

Ted had already caught me taking a second liquorice allsort from the covered china dish on the table in the hallway. Aunt Ella always uncovered the dish for us when we came to visit. But before we got out of the car, our mother told us we could only take one each.

I would look and look at the candies, trying to decide. Don't take one of the ordinary little square sandwiches, I would tell myself. Take one of the wagon wheels rimmed in coconut, or one of the soft beaded cushions, or one of the white logs covered with liquorice bark you can skin off with your teeth. But then, when my mother said, 'For heaven's sake, just *take* one!' my hand would jump into the

9

dish and my fingers would close on one of the ordinary square sandwiches.

But this day, I couldn't stop thinking about the black and white skinnable logs. When nobody was looking, I sneaked back down the hall. I lifted the china lid and put it back without a clink. Then I peeled the little log I had taken, chewed the liquorice and popped the white part into the other side of my sweetening mouth.

That was when I heard Ted breathing behind me. I turned around and saw his slow smile already starting. 'Are you going to tell?' He turned his back. 'Are you going to tell?' He walked slowly toward the kitchen, where the grownups were. 'Are you going to tell?'

Of course he was going to tell. But he would take his time. He would wait until we were all home having supper. Just before our mother was about to put my dessert in front of me.

I was still wondering whether this new mistake I had made was calling Aunt Ella and Uncle George *you guys* or asking them if they were married, when I saw them looking at me. Their blue eyes were very round and young for a second. Then they both bent back down to their soup.

There was something muttering in a pot on a back burner of Aunt Ella's stove. I stroked each china knob with my finger, waiting for her to tell me not to touch. She didn't.

I was being left with Aunt Ella and Uncle George that afternoon while my parents and brother went somewhere that I was too young or too small or too much trouble to go. 'Don't be any trouble,' my mother had said. I wasn't sure what trouble was, but I had promised not to be it.

Aunt Ella's stove kept fooling me into thinking it might be fun. It was big and old, with knobs and little clock faces that looked kind of like toys.

'We haven't any toys here, Daisy,' Aunt Ella said quietly, as if she could hear my thoughts. She had turned from scrubbing the kitchen sink. 'Not very exciting, George and me, for a little girl.'

I pointed to the can of Old Dutch cleanser in her hand. 'We have that in our kitchen.'

She looked at it, smiled and said, 'Well, yes, I guess just about everybody does.' She had a gold tooth on the side.

I came up to the sink to watch, standing on tiptoe, mashing my lips against the edge. The white powder turned into a blue paste as Aunt Ella scrubbed the bottom and sides of the sink with a blue cloth. My mother always did this fast, lick and a promise she called it, ending with a short blast of water from the tap. But Aunt Ella loved the stains she was scrubbing out. And she ran the water slowly afterward, swishing it in little waves with her cloth, rinsing away every speck of cleanser, then rinsing the cloth and hanging it up.

'There. Isn't that lovely?' she said shyly. And it was lovely, the whiteness of it, the gleaming.

'Now I make tea for George. He sits in the sunroom in the afternoon and reads his paper.' Aunt Ella gave me a tea bag to look at while we waited for the kettle to whistle. I liked the soft paperiness of it, the whispery sound it made, and the way its shadowy insides shifted when I turned it.

I decided that the afternoon in this house was longer than the afternoon in my own, and that the same things happened here in the same order every day. This was a comfortable thought. I thought it over and over while the kettle whistled and Aunt Ella poured the boiling water glugging into the teapot.

In my own house, my brother went off to Cub camp, then came home, then went somewhere else. My father was always sawing and hammering upstairs, because Ted and I were going to have to sleep up there when we were bigger. And my mother said she couldn't wait for a brand new kitchen. There was always somewhere in our house that was covered in plastic or smelled of sawdust. And every few months, I had to go to a store full of shoes where a man measured my feet. 'You're growing *so* fast,' my mother always said, shaking her head, opening her purse.

But nothing changed here. No matter what the pictures in the hallway said.

'That's George,' Aunt Ella told me, pointing a purple finger at an old brown photograph. We were waiting for the tea to steep. The photograph she pointed to was of a baby dressed in ruffles and ribbons.

'That's not Uncle George!' I said. 'That's you!'

'Oh no it isn't, child. No. Surely you can see that it isn't me.' I looked and looked. Then I saw. The baby's face was all the same colour.

There were so many old pictures of Uncle George, in short pants, long pants, a cap, a straw hat. Pictures that changed from brown to black and white.

'Where are the pictures of you?' I asked. She didn't answer. I asked again.

'Well, they didn't. My parents just didn't, you see. They didn't think it fitting.'

I tried to imagine what it would be like never to have my picture taken. I didn't think I'd mind. But maybe Aunt Ella did mind, because she said, 'There is *one* of me.' She pointed, this time with the white hand, to a small, cracked photograph in a round frame. It showed a lady in a long-sleeved white dress pulled tight in front and bunched out the back. She had on a white hat with flowers. The hat made a shadow over her face.

'George took that one,' Aunt Ella said, sounding shy again. 'I was twenty. I remember that day. We were all set to go out hunting eggs.'

'Easter eggs?'

I could hardly feel the hollow shell on my palm. A breath would roll it off onto the hardwood.

We had brought Uncle George his tea in the sunroom, and Aunt Ella had said, 'Lady here to see some eggs, George.'

They were in shoeboxes, bedded down in cotton batting. Robin's eggs like drops of sky. Speckled eggs, the speckles blurred as if somebody had dabbed them onto the shells with a watercolour brush.

'We'd go off, Ella and me, whenever we could get away together,' Uncle George was saying. 'We'd take a blanket and pack a picnic lunch.'

'What do you mean, *we*?' Something giggly in Aunt Ella's voice made me look up at her. 'I'm the one who packed the lunches. You never so much as made a sandwich.'

'Oh? And who carried the heavy basket, miss, and helped you over the fences, and swatted bees away from you?' There was a laugh inside Uncle George's voice too.

'We'd be out sometimes sunrise till dark,' he said more quietly. 'Some days the sun would be so hot even the bees would be heavy and slow with it. So we'd leave the blanket spread after lunch and just sleep. Sleep for hours some days. I remember us waking once when the day had cooled and the dark was just beginning to fall.'

They were quiet for a long time. I began to think they had forgotten I was there. I reached and picked up a grey-and-brown speckled egg.

'You like that one?' Uncle George asked. I nodded. 'Hen that laid that one,' he said (he had already explained that all lady birds were hens), 'knew a pretty good trick. And we saw her do it, didn't we, Ella?'

'We did. I remember.'

'She'd hidden her nest pretty well, way back deep in the shadows. But as soon as we got near it, she came right out of hiding and pretended to have a broken wing. Flopped around on the ground to lure us toward herself. And once we were a safe distance from the nest, she took off. Flew straight up and away into the sunshine.'

'Who showed her how to do that?' I asked.

'Oh, she just seemed to know, all by herself.'

'Perhaps God taught her, George,' Aunt Ella prompted, glancing at me.

'Well, yes, come to think of it, I guess that's what happened.'

I yawned. The sun in the room was making me sleepy. Aunt Ella sat down in a chair and pulled me up onto her lap. I leaned back against her, my eyelids heavy. Her hands were clasped in front of me, purple over white. I reached a finger and touched the purple skin. Then I touched the white skin. They felt the same.

'Am I being trouble?' I asked, pulling my finger back. Maybe it was a mistake to touch purple skin. Uncle George grinned at his sister. His teeth were as white as his hair, but he hadn't any gold ones.

'No,' Aunt Ella said. 'You're not.'

Music was coming in the window. Tinkly, one-note-at-a-time music. 'Carillon,' Uncle George said, checking his watch. 'We hear it every afternoon. Comes from over there.' He pointed out the window to a steeple poking up above the trees.

'Shhhhh!' Aunt Ella sat up a little. I turned and looked at her face. Her chin bobbed with each note, and her eyes were sad and happy at the same time. Uncle George was leaning forward in his chair now, his good ear cocked to the window. Almost together, they said, "Blessed Assurance". Then, in a high, shaky voice, Aunt Ella sang the words in time with the picked-out notes. I could feel the singing in her body as I leaned back against her.

I fell asleep. Not a deep sleep, because as I was dropping off I remembered something that kept me floating near the surface. I remembered my father telling my mother that as soon as they were grown up, George and Ella quit going to church. Just quit all at once. Never went back.

When the noise of my parents and brother coming back woke me, it was as if all three of us had fallen asleep, and still were. Aunt Ella kept hold of me, even when my mother called, 'Hello? Folks? We're back!' I had a strange, half-awake thought. That it was a mistake for them to be my family. That this was where I really lived.

Aunt Ella still held me. At last Uncle George looked at her. She unclasped her hands. He began struggling up out of his chair.

All of a sudden I remembered the eggs. I didn't know why, but I was afraid for them. They were like a secret between Uncle George and Aunt Ella and me. But the eggs were gone. Uncle George must have put them away while I was asleep. Or maybe I dreamed them.

'Did you say thank you to Aunt Ella and Uncle George?' my mother asked me as we were going down the porch steps on our way to the car. I didn't answer. 'You *didn't* say thank you, did you?' She could always tell every single thing I had done or not done, just by looking at my face. 'All right then, we'll wait for you in the car. March back inside and do it.'

But that house was for tiptoeing, not marching. I made no noise at all as I went down the long hall, hardly glancing at the covered dish of liquorice allsorts. I stopped near the door to the sunroom, where they both still were. They didn't see me.

Aunt Ella was standing behind Uncle George's chair, arms around his neck, cheek resting on his white head. He took one of her hands in his and kissed the fingers. Then he turned it over and gave the palm a long, slow kiss. She slid the fingers of her other hand inside his shirt collar. Very slowly, in bigger and bigger circles, she ran her fingers round and round on her brother's neck and shoulder and chest.

I held my breath. Then I began to back away from the door to the sunroom. They still didn't hear me.

All I knew was that I had found something nobody was supposed to find. And the tiniest noise from me would shatter it. When I was halfway down the hall, I turned and ran the rest of the way on tiptoe.

In the car my mother looked at my flushed face and said, 'What? What is it?'

'Nothing.' I ducked my head. Now Ted was looking at me too. I could feel my cheeks getting hotter.

My father was about to turn the key and start the car. My mother put a hand on his arm to stop him. 'Now come on,' she said. 'Something happened in there. Did you break something just now? Were you any trouble for Aunt Ella and Uncle George?'

'No!'

'Well,' my mother said, 'I'm going back in there and ask them.' Her hand was on the door handle.

'I *did* do something,' I said. My mother turned and looked at me. Her hand was still on the door handle. 'All right,' she said slowly, 'you'd better tell me what.'

'I took another liquorice allsort! I took one of the little logs! And I ate it!'

My mother took her hand away from the door handle. She glanced at my father, and for a second the two of them looked as if they were trying not to laugh.

Then, as my father started the car and my mother took a deep breath, getting ready to give me a talking-to, I began to feel light. I felt lighter and lighter until soon I was so light that if there had been no top on the car, I would have been flying.

# Brébeuf and Lalemant

'YOUR HEAD'S LIKE A STOVE ELEMENT,' my mother says, touching my hair. 'Put your hat on.' Then she spots a bump on the ground that she's missed. She goes to it and starts stabbing at it with her fork. She'll go over the whole field that way, digging for a minute, straightening up, spotting some new patch and running over to dig there. My father is different. And not just because of his leg, either. Even if he had two legs, he would probably still pick one place, sit himself down, mark out a square of dirt, then sift through every inch of it with his spoon until it was time to go.

It won't be time to go for hours yet. The bug that buzzes when it's hot is doing it right now. It's the *fif*teenth day of the *eighth* month of the year one *thou*sand nine *hun*dred and *six*ty. That's how Walter Cronkite says it on TV. I wonder if Walter Cronkite talks that way at home. Would you *kind*ly *pass* the pota*to*es *please*.

I don't want to think about Walter Cronkite. I brought along a whole stack of *Little Lulus* and *Caspers* and *Little Lottas* to get me through the day, but I've already read them all. I almost wish Ted was here. But he's at Scout camp. There's nothing to do but sit and watch my mother and father dig up the field, her with her fork and him with his spoon. I don't know which of them finds more stuff. But they both think that their way is the only way to look.

I never look for anything. But I once found a little tube that my father said was part of a pipe-stem. And another time I found a round clay bead. It was lopsided and had a hole poked through the middle for a string. No, for a rawhide, Ted said when I showed him.

I don't know how I find things. Sometimes I just get a feeling that I'm going to see something before I see it. So I look down, and there it is. A shape that doesn't fit. Like finding a four-leaf clover.

My father has found something. Just now. I can tell, even though he doesn't move or make a sound. And in a second my mother can tell too. She looks at him, then looks again, then says, 'Bill? Bill, what is it?'

'Come and see.' His mouth sounds like it's all sticky inside.
We go and look down at his square of dirt. 'Oh, *Bill!*' my mother
whispers. 'It's all in one piece!'

The rim of a clay pot is sticking up about half an inch out of the
ground. The clay is the exact same colour as the dirt, so you have to
look twice to see it. But it's there, and it really is all in one piece.
Most of what we find is broken, because the field we're digging
up was once ploughed. Grass and wildflowers are growing in again,
but if you stand on the little hill at one end and squint, you can still
make out the marks of the plough.

Ted takes the broken pieces we find and wires them to boards
painted white. Then he labels every piece in black India ink, so it
looks just like something in a museum. My bead is wired to a board
now, with *Clay Bead, Probably Huron* printed underneath.

Now I wonder what Ted's going to do with a pot that's all in one
piece. At least it will be, if my father can get it out of the ground
without breaking it.

Very slowly, my father pokes his spoon into the dirt inside the
rim. He pries up a spoonful of dirt and lifts it out.

'Be careful!' my mother whispers.

'I intend to be, June.' He takes a spoonful of dirt from outside the
rim, just as slowly as he took the one from the centre. Then he takes
from the centre again, then from the outside, from a spot right
across from the first spoonful.

My mother says, 'Why don't you just hollow it out? The way
you're going, it'll take you all day.' She isn't whispering any more.
'That's what I would do. Hollow it out. See what I'm dealing with,
for heaven's sake. How deep it is. What shape it is.'

'Right, June, and you'd end up with a pile of broken pieces.'

'Oh, I would *not*. The earth around the outside would hold it
together, and you know it.'

'That's where you're wrong,' my father says in that slow way that
I know drives her crazy. 'The earth around the outside would cave it
in. When something's been in the ground this long, you have to keep
the inner pressure and the outer pressure equal, or else you'll –'

'Sure, sure, listen to the expert.' She feels my head again, just to
ignore my father. 'Daisy, didn't I tell you to put on your hat?' She

makes a show of spotting another bump in the ground, going to it and stabbing it with her fork. She pulls up clumps of grass, and the tearing roots make a ripping, popping sound. Then she straightens up, shades her eyes with her hand and heads for another bump farther away.

'No system,' my father says, shaking his head and keeping his eyes on what he's doing. He's back to the middle again, prying up another spoonful of packed dirt, steadying it with his fingers. 'You can't just go off half cocked with this kind of thing. You tear into it like a kid on Christmas morning, and you'll wreck it.'

I don't know whether my father is talking to himself or to me. And I don't know whether I should listen or not. But in a little while I'll follow after my mother and listen to her complain about him, so maybe it all evens out.

Probably nobody else's parents would fight about how to dig up a pot. Mine can fight about anything. My mother talks and waves her arms and stomps around when she fights. But my father just gets very quiet and still. Maybe because he can't stomp.

I asked him once if his leg hurt, the leg that got cut off when he was a boy. He said it hurt once a long time ago, but not any more. Lots of things have happened to my father, but you would never guess it to look at him. Except about the leg. His little brother Theodore died. That's who Ted's named after. And his mother died when he was only fourteen. I asked my mother once why my father never cried about all the things that have happened to him, and she said that he was crying all the time on the inside.

Right now he's whistling 'Would You Like to Swing on a Star', a song that drives me nuts when it comes on the radio. I try to block it out and just watch what he's doing, but what he's doing is so boring I don't know how he can stand it, how he can face a whole day of spooning dirt, even if he is going to have a clay pot all in one piece at the end of it.

We've been coming to this field since before I can remember. That's why I'm the only kid in my class who knows words like petrified and relic and fleur-de-lis. I can tell if a rock is just a rock or if it was once a skinning stone. And I've felt how sharp a flint edge is, even after it's been buried for hundreds of years.

19

My father glances up from his spooning. 'I thought I heard your mother telling you to put your hat on.'

'It's not that hot,' I say, feeling the top of my head. The bug that buzzes is buzzing louder. My head really is pretty hot, but not as hot as my mother says, not like a stove element. I know how hot a stove element is. I touched one once when it was bright orange, just to find out. I snatched my finger back right away, but it was already red, and a blister was filling up.

I did it because I was thinking about Brébeuf and Lalemant again. I was wondering what it would feel like to have a necklace of red-hot tomahawks put around your neck, so that they stuck to your bare chest. My mother had told me to stop thinking about Brébeuf and Lalemant. She said I *dwelled* on things.

This all started the day I asked her whether, if somebody cut your heart out and ate it, you would still be alive. She had a Dad's oatmeal cookie halfway to her mouth, but she put it down and said, 'Good God, what are you reading *now?*'

I was reading my reader from school. I was reading ahead to the Indians section. We're not supposed to read ahead of where the class is. But I always do, and then when the class catches up to where I am, I just pretend to be reading it all for the first time again.

The Indians section had 'Hiawatha' and 'The Song My Paddle Sings' and a story about the Maid of the Mist, and 'The Huron Carol', by Father Jean de Brébeuf. Under the carol there was a painting of Brébeuf and Lalemant being tortured to death, and a list of the things the Iroquois did to them. That's how I knew about the tomahawks, and about the heart business.

I found the same painting, only big and framed, in the museum at the Martyrs' Shrine in Midland, where we went last summer. I stood in front of it until my mother said, 'Come away from there. Why would you want to stand and look at something like that, any-way?'

I don't know why. And it's not that I want to look at it. Not exactly. It's more that I can't *not* look at it.

My mother likes to look at quill boxes and beadwork and little clay dolls. She doesn't mind looking at arrowheads and skinning stones, she says, as long as she doesn't think about what they're for.

One time on a dig she handed my father something she had dug up with her fork. 'Bill? What would this be, do you think?' It looked like wood, but it was shaped like something made of clay. He took a good look at it, weighed it in his palm and gave it back to her. 'It's the rim of an eye socket,' he said. 'With a bit of cheekbone attached.'

'Yaaah!' She sent the thing flying. 'Why did you have to *tell* me?'

'Because you *asked*, June. You *asked*.'

I went looking all around where my mother had thrown the piece of skull, but I couldn't find it. I didn't know why I was looking, or what I was going to do with it if I did find it. I couldn't imagine Rebecca Goldsmith or any of the other girls in my class trying to find an eye socket. When I told Rebecca about digging up relics, she wrinkled her face and said, 'Don't you get *dirty*?'

My father has taken a few inches of dirt out of the pot, and the same from around the outside. The mouth of the pot is wide, but the neck is narrow. There are markings in the clay. It looks like somebody has taken a twig and poked little holes to make a spiral design, going round and round into a centre, then round and round back out again.

'Somebody's put a lot of work into this,' my father says, pulling his cap off, scrunching it, swabbing his forehead with it, then putting it back on.

I should have asked my father about cutting out a person's heart and eating it. No matter what I ask him, even if he's having supper, he just finishes chewing, swallows and answers.

In my reader, it says that Brébeuf didn't move or make a sound the whole time he was being tortured. That's why the Iroquois ate his heart, because they wanted to be brave like him. But Lalemant was smaller and weaker, and they knew it. So they made him watch them do things to Brébeuf before they did the same things to him.

I'm *dwelling* on things again, just like my mother says. But I can't help it. I want to know how Brébeuf could stand still and not make a sound. Especially since I hopped around and shook my hand for a whole minute when I burned my finger. And that's nothing compared to a necklace of red-hot tomahawks. If I was tortured, Brébeuf is the one I'd want to be like. But I'd probably end up more like Lalemant.

In the painting, Lalemant is looking up at a pot of boiling water somebody's about to pour on him, and his eyes are as big as two eggs. But Brébeuf just stands straight as a tree, wearing his necklace of tomahawks as if he's proud of them.

*Brébeuf* even sounds like *brave*. But *Lalemant* is a name like butterflies, like *fa la la*.

There are butterflies all around us in the field. Most of them are plain little white ones, but sometimes there's a black-and-orange monarch, and I call 'King Billy!' and point until either my father or my mother looks up and nods.

You're supposed to share a King Billy, the way you're supposed to make butter under somebody's chin with a dandelion, then flick off its head with your thumbnail and say the rhyme about Queen Mary. And there's something else you're supposed to do with Queen Anne's lace, but I forget what.

It's time to visit my mother. The pot is starting to get interesting, but it'll be ages before I can really see it. And I'm wondering if my mother has hurt feelings because I stayed with my father after she left. But if I'd gone with her right away, maybe now my father would have hurt feelings.

'You hurt my feelings when you didn't stand beside me in choir!' That's what Rebecca Goldsmith said to me last Christmas. Miss French had decided that our class would wear Indian costumes and sing the Huron Carol for the Christmas assembly. She made each of us sing *doh* to a note she blew on her pitch-pipe, and that decided where we would stand in the choir. The best *dohs* were in the front row, most of the boys were in the back, and Rebecca Goldsmith and I were in the middle, but at different ends.

'I can't help it if Miss French puts me miles away from you,' I said. But Rebecca decided she had hurt feelings anyway, because it was her turn.

After a couple of days, when she was tired of having hurt feelings, she shared her recess cookies with me and said, 'I bet you just *hate* having to stand beside Angela Lumley in the choir.' So I told her that Angela's breath smelled like devilled egg, and she couldn't say her Rs, and I kept hearing, 'A wagged wobe of wabbit skin enwapped His beauty wound.'

Then about a week later, when it was my turn, I said to Rebecca, 'You hurt my feelings when you said I hurt *your* feelings!' We went back and forth like this all year.

'Have you found anything yet?' I ask my mother. She has just straightened up from forking a tuft of grass, and is pressing her hands to her back.

'Just this.' She pulls something out of the pocket of her slacks and hands it to me. 'There. That could be something, couldn't it?' I look at the thing she has found. It's a splintery bit of wood, shaped sort of like a capital T. 'I mean, if a piece has broken off the top there, then it could be a little cross, couldn't it?'

'Uh-huh. I guess it could.' But she can probably tell I'm just saying that to be nice.

She takes the bit of wood back from me. 'There were Jesuits all around here,' she says, sounding so-*there*. 'Teaching the Huron. They probably made all kinds of little crosses for them to wear.'

Maybe she's jealous of my father for finding the pot. I hope she finds something today. If I do, I'll drop it near her where she'll be bound to see it. Right now I look all around where I've sat down, but nothing jumps out at me. Nothing gives me that feeling I get when I'm just about to find something.

I haven't had that feeling since I was in the museum at the Martyrs' Shrine and my mother managed to get me away from the painting of Brébeuf and Lalemant. We walked into a room where a bunch of people were standing around a glass case. Even before we got near it, I had that feeling. I knew there was something in the glass case that I'd never forget. I wanted to see it, and I was afraid to, all at the same time.

My mother got there before I did and said, 'Oh, my God. Out of the frying pan.'

I didn't know what she meant until I saw what was in the glass case. It was worse than the painting of Brébeuf and Lalemant. So I knew I'd end up *dwelling* on it. Parts of it weren't so bad, but it hurt to look at the face, especially the teeth. My eyes kept jerking away, then jerking back again. There was a ball of black hair under the skull. The hands were just a tangle of little bones, and the feet were inside moccasins.

A card on the glass said this was an Algonquin maiden, about ten years old. The decorations on her clothing and the number of toys and gifts that were buried with her suggested she might have been a chief's daughter. There were beads all over her dress, kind of like the one I found. I wondered if her mother had sewn them on. My mother sewed my Indian costume for the Christmas assembly out of burlap, and she put coloured beads on it from the hobby store. Rebecca's mother took apart old necklaces, so her costume was covered with pearls, white and pale pink and pale blue.

You couldn't tell what colour the Algonquin girl's beads were any more. I looked up at my mother. I wondered how she could stand looking at the skeleton inside the glass case, when touching the eye socket had made her scream.

'Is your father still digging up that pot?' she says now, sounding like she doesn't want to ask, but can't help it.

'Uh-huh. He's about halfway down.'

She shakes her head. 'If I'd found something like that,' she starts, then doesn't finish the sentence. 'But not your father. The only time I've ever seen him really excited about anything was once when we were driving along the highway and his hat blew off.'

I can't imagine my father even getting excited about that. But my mother gets excited at least once a day. She gets excited about things she hears on the radio, or about tomatoes on sale, or about rain starting the minute she finishes hanging out the wash.

Now she says, 'Have you gone and lost your hat? Is that why you won't put it on?'

'Nope. It's over there with my comic books.' She glances where I point, and sees my father. She shakes her head again, bends over and begins forking another tuft.

Maybe my parents take turns hurting each other's feelings, the way Rebecca Goldsmith and I do. I told my mother all about Rebecca, especially about her hair. It's in little tiny curls, even the short bits, and her mother doesn't have to put it in curlers or anything, because it just grows that way.

'That's because she's a little Jewish girl,' my mother said, making her voice go soft on the word *Jewish*. She does that with other words too, like *Negro* and *elderly* and *hard of hearing.* 'Jewish people always have beautiful children. With curly hair and lovely big sad eyes.'

I didn't know Rebecca was Jewish. But she had to be, because she looked just like my mother said. 'Does that make it all right to be Jewish?' I asked. 'Because if you're Jewish you have beautiful children?'

'What do you mean?' My mother sounded mad all of a sudden. 'There's nothing wrong with being Jewish! No one in this house has ever told you there's anything wrong with being Jewish!' She thought for a second, then said, '*Jesus* was Jewish!'

I begin to wonder now if there really are little wooden crosses all over the place, the way my mother says. I start picking up bits of wood and sorting them into two piles, might-be-a-cross and couldn't-be-a-cross. After a while I have two might-be's and a whole bunch of couldn'ts. I give the might-be's a second look, put them on the couldn'ts pile and dust my hands.

I don't like the idea of Brébeuf and Lalemant making little wooden crosses and handing them out to the Huron to wear around their necks. I just think it would look kind of funny or wrong or something for the Indians to have crosses slapping against their bare chests when they ran through the forest or did their dances.

I saw Indians doing dances last fall at the Rockton fair. They were real Indians, from a real reservation. A bunch of them sat around a big drum and beat on it with sticks and sang, and another bunch did a shuffling kind of dance, bent over at the waist and looking at the ground. Every now and then an announcer dressed like a cowboy told us through a microphone that this was moose dance or quail dance or bear dance.

Watching them made me remember the Algonquin girl in the glass case. There was nothing on the card about how long ago she had died, or how long she had been in the museum with everybody looking at her.

When we were there I touched my mother's arm and said, 'If I was buried, would somebody come and dig me up?' I thought I was whispering, but the people standing around the glass case heard me and smiled. Then a man said, 'Oh, so you think *you* should be in a museum too, do you?' And that made them all laugh.

'This is corn dance,' the cowboy announcer said into his microphone. 'A dance of rejoicing for the harvest.' The Indians danced on and on, and the same guys beat the drum just like before. Even their singing was the same. It didn't sound like rejoicing to me. It was a loud, sad wailing sound that made me think of winter.

*'Twas in the moon of wintertime,*
*When all the birds had fled...*

The Huron Carol is the only Christmas carol I can stand to think about, let alone sing, in the summer. I sing it now very softly, almost in a whisper, and I leave long pauses between the lines.

*That mighty Gitchi-Manitou*
*Sent angel choirs instead...*

My father is at the other end of the field, digging up his pot. My mother has wandered away again, forking bits of ground closer and closer to him. Nobody knows I'm singing.

*Before their light the stars grew dim,*
*And wond'ring hunters heard the hymn...*

'This is how Father Brébeuf made it easy for the Huron to understand the Christmas story,' Miss French told us at choir practice. 'He turned the shepherds into hunters and the wise men into chiefs. And he made the stable into a lodge of broken bark, and he told them that the baby Jesus was wrapped in a robe of rabbit skin, instead of in swaddling clothes.'

Sometimes at choir practice I would look over at Rebecca Goldsmith. She sang too, just like everybody else. But I wondered if being Jewish meant that she could never understand the Christmas story, not even if somebody like Father Brébeuf came along and changed everything for her.

'She can understand it,' my father said. I asked him, because I thought Rebecca might decide to get hurt feelings if I asked her, and it wasn't her turn. 'She just doesn't believe in it.'

'Do I believe in it?'

'Of course you do!' my mother said, sounding the way she did when I asked if it was all right to be Jewish.

'Father Brébeuf filled the carol full of things that the Huron saw every day,' Miss French said. 'Because he knew they had never seen a stable or a manger or a shepherd or even a sheep.'

I've never seen a stable or a manger or a shepherd either, except in pictures in Sunday school. But I have seen a sheep, at the sheep dog trials at the Rockton fair. I guess I was expecting to see little woolly white lambs like the one Jesus is holding in the picture on the wall at Sunday school. But these sheep were great big things, and they were really dirty, especially at the back.

'Father Brébeuf even let the Huron sing about their own Gitchi-Manitou,' Miss French went on, 'because of course they had never heard of God.' Her *God* was all soft, like my mother's *hard of hearing*.

*Oh, children of the forest free,*
*Oh, sons of Manitou ...*

This is my favourite part, so I sing it over a few times. Manitou sounds more like God's name than God does.

*Oh, children of the forest free,*
*Oh, sons of Manitou ...*

That could be a song all by itself, just those two lines. It's almost as if when I sing them, I'm calling to the children of the forest free. Calling to their ghosts.

All of a sudden I wonder if their ghosts are here. Watching me. Maybe they've been here for hundreds of years, watching their stuff get buried, watching the plough break it into pieces, then the grass and wildflowers growing over, then us coming and digging up the pieces and taking them home. Then Ted wiring them to boards. Maybe the ghost of the Algonquin girl is right here beside me. Maybe she watched herself being dug up and taken to the museum.

I'm not supposed to believe in ghosts, because there's no such thing. But I'm supposed to believe in the Holy Ghost, because he's everywhere, all the time. That's what Miss Urquhart says in Sunday school. I don't understand how anything can be everywhere all the time. But I can understand how the ghosts of the Indians could be right here, right now. Because they're giving me goose pimples.

I won't sing those two lines with Manitou in them again. I'll sing what comes after them instead, even though I don't like it as much.

*The Holy Child of earth and heaven*
*Is born today for you.*
*Come kneel before the radiant Boy*
*Who brings you beauty, peace and joy...*

Miss Urquhart says it hurts Jesus' feelings if we don't believe in him with our whole hearts. I don't want to make Jesus any sadder than he already is. He always looks so sad in the pictures I've seen of him.

Maybe the Huron worried about making Manitou sad too, when they started learning the words to the Christmas carol. So maybe they went right on believing in Manitou, and just kind of made room for God and Jesus. Because they didn't want to hurt Brébeuf's and Lalemant's feelings either.

*Jesus your king is born,*
*Jesus is born,*
*In excelsis gloria!*

There. That's the whole carol I've sung now. I think I'll go see my parents. They've gotten back together over by the pot. My mother is pointing and saying something, and my father is nodding. I'm halfway there when my mother waves to me to hurry up. She's excited again. When I get closer, I see why. The pot is standing free.

I stop and just look at it. It's like some wonderful, strange flower that's grown up out of the ground. And I have that feeling, that funny kind of ache. I want to look at the pot forever, and I want to run away and never see it again.

Very slowly, my father puts his hands on either side of it. Very

28

slowly, he brings them together. He almost touches the pot, then doesn't, then almost touches it, then doesn't, then almost touches it, then does.

That's when I know what's going to happen.

Too late, I put my hand out to stop my father.

He fumbles to catch the pieces.

One of them stays together when it hits the ground.

The other two smash.

'Shit!' my father yells. He picks up his spoon and stabs it into the ground. 'Shit!' He stabs again, then throws the spoon. He takes his cap off and slams it down, picks it up and slams it again. He scrunches it, looks like he's going to throw it after the spoon, but then puts it back on his head. He wipes his nose with the back of his hand, inhales some dirt and sneezes. He sneezes again and yells, 'Dammit, dammit, dammit to hell!'

When he starts to look like he's going to cry, I get scared. I think he's going to come apart the way the pot did, and all the crying he's been doing inside is going to come out in a flood. I wonder if my mother's as scared as I am. She's just standing very still, not making a sound.

He doesn't cry. And he doesn't come apart. In a little while, when he's just breathing hard, my mother crouches down beside him. She puts her hand on his shoulder. He shrugs, not hard enough to shake it off.

'You were careful,' she says. 'You were as careful as you could be. It must have been when it was moved. Maybe just that little bit of movement did it. Maybe even just the air passing over it, after all this time.'

'Yeah,' he says at last. 'It was probably cracked. There were probably hairline cracks all through the damned thing.'

'Of course there were. Nobody could have gotten it out of the ground in one piece. Not you, not anybody.'

I've never heard her talk that way to my father. Almost as if he was a little kid. She even looks older and bigger than he does. I don't like it. I don't want to see my parents acting that way. As if I wasn't there. As if they've jumped back to a time before I or even Ted was born.

I start to walk away, eyes on the ground, not sure what I'm looking for until I find it. Then I pick the spoon up and take it with me to the little hill at the end of the field. From there, I can see the old marks of the plough.

*Oh, children of the forest free,*
*Oh, sons of Manitou ...*

I sing those two lines over and over while I dig a hole with the spoon my father threw. I don't know why, just that it feels good to dig.

The bug is buzzing again. I imagine the ghosts of the Indians watching me. Jesus is there too, and the ghost of little Theodore, my father's brother who died. And the Algonquin maiden.

It feels like putting toys around a table for a tea party, the way I used to do. So I let the Holy Ghost come, and God and Manitou. And Brébeuf and Lalemant, and the Iroquois who tortured them. And they all watch me dig.

I still don't know what I'm digging for. When I finish, I haven't found anything. All I have is a hole, and you're supposed to put something in a hole. So I put the spoon in, because that's all I have. Then I push the dirt back over it and pat it as flat as it will go.

My father is picking up the pieces of the pot. And my mother is calling to me that it's time to go home.

# To Hell and Back

THE SUMMER I WAS ELEVEN, my mother screamed at my father one night for three hours, then didn't say a word to him for three weeks. She didn't say much in my direction either, except to talk through me. 'Go tell your father to start the car. We'll be leaving in five minutes.' That kind of thing.

It began when my father picked me up to bring me home from my piano lesson and said, 'Your mother and I are in the middle of something. You just go straight up to bed.'

Whatever the something was that they were in the middle of had left my mother sitting hunched at the kitchen table with her mouth frozen hard into a shape. I took one look at her and ran up the stairs to my room.

She started screaming the second I was in bed, as if she thought I couldn't hear lying down. *'Did you look into your daughter's eyes when you picked her up tonight? Your sweet little girl's eyes? After what you've done?'* Her voice sounded stretched and torn and wet. *'What about your son? Will you look at him when he gets home? Will you say to him, This is your father? This is the example you should follow?'*

My parents argued a lot, and my father usually matched my mother's words with noise of his own. Scraping his chair back hard from the table, or slamming a door. But this was a fight. It had torn something between them, as if their life together, and my brother and me, and our house, and everything I was familiar with had been a piece of paper that was now ripped in two. And though I couldn't see him, I knew my father was just sitting, letting my mother's words hit him like well-deserved slaps.

*'I won't be seen with you! I won't walk down the street with you! I won't sit beside you in church!'*

Except she did. Outside our house, for the whole three weeks, she did everything exactly the same as always, and so did my father. He drove her to the supermarket to get groceries. Picked her up and brought her home from the hairdresser. On Sundays I sat between them as usual, sharing my mother's hymn book, hearing her high little voice in one ear and my father's big rumble in the other.

But inside our house, I ate supper between two silences, my mother's like a fist, my father's like a hole. At night there were sheets and blankets and a pillow on the living-room couch. Though my mother bundled these up and put them away as soon as my father left for work in the morning, his bitter tobacco smell lingered while I sat with a bowl of cereal, watching Captain Kangaroo.

I was too old for Captain Kangaroo, but I couldn't kick the habit. To salvage my dignity, I snorted and made loud sarcastic comments about Mister Greenjeans, Mister Bunnyrabbit and Grandfather Clock. It was exhausting work, and during the three weeks of silence in our house I lapsed back into just watching like a little kid.

I wished I was a little kid again. I even wished I was a baby, so my father could tell himself I hadn't understood the things my mother had yelled at him. Then maybe his eyes would stop sliding away from mine whenever I tried to look at him. But when my mother sat at the kitchen table with her cup of tea, staring out at the back yard, trying to keep her face still to hide that she was crying, I wished I was older than eleven. Then maybe she could tell me what my father had done. Because for all her screaming, she had never let that slip.

The police didn't come to the door to arrest him, so I knew he hadn't broken any laws. But that was as much as I could figure out on my own. My brother Ted, who was fifteen and sometimes grudgingly explained things, was away on a month-long canoe trip. And Sigrid Kiraja, who lived next door and was six months older but still played Barbie and Ken with me, was away at Estonian camp.

I wouldn't have told Sigrid, anyway. Sigrid and her family, I believed, lived lives that were sparkling clean, spotless and smelling faintly of bleach, just like their kitchen sink. I could not imagine Mr and Mrs Kiraja even having a mild argument, let alone building a wall of silence between them, brick by brick, day after day.

The silence between my parents was a dirty thing, a shameful thing. A thing to keep secret, no matter what. I didn't know what the shame was or where it was coming from, but I breathed it in with the air inside the house. I carried it on me the way I carried the smell of the house on my clothes and in my hair.

For a while, until I got used to the silence, my eyes felt dry because I kept forgetting to blink. In the mirror my mouth looked too small and white, and there was a gluey web between my lips. I started stuttering on the piano. I would go to press a key and my finger would jump away from it. I would try to press again and the same thing would happen. Finally my piano teacher covered my hands with hers and pressed them down to make a loud mess of a chord. 'See, Daisy?' she said. 'You can make a mistake. It doesn't matter.'

I stared at her. What did she know? What could I tell her? The blankets and sheets and pillow were still on the living-room couch, morning after morning. Whatever mistake my father had made was so bad that my mother was never going to sleep with him again.

I knew that meant more than just sharing a bed. I had known for almost a year. The graffiti inked into our hand-me-down textbooks at school was an education in itself. I couldn't open my reader without seeing blue U-shapes hanging from every female chest, blue lozenges growing out of every male crotch. Sometimes a lozenge would stretch across an entire page to connect with a female crotch decorated for the occasion with blue pubic hair.

So one day last summer Sigrid and I agreed to draw pictures of what we thought grownups did to make a baby. We couldn't say the words, not out loud, but we decided that if we both drew the same thing, then we had probably got it right.

We turned our backs to each other and drew. When we were finished we put our drawings side by side and looked at them. We had both drawn a naked man and woman, standing facing each other, a distance of what would have been a foot or more apart. Spanning the gap, growing out of the man, was a skinny bridge of flesh. Its end disappeared somewhere between the woman's legs.

Sigrid and I stared at each other. At last I said the unthinkable. 'Our parents!' We stuffed our fists into our mouths, fell over and rocked back and forth on Sigrid's rec room floor. When we had exhausted ourselves and were lying staring at the ceiling, the unthinkable once more occurred to us. I had a brother. Sigrid had a sister. She said it this time. 'Twice!' And we stuffed and rocked again.

Now I wondered if my father had tried to do it a third time, and that was what had made my mother so mad. I hated thinking about my parents ever doing such a thing, even to get a baby. But I couldn't stop. I kept seeing my mother looking up and away, her lips stiff the way they got when she was putting up with something that couldn't be helped. I couldn't imagine my father's expression. I didn't want to think about the thing between his legs, hanging down inside his trousers all day long, then reaching like a root toward my mother in the dark.

But the silence between my parents, my father's banishment to the couch, for some reason made it impossible for me to look at them without seeing them naked. And not just them, either. Whenever I saw a man and a woman now, I imagined his *thing* nudging into the woman's. *Things*, in fact, obsessed me. Every man and boy I saw – the mailman, the kid who delivered fish and chips on his bike – every one of them suddenly had a *thing* whose size and shape I couldn't stop trying to guess.

I took to undressing my Ken doll a dozen times a day, while Barbie languished in the same outfit. Ken's thing was a smooth featureless bulge swelling between his thighs. I kept running my thumb over it, and once even felt it with my tongue. Then, when my parents had gone a whole week without talking to each other, I stripped both dolls naked and put Ken between Barbie's legs.

Barbie had nothing between her legs, no hole, no hair. And Ken's rump was oddly hinged, like a ball and socket joint. The two of them lay nose to nose, inert and smiling, Barbie's legs straight up in the air like a V because her knees didn't bend.

I knew the word fuck, but I couldn't say it. So I just pressed Ken down on Barbie and put my teeth over my lip to make the *eff* sound. Then I clicked the *kay* sound in the back of my throat. Press. Eff. Kay. Press. Eff. Kay.

I pressed and effed and kayed over and over until I felt as if I was filling up with warm water between my legs. It was a nice feeling, one I woke up with sometimes. It got better and better until all at once I felt a throb between my legs, then another, then another, as if I was opening and closing down there. It felt good. It felt very good. Better than sneezing. Better than scratching an itch. But I got scared it wouldn't stop, or that I would damage myself and have to be taken to the doctor, who would know right away what I had been doing, and would tell my mother.

Then my mother would know I wasn't the sweet little girl she had screamed about to my father. And she would get that shocked, bruised look on her face and ask me why I would do such a thing, and what was the matter with me. *She* would never have done such a thing. *Sigrid* wouldn't. *No* girl would even so much as think of it.

So as soon as the serious throbbing started between my legs, I pulled Ken away from Barbie and dressed them both as fast as I could in their wedding outfits. I kept glancing over my shoulder, expecting to see my mother standing in my bedroom doorway. Or worse, much worse, Jesus standing there. Looking baffled and sad and hurt by what I was doing.

I had a complicated relationship with Jesus. My mother didn't talk about Him much, but when she did, she managed to give the impression that the two of them were on a first-name basis. That they got together now and then to commiserate over a cup of tea. I could see Jesus appealing to my mother as the kind of nice, polite, clean-cut young man she kept hoping my brother would turn into.

As for me, something in me loved Him achingly, the way it loved the abused collie in *Lassie Come Home*. But at least Lassie did come home. When I thought of that movie, what came to mind was the exhausted dog licking away Roddy McDowall's happy tears. But when I thought of Jesus, it was not the resurrection I pictured. It was the lash. And the thorns. And the nails.

I felt at once personally responsible for Jesus' agony on the cross and utterly incapable of doing anything about it. Church, especially hymns, did nothing to assuage my guilt.

*Thron'd upon the Awful Tree,*
*King of Grief, I watch with thee ...*

Jesus had died, I was told, to save me. Jesus had died for my sins. And what did Jesus want in return for spending six hours hanging with His full weight on nails that should, by rights, have pierced my wrists?

He wanted me. For a sunbeam.

And that wasn't all. I was to be a jewel, a precious jewel, a bright gem for His crown. Exactly how I was to twinkle and glitter and beam for the King of Grief thron'd upon His Awful Tree was never explained. All I knew was that Jesus bade me shine.

Now and then Miss Urquhart, our Sunday school teacher, would bleat out some practical advice, and I would prick up my ears. 'Jesus *knows!* He knows every single little thing you do! And He *remembers* it! Even if you do something small, like fetching a glass of water for someone, Jesus *sees* that and He *magnifies* it and it makes Him *happy!*'

This was reassuring until I realized that if my good deeds could make Jesus happy, it followed that my bad deeds could make Him sad. And surely, as King of Grief, He had enough making Him sad already.

I would torture myself with thoughts of the Second Coming happening in my lifetime, in my neighbourhood. I could see Jesus touching down in my very bedroom, in fact, and catching me going eff and kay with Barbie and Ken. The thought of the look on His face (and on my mother's when, naturally, He told her) was so awful that it made me bite my arm hard enough to leave teeth marks that lasted two days.

But it wasn't bad enough to make me stop. I had gotten to the point that just thinking about Barbie and Ken could give me that scary, delicious feeling between my legs, and make me hightail it upstairs.

I kept waiting for my mother to ask me why I was spending half the summer in my room, and to come out with her usual lecture about how next year, whether I liked it or not, I was going to camp too, like Ted and like Sigrid. But she didn't. She was too busy not talking to my father to notice much of anything I did.

At the end of the second week of silence, I locked myself in the bathroom with a pair of scissors. First I snipped away my pubic curls until the hair lay flat like fur. Then I soaped myself and borrowed my father's razor.

I had been growing armpit and pubic hair for almost a year, and I was starting to get breasts. It all embarrassed me so much that I could hardly stand to look at myself in the mirror. And just a month ago, when my mother said, 'We'll have to get you a bra before you start back to school in September,' I turned and ran out of the kitchen and up to my room.

I couldn't remember deciding to shave myself. Didn't know what I was doing or why. But now it was done.

I had forgotten what I looked like down there. The cleft mound of flesh, the odd little vertical lips. The naked skin felt like somebody else's.

Automatically, I looked over my shoulder. No mother, of course. The door was locked. But no Jesus either, though I seemed to remember a Bible story about Him showing up in a locked room.

Still, it was hard to imagine Jesus ever coming into the bathroom, even to check up on me. And to tell the truth, I was starting to get fed up with Jesus poking His nose into every single thing I did.

I wasn't even sure any more that He really did know what I was up to. My mother didn't, so why should He? I had stopped believing in Santa Claus when it dawned on me that nobody could slide down all the chimneys in the world in a single night. So why did I think Jesus could keep tabs on who was doing what, every second of the day? Because Miss Urquhart said so?

My new thoughts scared and thrilled me as much as my new, secret baldness. When my pubic hair started to grow back in, the prickle and itch led to scratching and exploring which, I discovered, could produce that breathtaking open-close throb without benefit of Barbie and Ken.

I stopped worrying about Jesus altogether. What was the point? Chances were He didn't even know what I was up to. Or if He did, He wouldn't want to have anything to do with me now. Not since I had started doing this thing I couldn't put a name to, but that I suspected had something to do with the secret world of adults. With the blankets and sheets on the couch. And with the silence that hung heavier by the day between my parents.

In the third week of my mother and father not talking to each other, I went to hell and back.

There must have been a box of Kotex in the house. But wherever my mother had hidden it, it was so well hidden that I never so much as saw it. I did see the 'Modess ... Because' advertisements in magazines, but I assumed they were ads for dry cleaning those gorgeous gowns the women always wore.

So when, in the third week of silence, my probing fingers went in a little deeper than they ever had and came out covered with blood, I had literally no idea what was really happening.

I assumed at first that I had scratched myself with a fingernail. When the bleeding got heavier, I lined the crotch of my underpants with toilet paper. Then, when I bled through double and triple layers, I knew that this was not a fingernail scratch. With all my poking around, I had done serious damage to myself. I might even be bleeding to death.

I tried to imagine dying. Being dead. I couldn't. What I could imagine, and what really scared me, was the possibility of being discovered. I was afraid blood would leak through the toilet paper onto my underpants, where my mother would see it the next time she did a laundry. I was terrified of her questions, of her dawning realization of just exactly what kind of a daughter she had, and of her added grief.

So the Saturday morning I woke up to find that I had not only soaked through the toilet paper, my underpants and my pyjamas, but had also stained my bottom sheet, I knew I had to leave my mother's house. I couldn't possibly sit beside her in church the next morning. And Monday was wash day.

It was easy to get away unnoticed. My father was home on Saturdays, so my mother was busier than ever not talking to him. I didn't pack anything or have any kind of a plan. I didn't even know where I was going until I got there.

Just below the edge of the escarpment was the abandoned Toronto, Hamilton and Burlington railroad. My brother had told me the letters T. H. & B. stood for To Hell and Back. The tracks, unused for years, were nothing now but miles of rusted rail, furred with milkweed and daisies and plants with no name.

Sigrid and I had walked along the tracks once, and had sworn each other to secrecy about it. Though nobody had ever actually told us not to go down there, we could guess from the discarded, abandoned look of the place that the tracks were forbidden territory.

But there I was. I had walked down the wooden steps of the escarpment face with the same feeling of not knowing why that I had had when shaving my pubic hair. It was hot on the tracks, and the heat was making things shimmer. I walked and walked, with no idea of where I was going. Just walking, just putting distance between myself and home, was a comfort.

Vaguely, I thought I might walk myself to death. Except I had eaten a good lunch and didn't feel as if I was dying. Or maybe, if I wasn't going to die, something might happen to change everything. It could be that I was wrong about Jesus, and He was watching me after all. Waiting for me somewhere along the tracks to give me a good talking-to. Then order me to go home and tell my mother the awful things I had been doing.

And then maybe my mother would take me to the doctor, who would tell her she had caught me in the nick of time, and would stitch me up or something. And then maybe I would have to do time in reform school. But they would let me come home for Christmas. And eventually I'd get out.

I had no idea how long I had been on the tracks when I heard a scraping, sliding sound behind me, like a miniature avalanche. I turned around and saw a boy of about my age standing there. He must have been following a trail somewhere above, and had slid down the gravelly side of the escarpment. The minute I turned and saw him, I heard a noise behind me exactly like the first noise. I turned again and saw another boy. This one said, 'Let's see it.'

I felt a stinging blow between my shoulder blades and turned again. The other boy had whipped a stone at me. 'Let's *see* it.'

At first I thought they must be brothers. But no, they just had the same smile. A pure grimace, a stretching and twisting of the lips. Nothing in the eyes.

Another stone. This one caught me on the shoulder. Stupidly, I turned and got a third stone on the buttock from the boy behind me. 'I got her on the ass!' he screeched. 'I got her on the ass!'

'What do you want?' I managed to say.

'What do you *want?*' they sang together in falsetto. 'What do you *wa-a-a-a-nt?*' One of them grabbed my shoulders hard in his hands and said, 'We wanna see your cunt.' Then he pushed me, and, oldest trick in the book, I fell backwards over the other boy who had crouched down behind me.

I lay winded on the tracks. All I could think was *cunt*, a word I had never heard or seen written, but somehow understood. A *cunt* was what I had down there, what I had been trespassing in, what I had caused to bleed. And because of what I had done, a *cunt* was what I had become.

So whatever these boys did to me, they would be doing it to a cunt. I would be getting what a cunt deserved.

'Make her pull her pants down,' one of the boys said, his voice tight with excitement. The other boy kicked me in the thigh. 'Pull your pants down,' he ordered.

I tried to sit up and wrap my arms around my knees, but he put his foot on my chest and shoved me flat. Then while the other boy came round to my head, held my arms down and knelt on my shoulders, the first one reached for the elastic waistband of my shorts and began to pull. When I locked my thighs together, he grinned and thrust his arm down the front of my pants.

'I got my fingers in her crack,' he said. 'I got my fingers in her crack.' His voice was breathless. He looked wonderingly at the other boy.

'What's it feel like?' the boy holding me said.

'Feels gooey. Feels like snot.'

I had died already and gone to hell, and these two were the devil. That's what must have happened. I stretched my eyes, searching the sky for Jesus coming again, just in the nick of time. I wanted Him back. I wanted my mother. I wanted to be a sweet little girl. With pubic hair. I started to cry, and my thighs moved apart. The boy with his fingers in me reached with his other hand and pulled my shorts and underpants down to my knees.

The crotch of my underpants was soaked with blood. A long wick of bloody toilet paper stretched from my underwear to me. The boys went silent and still.

'What *is* it?' the boy with his knees on my shoulders whispered at last. 'What's the *matter* with her?' His knees slid away. I didn't move.

40

I was too afraid even to pull my pants back up.

'Aw shit, it's on my *hand!*' the other boy said, sounding as if he was going to cry. '*Shit!*' He got up and ran to the side of the tracks where he began frantically scraping his hand clean in the grass.

'She must *have* something,' the other boy said. He was standing now, watching his companion. 'Maybe it's a disease. Maybe it's catching.' I could tell he hoped it was, and that he was glad he wasn't the one who had put his fingers in me.

'*Shut up!*' the other boy screamed at him, still wiping his hand.

'Maybe you're gonna *die*,' his companion crowed. ''Cause you touched her cunt. Maybe blood's gonna come outta your *cock* now.'

'Fuck *you!*' the other boy screamed, throwing a stone. The laughing boy turned and started scrambling up the face of the escarpment. The other went after him, but not before looking furiously at me, bending and picking up a handful of gravel. I curled up in a ball and covered my face just as the rain of stones hit me.

'Dirty cunt!' he screamed. Another rain of gravel. 'Dirty bloody cunt!' He had started to cry. 'Get your blood on *me*, will you? Get it on *me!*' A final rain of stones. Then the sound of scrambling up the cliff face. Then nothing.

I lay there in a daze. I had a curious, peaceful feeling that I had been punished, and punished enough. For whatever I had done. Just then, I couldn't quite remember what I had done. But in time I came out of my daze and did remember.

I couldn't know, then, that after pulling my clothes back up and crying myself dry I would start to feel hungry. That I would get up and walk back the way I had come, thinking that maybe it was best to die at home. After supper.

And I couldn't know then that when I got home I would feel a change in the very air inside the house. That I would hear my father whistling 'Sweet Georgia Brown' at his workbench in the basement, and would find my mother in the kitchen, baking a cherry pie, his favourite. That I would glance into my parents' bedroom and see their bed unmade, in the middle of the day.

And that my mother, seeing the blood caking on the tops of my socks, would burst into tears. Then fill a tub for me, and put in bubble bath, and sit beside me while I soaked. And, flushed and happy and young-looking as she had not been in weeks, explain what was happening to me, and that it happened to every girl on earth, and always had and always would.

'Has it happened to Sigrid?'

'Last year. Mrs Kiraja told me.'

'Why didn't Sigrid tell *me?*'

'Because I asked Mrs Kiraja to tell her not to. I wanted to tell you myself. And I was just saying to your father a month or so ago that I should talk to you about it, but then –'

She stopped and looked away. The fight between her and my father was over, the silence broken. But she was never going to tell me what it had been about. That much was clear.

And I couldn't know, while I sat on the tracks, that in less than an hour I would learn that what had frightened me almost to death held no danger and no mystery, except for myself and the two boys I had met. My mother had known all about it, and so had Sigrid, and so had even my father. Probably Jesus had known about it too. And Miss Urquhart. The whole world had known, the whole time I was making ready to die. Had watched every step I took along the tracks. Had watched the boys, too, as they first stripped then stoned me.

I couldn't know that I would start to feel a strange kinship with those boys. That I would never tell anyone about them, would come to think of the three of us as partners in a secrecy of our own.

That when my mother asked me how I had gotten so dirty, and why I was so scraped and bruised, I would stare down at my naked body through the disappearing bubbles in the bath and say nothing. That I would feel a huge silence gathering in me, filling me. That I would fear to open my mouth and break the silence. For surely if I did, lightning would fork out from between my lips and hit the water and electrocute me, and then her, and then my father and Sigrid and the whole world.

No, I couldn't possibly know any of that then. All I could do was sit on the side of the tracks and cry. I was still guilty as sin, still bleeding to death. And still wondering whether Jesus or the devil would come and get me first.

# Missing Person

---

*Elvira is walking to the sea. She keeps her eyes on the grey horizon. She smells a cold, alien smell and hears a sound like the slow clashing of cymbals.*

*The dust of the road becomes sand under her feet, dotted with crunching bits of shell. The sand smooths and darkens near the water. At the frothing edge of the sea it is almost black.*

*Elvira stands looking at the moving waves. Her feet are hot and hurting. She stoops and unlaces her shoes. One of the laces has broken twice, and has been knotted twice. She eases the shoes off, careful of the raw spots on the backs of her heels. Then she lifts the hem of her skirt, unfastens her shredded stockings and rolls them down.*

*The breeze is cool to her bare feet. The dark sand has the texture of brown sugar. Her footprints are tiny lakes that fill up from below.*

*At the foaming edge, she stops. She looks around. There is a house in the near distance, but no one watching at any of the windows. She bends, scoops up water in her calloused palm and touches the tip of her tongue to its surface. The taste of salt makes her throat knot up.*

*The water is inching away from her. It leaves lines of dirty foam and frayed seaweed to mark where it rested before moving on. She imagines the tide inundating some far shore, then swaying back like a huge bell.*

*First she puts one bare foot in, then the other. Salt sizzles in the backs of her heels. The undertow is surprisingly strong. A rope of seaweed, caught on her ankle, snakes away after the tide. She hesitates. Then begins to follow it.*

'That's Mister Bunnyrabbit, Elvira. And there's Grandfather Clock in the corner. And see that guy coming in? That's Mister Greenjeans.' As I licked a molten dollop of peanut butter from my toast, Elvira would have nodded solemnly beside me on the couch, saying a careful, 'Oh yes. Yes. I see.'

It was easy enough to talk to Elvira. Nothing I said ever seemed to matter. She wasn't like other adults. She didn't ask me to call her

43

Miss Tomlinson or Aunt Elvira. She didn't fuss over me or make her voice go tinkly when she talked to me, either. She didn't seem to know I was a child. Maybe because she had no children of her own. She was the only woman I knew then who wasn't a mother.

With Elvira, my mother never had those whispered, womanly conversations that she had with my Aunt Heather. The kind that ceased the minute I wandered into the kitchen for a cookie. No, my mother removed her apron when Elvira came to visit, and sat with her in the living room. What the two of them said to each other was safe enough to say in front of me, and so boring that not one word of it stands out in my memory.

Elvira was the perfect guest, nodding and smiling and wearing her manners like gloves. She lived in Toronto and came to Hamilton once or twice a year to see us and Grandma McEwen and Aunt Heather. Then, as my mother put it, she knew when to leave.

I didn't know what to call the way she looked. I didn't know then that a woman could be handsome. Her thin, mobile lips pronounced each word precisely, finishing it completely before going on to the next. Her speech didn't slip and slide around the way ours did. She didn't say things like y'know and okay.

She sat very straight, even on the couch. She always wore a suit, and a silk scarf pinned at the neck with a brooch.

*But now she is wearing a second- or third-hand dress. She is wading thigh deep in the water, just at the point where the shallows become the depths. The sun is still burning her shoulders, but the water is numbingly cold. She cannot feel her feet, though she can see them, greenish white and moving. All she can feel is the pull of the tide.*

*Drown, she thinks. She is going to drown. But how will she do it? Is it something she will in fact have to do, or will it just happen to her?*

*The water is up to her waist. There is a tickle of cold where it laps at her body. She can't see her feet any more. Will the water simply open her up and flow into her? Or will she have to do it, have to decide, have to consciously, deliberately, open herself?*

*She can imagine herself dead. Floating like weed, less and less of her, eyeless and eaten away. Washing up on a shore somewhere. Being found. Perhaps even identified.*

*But that will be someone else's worry. She is not worried about being
dead. What worries her is dying. The moment that it happens. The doing
of it.*

Elvira walked to the sea before I was born. Before my parents were
married, or had even met. When my mother was still living at home
with her own parents, listening to Rudy Vallee on Sunday nights on
the radio.

'Now, listen, Daisy. Don't ever let on to Elvira that I told you this.
Okay? Promise?'My mother would have glanced out the kitchen
window, as if checking for neighbours cocking their ears.

I can't remember her telling me the story. But I know she did,
probably when I was about nine. At nine I was young enough to be
my mother's friend. Too young to guess just how badly she needed
one.

'Promise you won't let Elvira know that you know?'

I would have nodded hard, skidding my elbows forward on the
red-checked oilcloth. I was about to be told some *business*, and business meant secrets, and adults kept the oddest things secret. *Don't
tell any of our business*, followed me through the screen door whenever I was on my way to a friend's house. *That's none of your business!*
could swat the most innocent question like a fly.

'I've told you about the Tomlinsons? Elvira's family? How they
were part of the old neighbourhood? There since day one? Just like
my folks?' I nodded to every question, wanting her to get to the well-
what-I-*didn't*-tell-you part.

'Well, what I *didn't* tell you was that when Elvira was only around
ten, Mr Tomlinson, the father, left them all. Ran off one morning
with a Chinese cook.'

It always amazed me to hear about adults misbehaving. Growing
up, I thought, was a kind of drying-out process, whereby all the bad-
ness evaporated away. Somehow, magically, the loud, rowdy boys in
my class would change into silent men like my father, wearing fedo-
ras and going to work in the morning. And the girls, including me,
would stop giggling and become women like my mother, aproned
and finger-waved, living most of our lives in kitchens.

Yet here was Elvira's father leaving his perfectly good wife. I saw

Mr Tomlinson as a stubbled, nasty-looking creature, sneaking off in a foggy dawn with the Chinese cook, a little woman wearing a conical hat and carrying a spatula.

'And if that wasn't enough,' my mother went on, 'when Elvira was just fourteen and the youngest of the four boys was, oh, about your age I guess, Mrs Tomlinson had a stroke. And died.'

I didn't know what a stroke was. But from the way my mother said the word, and judging from the cartoons I had watched, I could imagine Mrs Tomlinson seizing her throat, keeling over stiff as a board and raising a cloud of dust as she landed.

'So there was Elvira,' my mother went on, picking at a hole in the oilcloth and shaking her head. 'All of fourteen. No father. No mother. And four little brothers needing to be looked after.'

'So what did she do?'

'She looked after them. She raised them. Did the cooking, the washing, the ironing. Helped them with their homework and got after them. Year after year. All by herself.'

'How did she go to school?'

'She didn't. She quit. At fourteen. Well, you could quit whenever you wanted to back then.'

'Did she want to?'

'I don't know. I doubt it. But she couldn't just do what she wanted any more. She had to grow up, right then and there. She had to do what was right.'

I imagined myself in Elvira's place, my own mother suddenly dead. I saw myself having to grow up right then and there, having to do what was right. Hanging my brother Ted's damp bluejeans out on the line. Opening cans for supper. Cleaning the canary's cage.

'Bit of a shame, y'know,' my mother was saying, 'about Elvira quitting school. She did well at school. And she used to sing. Whenever there was an assembly or commencement or something, they'd always get Elvira to sing. Most of the time, it was a hymn. Once though, she sang 'The Last Rose of Summer'. Up on the platform. In a white dress.'

I was mentally trying to iron one of my father's white shirts. Getting a sleeve all smooth and stiff, then peeling it off the board and turning it over to find a zigzag crease on the underside. The kitchen blurred. In another second, I was going to cry, and my mother was going to say, what's the matter with *you*, and I was going to say, nothing, and she was going to say, it *can't* be nothing. And then I was going to have to tell her about imagining her being dead, and feel stupid.

So I made myself look hard at my mother, alive and sitting across from me in her rickrack-trimmed apron. Her arms were bare for the summer, her shoulders freckled brown. The sun had given her hair that blond streak on top that she made into a wave and held in place with a bobby pin.

'The neighbours pitched in, of course,' she was saying. 'Saw to it that the boys had after-school jobs. My mom was awfully good to Elvira. Used to send me over with pots of food all the time. Knit sweaters for all the boys one winter.'

'Did she knit one for Elvira too?' I asked.

'Oh, probably. But Elvira was pretty proud, y'know. She'd take things for the boys, but it was hard to get her to accept anything for herself. My mom would have offered her stuff. Anything your Aunt Heather or I didn't wear any more. Your grandmother would never throw anything away. Still won't. If you give her a present, she saves the paper and turns around and wraps something for you in it.'

'So, what's the part I'm not supposed to *know*?'

'I was just going to tell you. But first I'll get myself another cup of tea. Do you want a Fizzy?'

'No, thanks.'

'It's hot. You should drink lots of liquids.'

'No.'

'There's orange. Lime.'

I shook my head.

'There's grape.'

'Okay.' I hadn't tried grape.

I didn't really like Fizzies, that is, I didn't like the drink they made, which was even sweeter than Kool-Aid. But I never got tired of dropping the little happy-face tablet into a glass of ice water and watching it dissolve like Alka-Seltzer.

Today's tablet was pale mauve. It sank to the bottom of the glass and began to boil up a furious purple. I thought of squid ink, and earthquakes happening at the very bottom of the sea.

*Elvira is chest deep in the water when she steps into a hole. The sky disappears. Green soundless cold. Water up her nose. Salt water like a fist in her mouth, punching down into her stomach.*

*She thrashes, climbs an imaginary ladder. Her head breaks the surface. Her feet scrabble for a foothold. Find it. She stumbles back into the shallows against the tide, stands knee deep in water, sneezing and retching and scrubbing at her eyes. When she can see, she sees that she is facing the shore again. The water has taken her, turned her around and thrown her back.*

*She can still feel the pull of the tide, dragging her dress skirt away from where it is plastered wet against her legs. Its pull is not as strong as before.*

*And there, sitting neatly side by side on the drying sand, are her shoes. One of her bloodstained stockings is still rolled up inside its shoe. The other has unrolled itself in the breeze and, held aloft by a lone spike of parched grass, is waving merrily at her.*

My mother was taking her time with her tea, adjusting the cosy, sniffing the milk. The cup she was using was one she had pulled out of a box of Tide. It took ages to collect even a single place-setting, and the plates were chip-scalloped by the time she got around to the completer set. But my mother liked things that took time, that happened bit by bit. Chances are, if the detergent box method of collecting china had been unknown, she would have invented it.

So all I could do was wait and drink my grape Fizzy. 'This Old House' was singing from the pink plastic radio on the counter beside the sink. The chicken clock was pecking away the time on top of the fridge. There was a barnyard scene painted on the clock face, and a rhythmically moving chicken in the foreground. For as long as I could remember, this chicken had pecked the ground in time with the ticking seconds, while her painted-on chicks looked up at her in frozen astonishment.

'Anyway,' my mother resumed over her fresh cup of tea, 'when Elvira was, what? Twenty-two? Something like that. Because she's a few years older than me. So she would have been twenty-two or so, and the youngest boy, oh, maybe seventeen. Old enough not to need her any more. Or maybe he was younger. Because kids grew up faster then, especially –'

'What *happened?*' I said. My mother was filled right up with words, words she heard, words she read, words she was thinking, and she needed to talk them out. She couldn't even read silently to herself. 'Just two lines!' she would promise, then read three paragraphs aloud while we all groaned and pleaded. She sang along with the radio, phoned in to talk shows, whistled at the canary, lectured the cat.

'Okay, okay. What happened? Well, one day, without saying a word to anybody, Elvira took what little housekeeping money she had, went down to the train station and got on a train going east. Her brothers called the police once she'd been missing for a whole day, and the police checked the train station, among other things. And they found out that a tall, kind of strange young woman had bought a one-way ticket east, out of the province. So that got the Mounties involved. And the Mounties checked with all the train porters and ticket-takers or whatever they're called, and they found out that this very quiet young woman who looked the way the brothers said Elvira did had sat up, night and day, right to the end of the line. Nobody could remember if she'd had anything to eat, but everybody remembered that she didn't have any baggage with her. Not even a purse.'

My mother paused for a sip of tea, her mouth becoming a round O exactly like that of the Dutch-girl string-saver. The Dutch girl had hung on the kitchen wall as long as the chicken clock had sat up on the fridge. Her ceramic lips were puckered around a hole that made her look like she was whistling. When my father needed string and couldn't find any, he would say, 'You've *got* a string-saver, June. Why don't you *use* it?' And my mother would reply, 'Oh, I put a ball of string inside her once, but she looked like she was eating spaghetti, so I took it out.' This always made perfect sense to me until I started to think about it.

'Did the Mounties ever find Elvira?'

'Oh, sure. The Mounties always find whoever they're looking for. They tracked her down to this big old house near the shore. She'd taken the train as far east as it would go, then she'd gotten out and walked the rest of the way to the sea. And that's where the house was.'

'Did anybody live there?'

'Uh-huh. A family. But Elvira didn't know them. She didn't even know if there would be anybody there.'

'So how did she get inside?'

'Well, I guess she just walked up and knocked on the door.'

'Was she scared?'

*The house is a big old clapboard with blistered white paint and a wraparound screen porch. In the middle of the roof is a tiny gable. Elvira stands knee deep in the water, looking at the window beneath the gable, then at the warped steps leading up to the porch's screen door.*

*She remembers looking at this house just before she walked into the water. Checking to see if anyone was watching from a window. Now she wishes someone was. Whether the face was welcoming or forbidding, it would make it easier, somehow.*

*After a long time she puts one foot toward shore, feeling for sharp stones. She didn't feel any on the way in, but her feet are suddenly tender again. In a little while, she puts another foot carefully toward shore.*

*She walks slowly up to her shoes. The unrolled stocking is no longer caught on the spike of grass. It has tumbled a little way down the beach in the wind. As Elvira watches, it sidewinds like a snake into a crack in some rocks.*

*She could run and catch it. But she won't. She'll go barefoot. And she won't think about what to say until she gets there. She will just go up the steps, knock on the door, then open her mouth.*

*When she reaches the porch steps, her dress hem is still dripping but her feet are dry and powdered white with sand. The steps are grey. A lining of cobweb shows through the slats. Her feet ascend slowly, leaving white prints.*

*On the top step, she pauses. The inner door of the house is open. She can hear kitchen sounds through the screen, and can smell food cooking. After a long time, she makes a fist and raises it to the door frame.*

*Footsteps approach from within. A blurred face looks through the screen. There is a pause, then the latch is lifted. The door creaks on its hinges. A small child, round-eyed and solemn, pokes his head out from behind his mother's legs.*

*Elvira tries to smile at him, but her lips are cracked from the sun and crusted with salt from her near-drowning. Her eyes go from the child to the faded print apron skirt he is clutching in his fist. She doesn't dare look up at the woman wearing the apron until a movement catches her peripheral vision.*

*The woman has raised her hand to touch her own hair. Her hair is pulled back and pinned. Probably no time for more. Still, when she sees a stranger, a strange woman, even a woman dripping wet and barefoot, her hand goes up to her hair in a token tidying gesture.*

*It is this small tribute that breaks Elvira down. Her lips stretch, crack, burn. Sounds come out of her, not words, sounds like the waves make, like the gulls make.*

*Then there is nothing but the bib of the apron against her face, the hand unmoving on the back of her head.*

'It took the Mounties two weeks to find her. She was upstairs in that big white house, in a nice little room. You know? The kind with one pointy gable that pokes up? From the middle of the roof?'

I nodded and nodded, urging my mother on. Without these constant affirmations, she would sit and spin her wheels forever.

'Well, there was Elvira, sitting in a rocking chair in a patch of sun. Rocking away. Just looking out the window. Peaceful as an egg.'

'What's that mean? Peaceful as an egg?'

'Oh, I don't know. It's just something my mom always says. Probably her mother said it. Stands to reason, though, doesn't it? I mean, you can't get much more peaceful than an egg.'

This was another of my mother's sayings that made perfect sense on a level inaccessible to thought.

'Anyway, all along the window sill in the room were stones and shells Elvira had collected. That's all she'd done. Walked along the beach every day picking up shells and pretty stones.'

'Did the Mounties put handcuffs on her?'

'Oh no. Nothing like that. She hadn't done anything wrong. She was just a missing person. So they weren't there to arrest her. They couldn't even make her come back if she didn't want to.'

'So why did she come back?'

'Well, I guess she wanted to.'

'But why?'

'I don't know,' my mother said, and paused, looking down into her cooling tea.

I wondered if she was seeing what I was seeing. That little sun-warmed room with the rocking chair and the shells. Dust motes made into jewels by that long-ago light. I tried to imagine Elvira sitting and rocking, calmly waiting for the authorities to catch up with her. I couldn't. The room had nothing to do with the scarfed and suited Elvira I saw once or twice a year. But neither did the train, or the walk to the sea, or the knocking on the door of the house.

'Did she ever go back?' I asked. 'To the house?'

'I don't know. I don't think so. She's never said, anyway.'

'Does she want to go back?'

'I don't know that either. And I would never ask. And don't you go asking either, Daisy. It's none of our business.'

*Elvira does not know whose room this used to be, whether a departed boarder or a dead child. In the last few days she has memorized its details, giving them to herself like gifts. The honey-coloured hardwood floor, the round braided rag rug, the sloping ceiling, the window facing the ocean. Through this window, day and night, comes the huge breathing of the water.*

*In the morning, the sun teases pinkly through her eyelids. She is already awake by then, having felt the day's beginning far beneath her in the house. She pulls the sheet and quilt over her head. Though clean, the bedclothes have that deeply personal smell that comes of much using and washing.*

*She is afraid. The fear is like a cold fingertip pressing right where her ribcage forks. She wakes to it, goes to sleep with it. Maybe she has been afraid like this for years, but all the other fears, what will we eat, what will we wear, how will we stay warm, kept her from feeling it.*

*All she knows is that one morning last week she woke up to the boys already gone to their day, gone to their lives, and the fear there in bed with her, its cold penetrating the cave of warmth under the sheets. She carried the fear around inside her like a pain all that day. She told herself there was nothing to be afraid of. The boys were all working. Earning. They could look after her now, and they would. So she had nothing to fear, for the rest of her life. Nothing.*

*She did not know how much a train ticket would cost. It turned out she had just enough in silver and coppers, knotted up in her handkerchief.*

*Elvira pulls the bedclothes down and opens her eyes. She does not know the surname of the family stirring below. She has no idea what the woman who opened the door to her told them all, only that not one of them seemed surprised by her presence at their table.*

*She is still afraid. But the fear is at home here, in this house. It is less like a pain and more like a presence. More like something she can negotiate with, silently.*

*It is a blessing not to have to speak. Her tongue lies soft in her mouth. This room is a blessing too, and her place at the table, and the plate of warm food all her own.*

*The plate is set before her in such a way that it makes no sound when the china meets the wood of the table. She looks forward to this gesture, this tenderness, as much as she looks forward to the food she did nothing to prepare but which is still, miraculously, hers.*

*The smell of breakfast cooking has reached her, filling her mouth with water. She sits up and swings her bare feet out onto the rag rug. Today she will walk along the beach again, and stoop and pry up half-buried shells, and swish them in the water, and carry them up to this room and put them on the window sill for the morning sun to bleach clean.*

'Now, don't go screaming yourself sick,' my mother said to me across the kitchen table.

'I *won't.*'

'And don't stand too close to anybody who is screaming themselves sick, because you could get ear damage.'

I glowered. She meant my new best girlfriend, Michelle. Michelle probably would scream herself sick, come to think of it. And cry, too, and maybe even faint. She was better than me at everything else, so why not this?

'And the two of you stay *together.* If you get separated or if something goes wrong before Michelle's parents can pick you up, find a policeman. There'll be police all over Maple Leaf Gardens, thank God. So find one of them if you need help. Don't go walking the streets of Toronto.' She might have been saying, the streets of Sodom.

'I'm not stupid,' I said.

'Oh, I know *you're* not.'

Another dig at Michelle. 'Michelle's father won't let her play Beatle records for a *whole hour* after he comes home from work,' I said fiercely. 'And when he saw her Paul McCartney haircut, he said, That's not coming out of my wallet, and then he made her *pay* for it. Out of her *allowance*.'

'This is the same man who stood in line for ten hours to get you both tickets to the concert.'

'He only did that to keep Michelle from doing it. Because she would have.'

'Oh, I know she would have.'

'She had her sleeping bag all ready and her bus tickets to Toronto and everything, but then her parents caught her sneaking out and they *grounded* her. Except for the concert tomorrow, she can't go *anywhere* for a *month*.'

'Somebody should get the Children's Aid after those two.'

I tried to sulk, but I was too full of emotional helium. The very next day, tomorrow, in just twenty-eight hours and seventeen minutes, I was going to be breathing the same air as John, Paul, George and Ringo. I had never heard of molecules, but I had a notion that that air would contain tiny bits of the Beatles that would somehow bypass the other thirty thousand screaming fans to enter my nostrils alone.

I would come home changed. In what way, I didn't know, but I would be different. How could I possibly be the same after breathing the dandruff of the gods?

'Excited?' my mother said, watching me.

I shrugged. 'A bit.' I stared down into my mug of milky tea. The mug was printed with a black-and-white photograph of Ringo Starr, and had cost $2.95. My mother had said that was highway robbery for a cup, but she had paid it anyway. I took a sip. I didn't like tea, but the Beatles drank it.

'You know you're getting pretty?' my mother said. 'In spite of that haircut?'

I rolled my eyes. I had had my hair cut like Ringo's. I didn't like Ringo's hair either, but I had to be loyal. *Somebody* had to love Ringo. Besides being the least attractive of the four, he had nothing witty to say to reporters, couldn't sing, and as far as I could tell, wasn't even much of a drummer.

I could have guessed that Michelle would go for Paul. She belonged with the best-looking of the Beatles. I used to imagine the two of us somehow meeting the four of them. I could see Michelle going right up to Paul, giving him that cool look she was starting to give boys. And there would be me in the background, finally managing to catch Ringo's eye.

I didn't know if I was getting pretty or not. But if I was, I wanted Michelle to tell me, not my mother. All Michelle ever said was things like, 'You know, it wouldn't *hurt* you to wear a pushup bra.'

'When I was fourteen,' my mother was saying, 'for me, it was Rudy Vallee.' She was using that shy, coaxing tone she used when she wanted us to talk. It made me itch with embarrassment, but it also made it impossible to get up and leave.

'He used to come on for Fleischmann's yeast on Sunday nights, and I used to dress up and sit in front of the radio.'

Oh, God.

'And one night, when he was singing, I lost a button off my blouse. It just popped off and went scooting across the kitchen floor. And my mother said, Well, *somebody's* heart's beating.'

'What did Grandma think of him?' If I asked questions I could at least steer the conversation away from anything truly nauseating.

'What did my mom think of Rudy Vallee? Oh well, he sang nice songs, and he always ended with a hymn, so she didn't mind.'

I had once seen a picture of Rudy Vallee singing into what looked like a giant lollipop. He had a face like Howdy Doody and a mountain range of hair parted as by a river. There was nothing there that I would scream at, let alone lose a button over.

'And she'd had kind of a crush on Maurice Chevalier herself when she was younger,' my mother continued, 'so she knew what it was like.'

'*Grandma?*'

'Your grandmother was a girl once, believe it or not. So was your mother.'

'I *know*.'

I looked up at the clock on top of the fridge. Twenty-seven hours and fifty-seven minutes to go. It was the same chicken clock, still pecking away. The Dutch girl string-saver still hung on the wall, still without string, despite my father's pleading. My mother continued to wear aprons, though I had told her not to, and she still got her hair done just like the Queen's.

'There might be something on the radio about the Beatles arriving in Toronto,' she said, getting up and going to the counter. At least the radio was new, a transistor. But she wouldn't throw out the pink plastic one. It was down in the basement with Ted's and my old toys and books.

'... pushing through the crowd ...' an excited announcer was saying. 'Security personnel are having great difficulty getting the Beatles safely to their waiting limousines. They are having to guide them, because they're bent over with their jackets up over their heads, and – What? Which one is it? Some fans have broken through the police cordon and have grabbed hold of one of the – Who? Ringo? Ringo Starr?'

My mother and I looked at each other. Her eyes were as big as mine felt.

'... Security personnel have pulled the fans away from Ringo Starr, and have gotten him and the other Beatles safely into the ...'

'Thank goodness,' my mother breathed when the broadcast was over and 'A Hard Day's Night' was belting out of the radio. 'They could really have hurt Ringo, y'know. Pulled out his hair. Grabbed his nose. He's got *such* a nose.'

I was suspicious of my mother's fondness for the Beatles. I thought it might have more to do with trying to be my friend than anything else.

At fourteen, I spent a lot of time analysing my mother, trying to determine exactly what was wrong with her. Her main problem, I had decided, was that she had no friends. She didn't go on shopping trips with other women, never had anybody in for coffee. She didn't join committees, either, or try to get a job now that Ted and I were growing up and didn't need her any more.

Instead, the lonelier she got, the harder she tried to make friends with me. Doing things like pretending to like the Beatles.

'Oh, they're *cute!*' she said the first time they were on the Ed Sullivan show. 'Their hair must be really *clean* to flip around like that.'

'I give them three months,' Ted said. 'Six, tops.'

'Jesus God,' my father whispered, raising his newspaper like a shield.

'Oooooh!' my mother was singing, trying to imitate Paul and John's falsetto. 'Oooooh!'

'Ringo must be Jewish, with that nose,' she was saying now.

'No, he's *not*,' I said. 'He's from Liverpool.'

'Well, there are probably Jews in Liverpool. There are Jews all over. I was reading somewhere the other day that there are even Chinese Jews.'

'But not all Jewish people have big noses.'

'I know. But lots do. Look at Elvira.'

'Is Elvira Jewish?' I pictured her high-bridged nose, her large brown eyes, the lids sliding slowly down when she blinked, then slowly back up.

'One of her grandmothers was. I forget which one. But look, don't mention I said that, all right?'

'I *won't*. Why would I?'

'People kept that kind of thing quiet back then. And then the war came, and they *really* kept it quiet.'

I hadn't said more than two words at a time to Elvira in years. The fact was, she had started giving me the creeps. The last time she had visited, I had come down the stairs on my way outside just in time to catch a glimpse of her sitting in the living room. My mother must have left her alone for a minute to go to the bathroom or do something in the kitchen. She was sitting absolutely still, in perfect profile, as if cut from paper. I suddenly got spooked by the idea of her turning and seeing me. I tiptoed out the side door so she wouldn't.

*Waiting*, my mouth said all by itself once I was safely outside. She had been *waiting* for something. Almost as if she believed that if she just sat perfectly still for long enough, she would find it. Or it would find her.

*Elvira has found a beach of stones. It is low tide, very sunny and hot. Tidal pools are forming and the gulls are circling down to feed on whatever is trapped inside them. Weeds like bunches of tiny dirigibles crunch and pop underfoot.*

*Elvira picks her way across the slanting, tippy surface with the help of a stick. The stones of the beach have been rolled by the waves into egg shapes. The boulders are like the eggs of dinosaurs; even the pebbles are pointed at one end, round at the other.*

*Her dress pockets are already full of stones. They knock softly, insistently against her thighs, like the fists of small children.*

*She'll empty them when she gets back to the room. She'll arrange the stones on the window sill, perhaps by size, big to small, or perhaps by colour, grey, salmon, speckled, striped.*

*Her ankles begin to ache for a flat surface. Bracing with her stick, she steps over a tidal pool onto a huge egg half buried in sand. She sits down and rests her stick in a pebbled groove beside the stone. Then she draws her knees up and circles them with her arms.*

*She looks around at the seashore and laughs silently to herself. She should abandon the idea of putting her stones in any kind of order on her window sill. There is no order here, or none that she can discern. The seashore is a torn edge, a smelly mess at low tide. The waves and gulls make a racket that never lets up. Things are dying and being born everywhere, fish flopping in tidal pools, insects flying up out of the weeds, baby crabs skittering on tiptoe.*

*Maybe she was expecting the kind of thing she had seen in paintings. Postcards. The smells are another surprise, everything from this salty, fishy stink to the wintry smell of high tide. An awful smell, she thinks. Awful in the biblical sense of awful. The smell of a maker of stones into eggs.*

*The big stone she is sitting on has gotten so hot in its few hours in the sun that it seems to be generating heat from within. Elvira imagines it submerged at high tide, still warm at the centre, sending up shimmers of heat through the water.*

*A breeze cools her face for a second. It catches one of the waves and pushes it further and faster than the others. She watches the wave snake through the twisting waterways of the low tide shore and find her rock. Actually lick the toe of her shoe. Cold seeps in through the broken stitches in the cracked leather.*

*Lorna, the woman in the house, has given Elvira a new dress and underwear, well, new to her, but there are only enough shoes to go around in the family. She explained this softly, apologetically, while Elvira was stepping into the offered clothes. Elvira nodded and reached and touched Lorna's hand.*

*She still has not spoken. She knows she will talk, in time, when the time comes. At least, she will open her mouth and make a sound. She has no idea what the sound will be, whether words or singing or something she cannot even imagine. Her tongue is still resting soft in her mouth. She is very aware of her tongue, now that she is not using it. It feels oddly new, almost alien, a thing she must get to know.*

*Perhaps she will never get to know it. Perhaps it will keep changing, and she won't be able to keep up with the changes. She might wake up tomorrow morning with her tongue forked, divided down to the root, and herself speaking in tongues. Or she might find her tongue gone altogether, a small nub or nothing where it once was, and a hard beak instead of lips and teeth. She might sing like a bird.*

*Another cold wave licks her toe. She inches her foot up a bit higher. She notices that the gulls have stopped circling and feeding. They are sitting on the water now in bobbing flotillas, smiling long, thin smiles.*

*Her tailbone is starting to ache. She is not sure she has ever sat this long on a stone. Or on anything. Doing nothing. She knows she should be ashamed of herself. She isn't. Not that she's proud of herself, either. She couldn't say what she is, right now. Maybe she's lost her mind. She's acting the way crazy people act. She's done what crazy people do.*

*Well. If this is crazy, then it's very ordinary. Very simple. She eats, she sleeps, she walks the beach. Nothing surprises her. If the largest stones were to shiver and rock, hatching in the sun, and sticky baby dinosaur heads poke out, squealing for their mothers, she would not so much as blink.*

*Even the extraordinary kindness she has received, and in a dimmed, waiting part of herself she knows it is extraordinary, even that seems only natural, like water flowing into a hollow.*

*She feels hollow. Empty as the shells she finds. Maybe when you lose your mind you really do lose something, and there is a space left.*

*Her mind used to be so full and hard and tight with all she had to do, had to make happen, had to keep from happening. She had to stretch a loaf of bread. She had to find a dollar. She had to see to, look after, make sure.*

*And she did. She did what was right. She did all the things she was raised to do. Have pride. Not ask. Mind her own business. Never beg. Keep control. Hold in. Not let on. Never break down.*

*Where did all that go? Did she leave it in the station like a lost suitcase when she boarded the train? Is it waiting for her?*

*A wave washes right over her foot. She reaches for her stick and touches wet. Her stick is floating. She watches it lift free of the pebbles it was resting on, watches one end swing toward shore, and the whole thing begin to move with the incoming tide.*

*She grabs the stick while she can, then stands up on the half-submerged rock, rubbing her numb backside. She had better get back to the house. Her stomach tells her it is time to eat.*

*She smiles, walking the stones with the aid of her stick. Her cracked lips have healed, thanks to a homemade balm Lorna gave her. Her tongue moves in her mouth, as if with a life of its own. The time is coming to sing.*

My mother seemed to know that 'She Loves You', the first song I ever saw the Beatles perform on the Ed Sullivan show, had a religious significance for me. She said nothing until the last 'Yeah' had died away and I had stopped the almost Hasidic rocking that took over my body whenever the tune was playing on the radio.

'Did I ever tell you that your grandmother saw Buffalo Bill? In Glasgow? When she was just a little girl?'

'Grandma saw Buffalo Bill?'

'Uh-huh. She did. And all she ever said about it was that the Indians smoked cigars, and the horses looked awfully thin, because the poor things had come over in the hold of a ship.'

'What was Buffalo Bill doing in Glasgow?'

'It was his Wild West show. He took it all over Europe. So my mom and her family and the whole village came down on the train.'

I couldn't stand it any more. 'What made you think of Grandma seeing Buffalo Bill?'

'You seeing the Beatles tomorrow. I just thought it was kind of interesting. Buffalo Bill and the Beatles. Hey! Sounds like a song title, doesn't it? Buffalo Bill and the Beatles.'

I had to cut her off, or she'd start making up lyrics and a tune. 'Did Elvira like Rudy Vallee too? The way you did?'

'I don't know. I don't think the Tomlinsons even had a radio. And Elvira wasn't going to school, remember. She was just like a mother with four kids. So she didn't hear what all the other girls were talking about. She might not even have known who Rudy Vallee was. She didn't have any kind of a girlhood. No dances. No boyfriends. It was as if a great big apple corer had come along and just lifted all that stuff right out.'

'Is that why she's so weird?'

'How do you mean?'

I couldn't say. I kept thinking about the last time I had seen Elvira. That sense of waiting. There had been a terrifying patience to the waiting, like the patience of statues, the patience of portraits. Whatever it was, it had sped me out the door.

'It's like she's not *real*,' I said at last. 'Like she's not really *there*.'

'Well,' my mother said, 'she's very, very reserved. That can happen, when somebody's been through something. And Elvira's been through a lot. She's been scarred. And they say that scar tissue's tougher than skin. Maybe that's a good thing. Because nothing ever came easy to Elvira. She did everything the hard way.'

'What about walking up to that house?' I said. 'She got taken in. Just like that. For nothing.'

'That was luck. That was just pure luck. Happening to find the right kind of people. I mean, when you think about what she could have found. People who'd have set the dog on her. People who'd have had her jailed as a vagrant. Anything could have happened to her. She could have ended up in a mental institution. There were people who thought she'd gone crazy. And in those days, crazy was next to criminal. You didn't get any sympathy.'

'Why would anybody think she was crazy?'

'Well, look at what she did. Oh, I know. It looks awfully brave, going off on her own like that. That's how people think of it now. But then? A young single woman? Going away by herself? Without telling her family?' My mother shook her head. 'In those days what you should and shouldn't do was chiselled in stone, especially if you were a girl. And if you once did something you shouldn't, you were either bad or you were nuts. Take your pick. So if you think Michelle's parents are being hard on her for trying to sneak off to Toronto ...' She shook her head again. 'I don't know what was riskier for Elvira. Running away or coming home again.'

'What happened when she came home?'

'Well, overnight she stopped being the brave little girl who raised her brothers single-handed, and turned into the woman who ran off. Amazing how people can drop one thing and pick up another without missing a beat.'

'Is that why she moved to Toronto?'

'Oh, she didn't move then. She couldn't have gone anywhere then. She didn't have one red cent to her name.'

I thought of the quality of Elvira's suits, the silk scarf always at her neck. 'So where did she get her money?'

'She worked for it. Starting with a little nothing job she managed to get somehow. Remember Bing's Variety? Down on Commercial?'

'Yes.'

'Where we used to get ice cream?'

'Yes.'

'And now it's a drug store?'

'Yes!'

'Well, Leonard Bing hired Elvira as a clerk. There was talk about that too. The theory was that Bing figured people would come into the store just to get a look at the woman who ran off. And he was right. So help me, people would come in and buy some silly little thing, a spool of thread or a pair of shoelaces. But they'd really be there to look at Elvira.'

'So what did Elvira do?'

'She counted out their change and looked right back at them. Oh, there was talk. My mom went to a Ladies' Aid meeting where Elvira might as well have been the only thing on the agenda. And the talk didn't stop until some pillar of the church announced that she for one had not been born yesterday, and she was keeping an eye on the girl's waistline and just waiting. And that's when my mom stood up and said if they didn't all quit tying their tongues in knots about Elvira, she'd quit the Ladies' Aid.'

'Grandma said *that?*'

'Hey, listen. Your grandmother doesn't open her mouth much, but when she does it's to *say* something. Besides. She had a lot of clout with the Ladies' Aid back then, and she knew it. It was bazaar season when all this happened. And she was their champion knitter.'

*'Lorna? My name is Elvira. May I sit down?'*

*Lorna's heart jumps at the sound. The words were dry. Sticky-sounding. But they were words. So she has a voice after all. And a name.*

*She knows she should be relieved to hear the woman speak at last. But she's actually a little sad. There was something childlike in the silence. Trusting. But of course, it couldn't last. That kind of thing never does.*

*The two of them sit carefully at the kitchen table, facing each other. Elvira has eaten with Lorna at this table three times a day for more than a week. She has slept in a bed whose sheets Lorna has changed. She has shared the privy with Lorna and her family.*

*But now they are beginning all over again. With words. The words will be a difficulty, at first. A thing to get used to.*

*'Lorna, I'm going to have to go back where I came from soon. They're looking for me. I can tell. I can feel them getting closer.'*

*Lorna nods, gets up and pours Elvira a cup of tea. She moves slowly, deftly. There is listening in every gesture.*

*'Something like this happened to me once before,' Elvira continues. 'When my mother died. I woke up one morning, and my whole life was gone. Just like that. But there was another one waiting for me. The boys were hungry. The boys were scared. The boys needed clean clothes. So I got through that day. The next day, they were hungry and scared and dirty all over again. So I got through that day too. And the next one. And the next.*

*'But the boys are men now. Whatever they can't do for themselves their wives will do. I've lost my life again. It's gone. Just like it was before. Only this time, there's no other life waiting for me.'*

*There is a time to speak. Lorna knows that. It's a very precise time,* very exact. She can feel it coming now, like a wave still far out to sea. Speak too soon, and the wave dies. Too late, and it's already crashed.

'I'm afraid, Lorna. I keep telling myself there's nothing to be afraid of. But it's the nothing that I am afraid of. And the nothing is me.'

The time is now. Quick, before the crash. Lorna prays, no more than a breath, then says, 'What do you love?'

It was the right question. Elvira's cheeks darken. In a rush, she says, 'Here. This place. This house. My room. The beach. The sea. The tides. The stones. The shells. The seagulls. The sound of the place. The smell.'

Lorna nods. Says nothing. Now it's time to be silent. That's about the only thing she knows, come to think of it. When to speak and when to be silent. She seems to have been born knowing it. She can remember, as a tiny girl, being astonished when people spoke during a necessary silence.

'Nothing else matters,' Elvira continues. 'I think of having to go back, and I do have to go back, I think of all the years to come, and it's nothing. It's like seeing my own ghost. It's like being my own ghost.

'But here? I know that I could be old here. No. It's more than that. I know I'm going to be old here. I can see myself old, picking up stones and putting them in my pockets. Keeping them for a little while on my window sill. Then bringing them back to the beach, and picking up different ones.'

She takes a deep breath. 'I could sing here. I haven't sung in years. Probably haven't any voice left. But I could sing here. Sing and gather stones.'

She looks down at her hands. In the space of a few days of no work, no dishes to wash, their redness has started to fade and their calluses to soften. 'But that's not a life. Singing and gathering stones. You couldn't plan for that. Live for it. Make a life out of it.'

Lorna says nothing. Elvira raises her head and looks at her. 'Could you?'

'Why don't you go back to school or something? Take art? You always wanted to go to art school.'

'Yes,' my mother said obediently, nodding over her mug of tea. 'I did, once.'

I had finally bullied her out of her Tide box china, and gotten her a set of lumpily glazed, earth-coloured mugs that crunched like concrete when they were set down. She used them when I was home from university, but I suspected that when I was away she reverted to her old chipped teacups and saucers.

'Well? Why don't you sign up for some courses or something? Dad's said he'll pay for them. And he worries about you having nothing to do, what with him at work all day and Ted moving out and me away at school.'

Actually, what my father had said was, 'Just chat with your mother when you come home. And try to keep it light. I think she's lonely.'

He had put my back up, saying that. He was her husband, after all. Wasn't it his business if she was lonely? And what did he mean by 'keep it light'? Couldn't he see that she was in a rut? That she wasn't realizing her potential? That she hardly knew there was a world out there? She was like so many women of her generation, I had told her, over and over, living in a time warp, clinging to roles that had become useless, meaningless. And if I didn't tell her these things, who would?

'You could even get your B.A.,' I went on. 'Lots of women your age are doing it.'

'I'd look like the Wreck of the Hesperus, sitting there in a class full of kids.'

'We're not kids. And most of the professors are your age or even older.'

'Well, anyway. I don't think I'm bright enough.'

'Yes, you *are!* Don't be *stupid!*'

We drank our tea in silence, save for the hum of the digital clock on top of the fridge. It had been my Christmas present to her, the only way I could force her to get rid of that damned chicken. The thing was probably still pecking away in the basement with all her other banished treasures. Probably she wound it, surreptitiously, every time she did the laundry.

I couldn't force a replacement for the string-saver on her, since she still didn't use it to save string. At least she had painted the Dutch girl's hat when she painted the kitchen, so it blended into the background a little.

But robin's-egg blue! Hadn't she heard of avocado? Or Chinese red? *Nobody* painted a kitchen robin's-egg blue. Except my mother.

My roommates and I swapped mother stories, shaking our heads, sipping cheap red wine, sharing a cigarette.

'Margarine. I kid you not. I go home. What's on the table? White bread. White sugar. And margarine.' The fact that these had been staples of our own diets as little as six months before was conveniently forgotten.

The chicken clock and string saver had me tied for first place with a girl whose mother still did her hair in pincurls. 'With bobby pins. Little metal crosses, all over her head. It looks like Arlington.'

Hats with flowers on them. White shoes and white gloves. But never before the twenty-fourth of May, we would remind each other, mock solemnly. And never after Labour Day.

In our waist-length hair, peasant skirts and pooka beads, we would groan as one. How lucky we were to have escaped the restrictions and conformity that ruled our mothers' lives.

'How long is your hair getting now?' my mother asked.

I bristled. 'Why?'

'I was just wondering. Did I ever tell you that your grandmother could sit on her hair when she was a girl?'

'I wear my hair long because I *want* to,' I said. I could never pass up an opportunity to educate my mother. 'Grandma had no choice in the matter. Keeping a girl's hair long in those days was just another way of turning her into a sex object and limiting her freedom. If she had chosen to cut her hair short, she would have been a social outcast.' I tried not to imagine my roommates' cool stares if I walked in with a pageboy or pixie cut.

My mother's lips twitched. She tried to stop them, but they twitched again.

'What?' I said. I hadn't said anything funny. Had I?

'Oh, nothing. Just something I've noticed lately. Now and then you talk like Elvira.'

I flushed. I didn't want to be compared to anybody else. I wanted to be unique. Everybody at school was trying to be unique. 'What do you mean?' I said.

'The way you pronounce things. Every single word a little jewel.'

I flushed hotter. Sometimes my mother could surprise me, and this was one of those times. She would show just a bit of grit, a cool-eyed touch of humour that had nothing to do with being a mother. It was as if she had a whole other self, a selfish self, one that could just get up and walk away from all of us and never look back. Except for these split-second glimpses, she kept it hidden. But it was there, and it could make me feel very young.

'What's Elvira doing these days?' I said, trying to change the subject without appearing to do so.

'I got a postcard from her. Just the other day. Tuesday? No, Wednesday. No, it would have been Tuesday, because –'

'Where was it *from?*'

'Just a minute. I'll get it.' She got up from the table and rummaged through the stack of coupons, bills, letters and junk mail that had always lived behind the radio. 'Here it is.'

I put my hand out. 'Don't read it to me. Let me read it for myself,' I pleaded. But she had already sat back down, holding the card and squinting at it.

'It's from Land's End. Where she always goes. Dear June, she says. I am taking my usual two weeks here. The sea and the beach are what they always are. I hope all goes well with you and your family. Elvira.'

'That's it?' I said.

My mother nodded. 'She never writes much.'

'Did she ever explain why she ran away from home that time?'

'No. She never talked about anything personal. And she hasn't even been to visit in a while. She's too busy. She was taking night school courses in business for a couple of years. On top of working all day. And now she's an office manager. For a big firm in Toronto.'

A momentary bafflement came into my mother's eyes. She had the entrenched Hamiltonian's combined worship and dread of Toronto. Why anyone would go there willingly to live was beyond her, as was the idea of a woman being an 'office manager' in a 'big firm'. One of my roommates was in large animal medicine, and my mother's only comment was, 'Imagine a girl wanting to be a vet.' She didn't disapprove. She just couldn't understand.

She couldn't understand my wanting to go away to Guelph, either, when I could have stayed home and attended McMaster. 'Why would anybody who has a home want to *leave* it?' she had asked rhetorically, over and over. Leaving home for marriage she could at least relate to. She had done as much herself. But all the years of her wifehood and motherhood, whenever she visited my grandmother, she called it 'going home'. And she had told me about lying awake in her childhood bed the night before her wedding, homesick in advance.

'Fugue,' I said. 'It's called fugue, suddenly running away for no reason.' I was taking Psych 100.

'I thought a fugue was something you played on the piano.'

'It just means flight.'

'It does? Fugue. Flight. Well, there's refuge.'

'And refugee.'

'And fugitive. Hey – remember *The Fugitive* on TV?'

Her cheeks were getting pink. She loved playing with words, always had. And she loved these talks, loved them more than I could comfortably admit. In a second, I saw all that she needed and wanted. Just some conversation with me. A bit of wordplay. An easy, uncomplicated kindness. Except it wasn't easy. Not for me.

'Let me see that postcard,' I said, reaching for it. She handed it over, hurt from my abruptness showing in her eyes for just a second.

I studied the back of the card. The handwriting was neat, almost unnaturally legible. A professional businesswoman's script. *The sea and the beach are what they always are.*

I flipped the card over and looked at the picture. Land's End. Typical east coast scene. Water. Rugged, stony shore. And far up the beach, tiny in the distance, a big old white house.

*Elvira is sitting in her room, rocking in her rocking chair. She is holding one stone. She has taken the others from the window sill back to the beach, but has kept this one. It fits perfectly in her cupped hands.*

*She lifts it near her face. Touches it with her lips. It is cool. Less smooth than it looks. She sniffs. Dust. She touches it with her tongue. Salt.*

*The stone's colour is subtle and complicated, a stippling of grey, blue and pale magenta. The spot where her tongue touched is darker, like meat, like blood. For just a moment, when she saw the stone under the water, she thought it was a heart.*

*She rocks in her chair, holding her stone. She hears a car pull up beside the house. A car door open. Shut.*

*The stone is getting warm in her hands. She imagines it dimly alive, with presence and awareness. It has been heaved into place by ice, rolled into shape by water. And now picked up and placed on a window sill by herself. She wonders if it knows where it is, what has happened to it. If it wants, if it can want, to get back to the sand and the waves.*

*She hears a knock. Hears Lorna getting up and going to see who's at the door. Hears men asking questions. Hears Lorna's answers, reluctant but truthful.*

*Elvira rocks and thinks. She could take the stone with her. Or she could leave it in this room. Or she could return it to the beach. What does the stone want?*

*Steps on the stairs up to her room. Heavy. Slow. Authoritative.*

*She brings the stone once more close to her lips. She whispers to it. Then she rocks and waits, listening to the steps, hearing them pause. She does not even turn her head to look at the uniforms filling the door to her room.*

*'Miss Tomlinson? Miss Elvira Tomlinson?'*

'I got a letter from her the other day,' my mother tells me. 'She's bought herself a big old white house. You'll never guess where.'

'No!' I say, slowly grinning.

'Yup. That's what she's gone and done. Worked hard and saved her money, all those years.'

She puts her hands flat on the kitchen table in front of her and looks down at them. She deliberately stretches and flattens them, I know, to check on the encroachment of her arthritis. The flesh of her face hangs a little forward, deepening the creases at her nose and mouth.

We are silent together for a little while. We often are now. Sometimes I'll ask her questions, to get her going on her old stories. Then I sit and listen to her digressions, which are becoming fewer and shorter. There are lapses and omissions, too. I usually remember the parts she has forgotten, but I don't correct her. I'm not sure that it isn't natural and right for parts of her stories to be falling away now, like petals.

'Didn't you tell me once that Elvira used to sing?' I coax. She glances up, her eyes round and young.

'Did I?'

'Uh-huh. You told me once that she used to sing in school. At assemblies.'

'Did I tell you that?'

'Yeah, you did. And you told me that once she had on a white dress ...' I go on encouragingly. The memory comes suddenly into focus for her.

'Oh, *right!* I remember now. And she sang – Damn it, what did she sing?' After a moment, she looks at me. 'When did I tell you that about Elvira singing?'

'Ages ago. I think I was just a kid.'

'Well, kid, you've got some memory. Funny. I can remember her singing, I can hear her voice, I can see her clear as anything. But I can't remember what she sang. And I can't remember telling you about it either. Funny.' She looks at her hands again, smiling a little to herself.

I have come for the day from Toronto, where I live now. I visit her more often than she visits me, though she can still manage the bus trip now and then. I meet her at the bus station and take her north on the subway. Each time we pass Wellesley Station, she says, 'Elvira used to live on Wellesley Street.'

Just once, early on, I suggested looking Elvira up and going for a visit. 'No, oh no,' she said quickly, her eyes taking on that frightened look that used to infuriate me. It is equal parts longing and fear, and in old age the fear is winning.

But there's more to it than that. My mother knows something about Elvira, has known it all along. And I'm beginning to think that I've known it all along too. You don't visit Elvira. She visits you. You do not haunt a ghost. You let it haunt you.

I suppose that's why, though I haven't seen Elvira in decades and will probably never see her again, hardly a month goes by that I don't search my mind and find her in it somewhere. Walking to the sea.

In my apartment I take my mother around, showing her my things. They are new to her each time, even the old things she has given me. 'Did I?' she asks wonderingly when I remind her that yes, she actually gave me the chicken-pecking clock, the Dutch girl string-saver and the pink plastic radio. She doesn't remember coming up from the basement during my last visit, wiping dust from something with her sleeve. And, when I tried to protest, pressing it on me, saying, 'Oh, come *on!* You *love* this old stuff!'

*Elvira is walking the beach. She walks with her head bent, looking for stones to pick up and take back to her house. Her hair is as grey as the sea.*
*She is singing. I strain my ears. I think I know what song it might be.*
*But the words and the tune are shredded to silence by the wind and the waves.*

# The Seven Solemn Vows of Friendship

### SOLEMN VOW THE FIRST
*To be best friends forever, forsaking all others*

*'That sounds like we're getting married.'*
*'Well, what's another word for forsaking?'*
*Sigrid shrugs. 'I don't know.'*
*'How about avoiding? Avoiding all others?'*
*'No.'*
*'Why not?'*
*'Because it sounds like we're never going to have any other friends, all our lives.'*
*'No. Just no other best friends. We can have second best and third best.'*
*'But what if one of us moves to Australia?'*
*'Well, what if we do? We can still write.'*
*'What if one of us dies?'*
*I have no answer for that. I can, with no effort at all, imagine myself in perpetual mourning, putting flowers every year on Sigrid's grave. In Australia, if necessary. But I'm not sure I can imagine her doing the same for me.*

It's her. Over there. A few tables from mine. Her hair still curves across her forehead the way it always did. That's what made me look, then look again.

She's with a man. Probably her husband. She got married when I was doing my master's at UBC. My mother clipped the wedding announcement out of the *Hamilton Spectator* and sent it to me. I remember, because there was no letter with it, not even a comment scribbled in the margin.

My mother's letters to me were usually full of little non-sequitur bulletins: *Remember Billy Pongress? Whose brother slipped off the dam and drowned in the Grand River? Well, he's a dentist now. Remember*

*Donna Phelan? Who lived with her grandmother because her parents were both in mental institutions? Well, she and her husband just bought a motel.*

In my mind I could hear her throwaway delivery of the final statement. As if the present, however fortuitous, could never make up for the past. There was no *remember?* tucked in with Sigrid's wedding announcement. And I sensed something grudging on my mother's part in the hasty, off-centre folding of the square of newsprint.

Well. My mother isn't here now, and I am. I should just get up, go over there and say, 'Hi. I'm Daisy Chandler. From next door.' We would sit and talk, the man smiling and being a good sport. It would all come back. The good things. Because there were good things. The two of us on the bus, clutching ourselves, afraid we would pee. Giggling as only eleven-year-old girls can, over an ad for Carter's Little Liver Pills. And the time we slept out in the backyard. Our mothers, two flashlight beams through the canvas. *Are you girls all right?* Then the surprise of morning. We had done it. Slept outside, all night long.

Sigrid Kiraja. My childhood friend.

She's leaning toward the man she's with, eyes generous.

*Did she ever look at me like that?*

Giving him each word like a little present.

*Did she ever talk to me that way?*

*My mother is ironing, a task that always puts her in a bad mood, especially in summer. 'Listen to me,' she says. 'I was a shy kid too.' She presses down with the iron. The damp shirt hisses, as if in pain. 'I was just as quiet and bookish as you are.' Press. Hiss. 'But I had more than one friend.'*

*So where are they all now? I imagine saying. But I won't gratify her with a single word.*

*She sprinkles the shirt, preparing it for more torture. 'You can bet Sigrid doesn't sit and mope when you're away someplace.'*

*I'm never away someplace.*

*'Anyway, this is the last time you're going to pull this. Because next year you're going to camp too.'*

*That's what she says every summer, when I drive her nuts hanging around waiting for Sigrid to get back from Estonian camp. We both know she doesn't mean it. I'd be no good at camp. At school, I can hardly get through recess. And I spend the whole year dreading Fun Day.*

*'Why don't you at least call on somebody else? Where are all the kids who were in your class last year?'*

*At camp.*

*I slump out into the back yard and sit on the swing under the willow tree. I'm too big for a swing, but I'm too big to watch Captain Kangaroo too, and I did that this morning.*

*The cuffs of my shorts are cutting into my thighs, and the edges of my thighs are pressing against the swing ropes. I hate summer, and not just because Sigrid goes away. I hate having to wear shorts and things with no sleeves. They make my arms and legs look like link sausages, pink and fat.*

*I stare through the curtain of willow whips at the Kirajas' back yard. Still empty. I lean back, hook my ankles around the swing ropes and let my head fall. The world always looks newer and cleaner upside down. The sky is a purer blue, and the leaves a shinier green. Sounds are sharper, too. The cicada drills a needle into the silence.*

*There's a tickle in my scalp from my hair just touching the ground. That means my mother will send me to get it cut again, any day now. I want long hair like Sigrid's, but my mother says mine is too thick to wear long. There's something else I can tell she's thinking, even if she never says it. Long hair only looks good if you're thin.*

*I wonder if Sigrid's hair will be shorter when she gets back. She was plotting to get one of the girls at camp to cut it for her. It's down to her waist now, all wavy and exactly the colour of Billy Bee honey. I don't know why anybody would want to get rid of anything so gorgeous. But Sigrid wants to look like Annette Funicello, and you can't do that with Estonian hair.*

*So every month we go through the new issue of Teen magazine until she finds something she likes. She's collected a whole shoeboxful of rollers and bobby pins and clips. I help her roll and pin her hair up to look like the photograph. Then I hold a mirror while she watches the pins work themselves out and the hair pull itself down with its own weight. 'Shi—' she says, just stopping short of putting the 't' on it.*

*When Sigrid almost-swears like that, it reminds me that she's six months older than me, just enough to put her a grade ahead in school. It's always made a difference, but it's going to make a really big difference in September.*

*I sit back up and turn in a circle, twisting the swing ropes as tight as they'll go. Then I lift my feet and spin. I do it again and again until, when I stop, the Kirajas' back yard turns like a slow-motion merry-go-round.*

*In September, for the first time in our lives, Sigrid and I are going to set out in the morning in different directions. I'll still be in public school, and she'll be starting junior high. I've watched the junior high girls walking together in bunches, all giggling and chummy. They tease their hair into beehives and wear white lipstick. Sometimes they even smoke.*

*Sigrid and I have been friends since before I can remember. We tried to be blood sisters once, but the bread and butter knife we sneaked out of her kitchen was too blunt to cut our fingers, and we didn't really want to try anything sharper. And last summer we wrote down Seven Solemn Vows of Friendship. Well, six. We couldn't think of a seventh, but we didn't like the sound of Six Solemn Vows. We memorized them, folded the piece of paper then wrapped it in Saran Wrap and buried it in my back yard. And we promised to come back when we were old and dig it up and add the seventh vow, which we probably would have been able to think of by then.*

*Sigrid tells me I'm her best friend. She's said so lots of times, looking straight into my eyes. I know she has other friends. She's popular at school. Her class sits in front of ours in assembly, and girls fight to sit next to her. 'Sit beside me, Sigrid!' 'No, sit beside me!' She just smiles and sits between them.*

*I've watched her, trying to figure out what she does to make herself popular. She doesn't do anything. She just is. Popular. One of those words that sound like what they mean. Kind of tall, and bouncy, and breezy.*

*But I'm still her best friend. She says so, and she lets me practise with her for when we have boyfriends. And that's something you'd only do with your best friend.*

*But sometimes, in the middle of it, I get a picture in my head of how we must look together, and I pull away from her. I can't help it. It isn't because I don't want to do it with her any more. It's because I don't know*

76

*why she would want to do it with me.*

♦ ♦ ♦

SOLEMN VOW THE SECOND
*To feel forever the way we feel about each other right now*

*'That doesn't make any sense.'*
*'Yes, it does. Why doesn't it?'*
*'Because you can't help how you feel. You just feel.'*
*'But you can feel friendship for somebody. Can't you?'*
*'Yeah, but if you do feel it, then you don't have to take a vow to. Because you already do.'*
*'But the vow is to feel it forever.'*
*'Well, you can't make yourself do that either. I mean, if you don't feel it right now, there's no point taking a vow to feel it forever.'*
*But we do feel it right now. Don't we, Sigrid? So we will feel it forever. Won't we?*

She's changed. Of course she's changed. She was twelve the last time I saw her. Her hair is short now, and the honey colour has darkened. She has a bit of thickening at the waist, and the hint of a double chin.

*You must not take pleasure in these things,* I tell myself, like a nun examining her conscience. I wish sometimes that having been a stubby, bespectacled child might have taught me charity. Or at least not to place importance in appearances. But it doesn't seem to work that way.

I'm always amazed whenever someone says, 'Daisy *Chandler?* I would *never* have recognized you!' Because I'm still stubby and bespectacled. But I have learned something, and the learning must make a difference. The secret to being popular, I know now, is to look people in the eye and silently ask the question, *Who needs you?* And I suppose I have Sigrid Kiraja to thank for that, however belatedly.

The man she's having lunch with is about our age, forty-five, forty-six. Thin. Dark hair. Balding at the back. Glasses. A lean, Jacques Brel-ish look to his face. I wonder what kind of a lover he is.

77

*Practising for when we have boyfriends.* I'd forgotten about that. The way we assigned purpose, gave practical justification, to this thing we had suddenly started to do. What girls of a certain age have always done. And it was so innocent. No clothes off. No hands even under clothes. Just her breath on my neck. My fingertips tracing her ear.

I can even remember what got us started. One Saturday night, on *Saturday Night at the Movies*, we watched *On the Waterfront* and fell simultaneously in love with Marlon Brando. For days afterward, we re-enacted the scene where he and Eva Marie Saint finally kiss for the first time, sliding down a wall and ending up on the ground. We didn't slide down a wall. And we didn't discuss who would be who, either. We didn't have to. I had to be Marlon Brando, because I couldn't possibly be the blonde, beautiful Eva Marie Saint. The very thought was so funny it hurt.

Sigrid's laughing at something the man has said. She loves him. I can see that in the way she leans into the space between them, in the soft, easy laughter she gives him, as readily as she would pass him the salt.

I drop my eyes to my plate. Take a sip of my coffee. Look back up through my lashes. I was sure, just then, that she was going to turn and catch me staring. But no. She's still talking to Jacques Brel.

Odd connection to make. I haven't thought about Jacques Brel in years. Now the song 'If You Go Away' is running through my head, and probably will for the next forty-eight hours.

Oh, well, at least it's a half-decent song. I once heard a recording of Brel singing it in French. His throat sounded dry, as if from tears.

I wish I knew more of the lyrics than I do. All I can remember now is *If you go away ... If you go away ... If you go away ...* And then the soaring, desperate, *But if you stay, I'll make you a day ...* What does that mean? I'll make you a day? Wait. Here it comes. *Like no day has been, or will be again.*

*My face is inches from Sigrid's feet. I'm under the tent in the back yard. Really under it, under its canvas floor. It's early evening. The grass is cool, and it tickles my stomach. The backs of Sigrid's heels are almost close enough to kiss.*

78

*The feet turn sideways. Then they face me, the toes toasted on top, pale on the sides. Then they turn the other way. This is the longest I've ever hidden from her. I always give myself away when we play hide and seek. I guess I'm afraid that if it takes her too long to find me, she might stop looking.*

*'Sigrid!'*

*Her mother's voice.*

*'Tule tuppa!'*

*I'm pretty sure that means, come in now, or time for bed, or something like that. I know Estonians say ordinary things to each other. But I like to think that they say them in an elevated, almost Biblical way, like the characters in the folk tales I'm always reading:*

*'Wife, is my dinner prepared?'*

*'It is, my husband. I shall summon your children to partake of it with you.'*

*I can't believe Mr Kiraja would ever say what my father came out with the other night. 'Y'know, I've been eating eggs all my life, and I don't see any reason to stop.' Or that Mrs Kiraja would answer, the way my mother did, 'Oh, terrific. All through supper, you don't say a word. Then when you do, it's about eggs.'*

*So now I imagine Sigrid's mother saying something along the lines of, 'Night falls, my child. Return to the hearth.' Sigrid answers, 'Ja ma tulen, Memme,' which I translate as 'I hear, my mother, and I obey.'*

*Then I watch her feet turn and start to walk home. She must know that I'm somewhere right near her. I wait for her to call to me. To say something like 'I have to go now, Daisy. Sorry I can't look for you any more.' But she doesn't. She doesn't say anything. Just turns and walks away.*

*'Let her go,' I can imagine my mother telling me. But I scramble up out of my hiding place, scraping my back on the edge of the canvas. 'See you tomorrow, Sigrid!' I call hopefully. Silence. She's already slipped through the hole in the backyard fence, turned the corner and disappeared into her house.*

*Sometimes Sigrid just does things like this. I can't tell if she's being mean, or just not being anything. I think I'd rather she was being mean. But either way, I have my work cut out for me. I have to take whatever she did and turn it into something I can stand to think about.*

*Okay. Maybe she forgot to say good night to me. No. Nobody's that stupid. And Sigrid's not stupid at all.*

*Maybe her mother's mad at her, and she had to leave right away, or else get into trouble. So she didn't have time to say anything. No. Her mother didn't sound mad. And how long does it take to say good night?*

*Or maybe she wasn't really looking for me. Because she knew where I was all the time, and she was just pretending to look. And she thought I knew that she knew. So she didn't have to say good night. So she didn't. So it's okay. I guess.*

*I know what my mother would say. 'Sigrid doesn't care about you, Daisy. She doesn't need you. So don't you care either. And don't you need her.'*

*Stupid thing to say. Like telling somebody not to be hungry, when they are. Or not to be thirsty, when they are.*

I appear to have slowed my eating to keep pace with Sigrid's and Jacques Brel's. What do I have in mind? Going out the door the same time they do, brushing against her accidentally on purpose, as we used to say, then appearing to see her for the first time? 'Sigrid? Sigrid *Kiraja*? Is that *you?*' Blasé. Breezy. In control.

Well, why not? There was more to my childhood than her. And there was more to our friendship than my offering up worship and her extending noblesse oblige.

But that's what I remember. First and foremost. Unless I make an effort, my default childhood memory is of waiting for Sigrid, who never comes. Wanting Sigrid, who doesn't want me. And it's always summer. The summer we were twelve. Just before she went away.

(*If you go away* ... There's that damned song again.)

♦ ♦ ♦

SOLEMN VOW THE THIRD
**To respect and uphold everything that each other stands for**

*'So what do we stand for?'*
*'Well, you could stand for Estonia.'*
*'I was born in England.'*

*'Yeah, but your parents are Estonian. You speak Estonian. You go to Estonian camp in the summer and Estonian school on Saturdays.'*

*'Don't remind me.'*

*I wonder what I stand for. For Canada? We stand on guard for thee. I don't know how to stand on guard. And I always think it sounds kind of silly. But if I don't stand for Canada, what do I stand for? 'Stand up for yourself!' my mother keeps telling me. But I don't know how to do that either. And I'm not sure it's the same thing.*

Even now, when the Baltics make the news, I pay attention. I can't let an article about post-*glasnost* Estonia go unread. I take an odd, vicarious pride in the way it kept its identity through centuries of oppression by Czars, Nazis, Soviets. The way it threw off even Gorbachev's easy yoke.

Estonia. A clean, cold stone under fast running water. Deeper than it looks. Too slippery to prise.

*Under water, Sigrid's lips are cold. We float in the pounding silence, arms out, legs spread. Joined at the mouth.*

*We can't stay down for long. A bump of noses, a hint of tooth, then back up into the screaming air, the chlorine, the bare feet slapping on wet cement.*

*It was my idea to try it under water. I like being under water. It makes me feel light and cool and graceful.*

*That must be the way Sigrid feels all the time. Maybe it goes with being Estonian. Her whole family is tall and thin and blond. Even the Grandmother still has bits of yellow in her grey braids.*

*My family is short and dumpy and dark. Last year I read* The Time Machine *and it made me think of the Kirajas as Eloi, and us as Morlocks.*

*'Well, let's see,' my mother started in when I asked her what we were. Right away I knew I wasn't going to like the answer.*

*'I'm mostly Scottish, both sides. Except my father's people had some Spanish in them. Because of the Armada. I mean, it sank just to the left of Scotland, and some of those guys must have swum ashore. That's why my father's mother's name was Isabella, by the way. Remember Isabella of Spain? Who gave Columbus the money to sail the ocean blue? In*

*fourteen hundred and ninety-two? In the* Nina, *the* Pinta *and –'*
'*The* Santa Maria*! I know! What about Dad?'*
'*Your father? Oh, he's a real mix. His father was English, you might as well say. English for generations, anyway. But his mother was Welsh by descent. She once went back to Wales and sang in an eisteddfod. Do you know what that is? An eisteddfod? It's –'*
'*I know!' I said, even though I didn't. You had to kind of herd my mother when you talked to her. 'So Dad's English and Welsh? Nothing else?' Please God, nothing else.*
*'Actually, he's French. Way back, I mean. Before his people turned mostly English. That's where the name Chandler comes from. It means candle maker. And don't pull a face just because I've told you that before. But you know what? There's even some Pennsylvania Dutch in your father. Somewhere. Because his people were Loyalists down in the States. And before they came up here, they must have rubbed shoulders with the Dutch down there. Because way back, he's supposed to be related to the seven Van Valleck brothers.'*
'*Who are the seven Van Valleck brothers?'*
'*People your father's supposed to be related to.'*
The way she said it, I thought there might be a statue erected to them somewhere. The seven of them, all in a row, cast in bronze. Clog-dancing against a frieze of windmills.

Sigrid still looks as Estonian as she ever did. There's the high-bridged nose I remember, and the firm jaw. And her eyes still have that characteristic Baltic tilt.

When we were children, it made perfect sense to me that if Sigrid and her little sister Elva had sandwiches for lunch made with Wonder bread, then there just had to be something essentially Estonian about Wonder bread. The same went for the clothes the Kirajas wore, the car they drove, their house. Their Estonianness filled them up and overflowed onto everything they touched.

In their living room, the carpet, the drapes, the frames around the few, carefully spaced landscape prints, were all the same colour. It was a light, neutral shade that made me think of the theme music from *Lawrence of Arabia*. 'Oh for God's sake, Daisy,' my mother said when I tried to describe it to her. 'That's beige.'

It was not beige. It could not possibly be beige. Secretly, I named it *Plains of Estonia*.

The bedroom Sigrid shared with Elva was pink with white trim, exactly like a girl's room in a magazine. Ballet prints on the walls. White bedspreads smooth as snow. And high up on a shelf, a huge, untouched doll.

There was a playroom in the basement of the Kirajas' house, where the girls were allowed to make a bit of a mess. That was where the balding teddy bears lived, the play farm with red, blue and green plastic animals spilling out, and the forever-naked Barbie surrounded by all her clothes.

But how wonderful, I would think, to have the untidiness corralled. To keep the mess confined to one place that visitors, ushered into that perfect living room, would never see. How *Estonian*.

My mother believed it was more important to read library books than to decorate. And a certain amount of clutter, she maintained, was homey. Natural. Normal.

Which was why I could never decide what was worse. Going from our house to the Kirajas', or coming from the Kirajas' house back to ours.

Our living room had blue floral drapes from Aunt Ella Chandler and a cranberry satin couch from Grandma McEwen. None of us could sit on the couch without my mother warning us not to bounce and not to spill. Meanwhile, the cat had shredded the lower edge to fringe.

One of the end tables had been made by my brother in grade eight shop class, out of plywood stained to look like walnut. The other was a blond Arborite split-level thing that hadn't made it to some aunt or uncle's cottage.

I had never seen the coffee table. It hid under stacks of *Redbook*, *Family Circle* and *Woman's Day* that Aunt Heather passed on to my mother, who bundled them, unread, to take to Grandma McEwen whenever a new stack arrived. Underneath it was the cat's bed, never slept in, a wicker basket with a cushion covered in McEwen tartan.

I decided at one point that my mother simply didn't know any better, and that it was up to me to teach her.

'Why do we always eat in the kitchen?' I asked, as patiently as I could.

'Oh, just because we do.'

'But why?'

'It's easy that way. The stove and fridge are there.'

'Couldn't we eat in the dining room? The Kirajas always do.'

'Well, bully for the Kirajas.'

'But couldn't we do it, just now and then?'

'We do when there's company.'

There was never company. Relatives might drop in, but in our family it was polite to make a big deal of getting up to leave as soon as it was suppertime.

I decided that if I beautified the dining room, it might lure my mother in the direction of gracious living. I rummaged in the linen closet, disturbing the sleeping cat, and found a lace doily to put in the middle of the dining-room table. Then I took a blue china bowl that had always sat empty on the bathroom window ledge, filled it with a bunch of artificial pansies that had been thumbtacked forever over my father's basement workbench, and put that in the middle of the doily. I spent my own money on two feet of yellow paper ribbon to tie back the plastic lace dining-room curtains.

'That's nice,' my mother admitted when I was done. She stood in the doorway and kept her face cool and slack. 'It's pretty.' Then she went back into the kitchen to set the table for supper.

Sometimes I used to imagine the Grandmother, smelling as she did faintly of bleach, marching into my bedroom and ordering me up off the bed where I was sprawled with a book. *Beds are for sleeping*, she would say in Estonian, which I would miraculously understand. *Books belong on a shelf.* She would make me take down the school projects I had thumbtacked to the walls, and put my drawings and stories in a scrapbook. Then she would promise to return next week for inspection.

*'So, where is your grandfather?' I whisper. 'Like, where does he live?'*

*'In prison,' Sigrid whispers back.*

*We have to be quiet. Sigrid is sitting in one of the pebbled paths that criss-cross the Grandmother's vegetable garden, pounding stones to bits*

84

*with a tack hammer. The Grandmother is a few yards away, furiously hoeing.*

'Does your grandfather wear a suit with stripes on it? Does he have a chain on his leg with an iron ball on the end?'

'I don't know.'

'So how do you know he's in prison?'

'He sends letters sometimes.'

'What does he say in them?'

'He says he's alive.'

'Doesn't he say anything else?'

'He can't. If he does, they cut it out.'

'Cut what out?'

*Sigrid rolls her eyes back. She hates it when I ask her about Estonian stuff.*

*But I can't help it. Every Sunday night, I hear Walter Cronkite talking about the Iron Curtain. Even though I know better, I see it as a miles-high curtain of heavy, cold iron mesh. And I see it crashing down in front of the Grandfather just as the rest of the Kirajas scramble out of Estonia.*

'They take scissors and cut the words they don't like out of his letters.'

'What words don't they like?'

'How should I know? They're all cut out.'

*... His letters looked like paper snowflakes ...*

*That just came into my head. It sounds like the start of one of my stories. I wonder if I should say it out loud to Sigrid. She used to like to hear me tell stories. But now she thinks they're childish. She gave me a look yesterday when we were exploring the new subdivision that's being built, and I said it was as if somebody had baked a loaf of house, then cut it off in slices.*

*I leave, slip through the hole in the fence and come back again with my father's hammer. When the Grandmother sees me, she claps a speck-led hand over her mouth and turns her back.*

*I sit beside Sigrid. Together we pound stones, the chunk chunk of our hammer blows uneven at first, then falling into a rhythm.*

'Why is she making you do this?'

'I skipped out of Estonian school.'

'But why is she making you pound stones?'

*'She thinks having to bust rocks is really horrible.'*

*'Why?'*

*'I don't know!' Sigrid says, forgetting to whisper. The Grandmother spins around and fixes us with her raisin eyes. We both start to pound furiously. Seeing me, the old lady turns away again, leans on her hoe and stands with her pointy little shoulders jerking up and down.*

*'Is she laughing at me?' I whisper after a while.*

*'Yeah, she thinks you're a scream.'*

*'Why?'*

*'Because,' Sigrid pauses. 'You're not thin.' When she sees my look, she says, 'There was a famine when she was growing up, and some of her brothers and sisters died.' Then, accusingly, 'She's always bugging me to eat more.'*

*I look at the Grandmother with new interest. The only famines I've heard about are in the Bible and the Brothers Grimm. The Grandmother hardly speaks English at all, and she doesn't even know my name. She calls me something that sounds like Margaret. More like Margretta. But I don't know her name either. I don't even know whose mother she is, Mr or Mrs Kiraja's. So I just think of her as the Grandmother. It's her husband who's behind the Iron Curtain. And she's the one who says Sigrid can't cut her hair. She's in charge of things like that.*

*We pound stones for a few minutes in silence. Then I whisper, 'Why did you skip out of Estonian school?' As long as I can remember, Sigrid has gone downtown to Estonian school every Saturday afternoon, even in the summer holidays.*

*'I hate it. And I'm not going back.' She pounds viciously with her hammer, sending a pebble ricocheting down the path.*

*'What do you do there?'*

*'Nothing.'*

*'You must do something.'*

*'We talk.'*

*'What about?'*

*'Nothing.'*

*'You can't talk about nothing. Come on. What do you talk about?'*

*'Estonia! What else?'*

*She shouldn't have yelled. The Grandmother spins around again and barks something. Estonian is a liquid language, more vowel than consonant. But the old lady gives it an edge that jerks Sigrid to her feet. The Grandmother thrusts the hoe into her hands and marches into the house. On the way, she looks at me, grins again and claps a hand over her mouth.*

*I go on pounding stones, looking up every now and then at Sigrid as she hoes. 'I'm sorry!' I finally stage-whisper. 'When she lets you go, do you want to come over and watch* I Love Lucy*?'*

*'I can't. I have folk dance.'*

*Once a year, I go to Sigrid's dance recital downtown at the Estonian Centre. She dances with a bunch of other blonde girls, all wearing Estonian national costumes. Hers is bright red with white lace. She dances in soft black shoes, and her hair is like a flame behind her.*

*I would take her folk-dance lesson for her, if I could. I would go to Estonian school for her, too. Even spend two weeks at Estonian camp every summer in her place.*

*But all I can do is sit and pound stones.*

◆ ◆ ◆

### SOLEMN VOW THE FOURTH
*To uphold and encourage each other
in the achievement of all our future ambitions*

*'Maybe it should just be ambitions,' I say. 'Not future ambitions. Because all ambitions are in the future.'*

*'No, they're not. You can be ambitious right now.'*

*Sigrid and I are sitting on either side of the Door to Below. Our bare toes nudge like small noses around its concrete edge. The Door to Below is the name I've given it, even though I know it's just a manhole cover. It's in the middle of the big empty lot at the end of our street where the new subdivision's being built. On the edge of the lot are three dead elm trees that I've named the Women of Grey. I hope they don't cut them down when they finish putting in the new houses.*

*Sigrid and I have been coming here as long as I can remember. We're here today to finish writing the Seven Solemn Vows.*

*'I'm going to be a scientist,' Sigrid says. 'And I'm going to find the cure for cancer.'*

*I wait for her to ask me what my ambition is. When she doesn't, I just go ahead and tell her anyway. 'I'm going to write children's books. And illustrate them myself.'*

*Sigrid smiles at me the way she hardly ever does any more. She used to like my stories. Maybe she'll listen to the one I've just started to make up, about the Women of Grey and the Door to Below.*

*Sometimes I imagine myself sort of fitting into Sigrid's family when we're grown up. Being kind of the way Elvira Tomlinson is to my family – not quite a relative, but more than a friend. Almost an aunt.*

*'Maybe someday your kids will read my books,' I say.*

*But Sigrid shakes her head. 'I'm never going to marry or have kids. I'll be too busy finding the cure for cancer.'*

*How can she do that? Just throw away everything that I keep trying not to hope for. Because nobody's ever going to want me. I'm pretty sure of that. But I've seen the way boys at the pool are starting to look at Sigrid when she walks by in her bathing suit. She could have anybody she wants. And she doesn't want anybody at all.*

To write and illustrate children's books. I'd forgotten about that. And I can't even imagine doing it now. I haven't drawn anything in years, and I doubt that I ever really had a children's book in me.

As for marriage and parenthood, I did come close once, so close I still get scared thinking about it. But the whole package has changed in my imagination from a prize I once despaired of winning to a land mine I just missed stepping on. I'm not even anyone's eccentric aunt, because so many of my friends are also single and childless.

*So many of my friends.* Now there's a phrase I once never thought I would use.

I wonder if Sigrid has children. I've spied a wedding ring on her left hand, so I'm pretty sure she and Jacques Brel are married. And if she has kids, what books does she read to them, I wonder. What stories does she tell them?

*'The Women of Grey,' I begin, 'aren't really dead. And they aren't still, either. They're moving all the time. So slowly that the naked eye can't see it.'*

*'So how do we know they're really moving?' Sigrid says, looking at the three skeletal elm trees.*

'We just know. We just have to believe it. Because they are.' I'm starting to feel a tightness across the back of my head. I had forgotten how
hard it could be to tell Sigrid one of my stories. But now that she's let me
start, I'm not going to stop.

'They're moving toward the Door to Below,' I continue, tapping the
manhole cover with my foot. 'Once, a long time ago, they grew around
the Door to Below, and they were leafy and green and birds sang in their
branches. That was when the Shining Ones lived on top of the earth. The
Shining Ones were people who heard music in their heads all the time,
and only talked in rhymes. But then something terrible happened.'

'What?'

'I haven't decided yet. I'll have to think about it. Anyway, something terrible happened, and all the Shining Ones had to go Below, down
through the Door. And the green leafy trees turned all grey the way they
are now, and were banished to where they are to this day.'

'That's not very far to be banished,' Sigrid says, still looking at the
elms.

'It is when you think about how slow they move,' I say. I really am
getting a headache now. 'Because that's what they're doing. They're
moving all the time, trying to get back to the Door to Below. Because
when they do get back to it, the Door will open, and the Shining Ones will
come back up to live on the earth, and the Women of Grey will be green
and leafy again, and birds will sing in their branches once more.'

'That's it?' Sigrid says after I stop.

'Well, I have to work on it. And then there'll be the pictures too.'

Sigrid looks back at the elms. 'You know something?' she says. 'If
those trees were really moving, there's a way we could tell.'

'How?' I say, though I don't really want to know. Sigrid has a way of
taking my stories and turning them into something else, something I can't
name. I just know that whatever it is, I don't like it.

'String. We could take a ball of string, and tie one end to one of the
trees.—'

'Women of Grey.'

'Yeah. Whatever. And then we could stretch it out to reach to the
manhole—'

'The Door to Below.'

'Right. And then every day, we could stretch the string out, and see if *the distance is getting any shorter. And we could snip bits off, and measure them. And that way, we could see how much the trees have moved in a day, or a week, or a month, or even a year.'*

*I don't bother to remind her that the trees are the Women of Grey. I hate what she's done. I can't put a name to it, but I still hate it.*

*'Hey,' she says softly, touching my knee. 'It doesn't matter. It's just a story.'*

♦ ♦ ♦

SOLEMN VOW THE FIFTH
*To be loyal and true,*
*and to do unto each other as we would have each other do unto us*

*'That doesn't sound right. Does it?'*

*'Sure it does. It's fine,' Sigrid says, looking bored. It was my idea to write the Solemn Vows, and we've been at it for three afternoons.*

*It's getting harder and harder to hold Sigrid's attention. I'll say something like, Do you want to play with Barbie and Ken? And she'll shrug and say, If you want to. It's the same with watching TV, or going to the pool, or reading Teen magazine, or anything I suggest. If you want to, Daisy. Or, I don't care, Daisy. Whatever you want to do.*

*I'm afraid to suggest practising for when we have boyfriends, even though we haven't done that in a long time. I don't think I could stand it if Sigrid shrugged and said, Only if you want to, Daisy.*

Sometimes I try to imagine what my mother would have written about me, if I had been the subject of one of her little bulletins: *Remember Daisy Chandler? Who was so pathetically grateful if anybody at all gave her the time of day?* Or: *Remember Daisy Chandler? Who was so easy to put down and push around that it wasn't even fun?* Or: *Remember Daisy Chandler? Who always brought a book to read at recess, to make it look like she really wanted to be all by herself?*

*Well, she's a writer now.*

No. Those aren't my mother's words. They're mine. They're my own indictment of the child I was.

The child I was could neither walk nor talk without worrying about doing it *right*. And *right* never meant what came naturally to me, what I would do without thinking. Instead, I would eavesdrop on conversations between girls in my class, dwelling on certain phrases, rehearsing them in my head. How did they know the right thing to say? And the right words to say it with?

In the classroom, where there were questions to answer and tests to pass and marks to earn, I was sort of in my element. But outside on the playground, I was a freak. A small adult, old from the neck up, soft and slow from the neck down. Flinching from thrown balls. Tangling my feet in turning ropes.

What tripped me up most painfully were the group dynamics of preteen girls. Their subtle politics, impulsive loves and hates, were as mystifying to me as the sudden, eyeblink shifts in direction of a school of fish.

*I think I've made Sigrid mad. When I came across the school play-ground to be with her and the grade six girls, her face went hard the way it sometimes does if she opens her door and it's me, and she doesn't want to see me just then.*

*I don't say anything, just stay on the edge of the circle they've formed. Up until grade five, it's all right to play games at recess. But once you're in grade six, you're supposed to stand in a circle and talk, like women.*

*They're talking about teachers I don't have yet, and subjects I won't study until next year. I know some of their names, though. Gillian, who talks the most. Anne Marie, who is the only one who smiles at me. Betty, who looks at me, then looks at Sigrid and smirks.*

*Maybe Sigrid's embarrassed. After all, I'm not supposed to be with her at recess. We walk to school together every morning, and that's all right. But once we're on the playground, she goes over to the grade six girls, and I'm supposed to stay with the grade fives. But today the grade fives were choosing teams for baseball, and the two captains got into a fight over who had to have me.*

*I hadn't brought a book to read, and nobody was skipping, so I couldn't go and offer to turn ropes. But I couldn't just stand alone all through recess. So I came over and tried to join Sigrid's group.*

*I can't blame Sigrid for being embarrassed. After all, it's not her fault that I can't throw, catch, hit or run. For a couple of mornings now, on the way to school, she'll walk too fast, keeping ahead of me the whole way, and not talking. I'll just hurry along behind, trying to catch up, hoping it won't be too long before she decides not to be mad any more.*

I'm looking at her now. This thoroughly ordinary woman, sitting having lunch and talking to her husband.

I suppose what's keeping me glued to this chair is the fear that if I go over there and show her what a poised, successful taxpayer I've become, she'll see right through it to the awkward, beggarly child I was. The one whose need was bigger than her pride.

My friends and I now brag about having been misfits and maladroits as children. We make it a point of honour to have been unpopular or funny-looking, alternately picked on and ignored. In fact, I don't think I even know anyone now who wasn't once a bully's delight. It's even possible that a miserable childhood is a prerequisite for being my friend.

So I join in when the bragging begins. God knows, I have stories to tell. But it's so safe, what we do. We frame. We edit. We show the scar, but never the wound. We're buffered by time. Accomplishment. Hard-won popularity. And the added convenience that none of us actually knew each other *when*.

I am a refugee from *when*. Every Sunday night, when my parents watched Walter Cronkite's *The Twentieth Century*, there would be jumpy, grainy film clips of refugees. Kerchiefed women, gaunt men, blank-eyed children peeking over the edges of wagons and wheelbarrows. Pushing, pulling, trundling, trudging. Forever running away.

When I dream about my childhood, the dream is jumpy and grainy, like those films. And I wake up thinking, *Oh no, not again!* Whole minutes go by before I can trust the sudden kindness of here and now.

Except I never entirely trust it. To this day, kindness astonishes me. Its grace and simplicity are those of the high-wire artist. There are so many ways to fall, and only one way to balance.

But at least I believe in kindness now. Back then, I could never accept it for what it was. I kept waiting for it to show its real face. Only cruelty rang true. Its origin mystified me, and I could never return it in kind. But I always knew it for what it was, and never doubted its reality.

Sigrid and Jacques Brel have finished their lunch. The waiter has brought them coffee. Soon they'll get up and go.

Who said, *May your first love be your last?* And is it a blessing, or a curse?

I have never loved anyone the way I loved Sigrid Kiraja. I have never since felt such hunger. Such thirst. Such gratitude for a crumb. A drop.

◆ ◆ ◆

SOLEMN VOW THE SIXTH

*To always know where each other is, and what each other is doing, no matter how aged we become or how far apart we do dwell*

*'Yeah, okay. So we'll write letters to each other. That's not a big deal.'*

*'But maybe we should decide how often we'll write. Like once a month?'*

*Sigrid shrugs. 'Whatever.'*

*I can't stand the thought of someday not knowing where Sigrid is, and what she's doing. It'll be bad enough when she starts junior high. But after that, there's high school. Then university. And it's not just different schools pulling us apart, either. There'll be new friends. Boyfriends. For her, anyway.*

*It doesn't seem to bother her at all, that everything's going to be different soon. Maybe she wants it to be different. Maybe she can't wait for it to start.*

So what am I going to do? Just sit here? Let her get up and go without even trying to make contact? Lose her all over again?

I don't know what I want to do. And I certainly don't know what she wants. Never did, come to think of it.

I have no keepsakes of Sigrid. No friendship ring, no lock of hair. If I wrote to her after she moved to Toronto, which I must have done, I don't remember her ever sending a letter back. And then, three years or so later, when her father was transferred back to

Hamilton, she didn't phone. Never tried to contact me again.

'You've always hated Sigrid, haven't you?' I say in what I hope are icy, Bette Davis tones. 'And you're glad she's going away.'

My mother sets the iron up on its end and looks at me. She has just finished telling me what Mrs Kiraja told her over the fence this morning. Mr Kiraja's company has transferred him to Toronto. The whole family will be gone before September, to give Sigrid and Elva time to settle in to their new schools. 'And don't look at me like that,' she finished up. 'I'm just telling you.'

No, she isn't. She's trying to make it worse. I can tell by the flat, matter-of-fact way she gave me the news. It was as if she was telling me some second cousin I hardly knew had died. So that's why I said what I said, about her always hating Sigrid.

'No,' my mother answers in a controlled, reasonable voice I'm not expecting. 'I haven't always hated Sigrid. I can't be bothered hating her. But I am glad she's moving. For your sake. Because of the way she treats you. And the way you let her get away with it. There. That's what I hate.'

She puts my father's ironed shirt on a hanger. Something in its mute white presence seems to ally itself with her. Agree, infuriatingly, with every word she has said.

'You're just jealous.' My words have an odd, wooden sound. They almost feel like pieces of wood coming out of my mouth, falling clunk to the floor. It would be so easy to stop. But I go on, as if reading lines from a script. 'Because at least I have a friend. But you want me to turn out to be just like you. Just staying in your kitchen all day long. Waiting for your husband and kids to come home. Or your mother to phone. Because there isn't anybody else.'

My mother pauses in hanging up my father's shirt, her back to me. Then she completes the gesture. Click, goes the hook of the hanger on the broom closet doorknob, no louder than it ever is. Then she turns and looks out the kitchen window. Opens her mouth. Takes in a breath. Lets it out.

My mother has always said that she believes in keeping herself to herself. Minding her own business. Not getting involved with the neighbours. She's always said that people who are in each other's pockets, who can't get through a day without visiting and gossiping, just don't have enough to think about or enough to do.

*I've always known what's underneath all that. I've always known how lonely she really is. But I've never said it. It was one of those things you don't even let yourself think, let alone say. Except now I have. And it's the worst thing I've ever done. And I don't know what's going to happen now. Everything's different. I take a breath, and I know that even the air has changed.*

*My mother finally turns to face me again. She doesn't say anything about what I've just done. But she looks as if she's made up her mind about something. 'Just tell me this,' she says, still in that controlled, woman-to-woman tone of voice. 'Did Sigrid get around to telling you she was moving to Toronto?'*

*I don't answer. Don't even shake my head no. All I can think is, Toronto. A city miles and miles from here. A city like an ocean, endless and grey.*

*'Because that's something else I found out from Mrs Kiraja. Sigrid's known for ages. Since before the summer even started. Did she bother to mention it to you?'*

*I just sit and stare at my mother. My eyes feel cold and dry. Come on, I tell myself. Come on. You can do this. There must be all kinds of good reasons why she didn't say anything. Maybe her mother told her not to. No. Because then why would Mrs Kiraja go ahead and tell my mother? Maybe Sigrid was too grief-stricken to say anything about moving. Too afraid of breaking down completely. But even I know better than that.*

*I can't think of anything else. I can't make up any more excuses for Sigrid. And all at once I feel very tired.*

*'What's it going to take, Daisy? How much proof do you need? Sigrid doesn't come running after you, does she? And she doesn't knock on your door night and day. Or phone you up and say, Please, please, please come over, can't you, can't you please? The way you do with her. Until it just makes me sick to hear you. And now she doesn't even let you know she's moving away in a matter of weeks. Maybe she thought you'd figure it out when you saw the moving van. Maybe she was going to send you a post-card.'*

*I wish I didn't have a face. Or that my face was carved out of rock. So that it wouldn't move all over the place, the way it's starting to do.*

*'Oh, don't. Don't. Stop it. Stop it right now. She's not worth it. So stop. Come on, honey. Don't. You don't need her. She's not worth it.'*

*I pull away from my mother and scream that she's lying, that I hate her. And I do. But not because she's lying.*

The waiter has brought their bill. Sigrid is looking in her purse, Jacques Brel in his wallet. They're comparing what they have, making change.

I never forgave Sigrid for not telling me she was moving. I couldn't forgive her, because I never blamed her in the first place. No, I managed to blame myself, not only for her silence, but for the very fact of her going away.

It had nothing to do with her father being transferred, I decided. It had to do with me. Sigrid was going away because I wanted her to stay. I was losing her because I wanted to keep her. And because I needed her more than I needed anyone else, she was the very person I was going to have to do without. It was all part of that monstrous cruelty I had always sensed lurking beneath the surface kindness of the world.

They're getting ready to leave. Pushing their chairs back. Standing up.

In time, I came to realize that there was something besides that cruelty. There was an equally monstrous kindness. And it was this kindness that had made my mother do what she did in the kitchen that day. But I never told her what I had come to understand. I would not give her the satisfaction. And so began the classic cold war of adolescence.

They're heading for the door. I wonder which way they'll turn, out on the street. I wonder where Sigrid lives, and what she does, and if she has children, and if she's happy.

*Let her go,* I hear my mother saying. *Just let her go away. Forget about her. Once and for all.*

◆ ◆ ◆

SOLEMN VOW THE SEVENTH

*Sigrid is all dressed up like a big girl. She has on her pink party dress that sticks out, and her black shoes with the strap across, and white socks and a pink bow in her hair.*

*I'm in my bathing suit that has a bib at the top and ruffles at the bottom. And I'm sitting in my round rubber pool that my mother filled with water from the hose. The water was cold at first, but now it's warm, and there's grass floating in it and ants.*

*Sigrid says she can't come in the water with me because soon she's going to go visit her God Mother and God Father. I think she must go up to heaven to visit them. That's why she's all dressed up.*

*I say, Can't you take your shoes and socks off and come in with your feet? But she says no, she's not allowed to. I say, Please? But she says no again. I say, Pleeeeeeease? and this time she doesn't say no. She pulls up her skirt and pulls down her underpants. Then she squats down and puts her bum in the water, just a little bit, dip dip.*

*It's the most wonderful thing I've ever seen anybody do. It's a lot better than feet. Her bum is round and white. And when she stands up, drops fall from it, plink, plink, shining down.*

'Margareta and Katrin,' Sigrid says when I ask what her daughters are called. 'Both Estonian names. That's something else I swore I'd never do.'

We're back in the restaurant, having coffee so we can sit and chat. I ran after them as they were going out the door, and caught up with them on the sidewalk. Her husband's name is Urjo. Up close, he looks nothing like Jacques Brel.

They met as youngsters at Estonian camp. They became friends because they both hated being there, and hated being Estonian, and swore they would never marry into the Estonian community.

Sigrid is a biologist, working in cancer research. Urjo is a house husband. Neither of them can stop talking about their children.

'Katrin's just started school,' Urjo says. 'She couldn't wait. She's been collecting rocks and leaves and bugs in jars practically since she learned to walk. Now she says she wants to be a scientist, like Mummy.'

'And find the cure for cancer,' Sigrid and I chime in together.

'Margareta's the creative one,' Sigrid says. 'The artistic one.' She pauses, as if she wants to say more about her oldest child, but wonders if she should. I get the impression there is something special about Margareta. A handicap, or some difficulty. Because Sigrid has changed. She has softened, and opened. Something has cracked the hard little seed of the girl I knew. Or maybe the girl I was has grown some shell.

But the moment passes, and she doesn't say anything more about her daughters. She asks me the titles of my books, and writes them down. Then we take down each other's phone numbers, and say what a great thing this was, and how glad we are that it happened.

Beyond that, we have nothing to say to each other. And I think we both know that we're not going to call, will probably never see each other again.

On the way home I hum 'If You Go Away' and stop at a little corner grocery store to buy myself a bunch of flowers. A sign says MAR-GUERITES $3.99 / bun. I prefer *daisy*, which comes from *day's eye*. The sun. The eye of the day.

They're my flower, and not just because I'm named for them. I like them because they're weeds. They're tough, and they're all over the place, wherever they can find a handful of dirt and a patch of sun. I can imagine them poking out of cracks in the Great Wall of China, nodding in the breeze as an emperor parades by.

I wonder what they're called in China. They probably have a different name in every country of the world. All I know is daisy, the English, and marguerite, the French. Why marguerite, I wonder. Maybe they're the flower of Saint Margaret. I'll look it up when I get home.

I look forward to looking it up. I have a feeling I'm going to find out about something besides the flower of Saint Margaret. I sense this other knowledge waiting, barely beyond my ken. A penny just about to drop.

*... Like no day has been, or will be again ...*

# Egypt Land

YEARS AFTER MY FATHER DIED, I dreamed that he was walking across a desert. His feet were in leather sandals, the ancient kind that loop around the big toe, weave across the instep, then strap around the ankle. In my dream, I could not take my eyes off my father's right foot.

I had never seen his right foot. I had never seen any part of his right leg, except the stump, peeking out of his swim trunks like a pink Parker House roll.

His artificial leg used to lean upright in a corner of my parents' bedroom when he didn't have it on. Its foot was smooth and featureless like a mannequin's foot, and its knee was bolted like Frankenstein's neck.

Yet here in my dream was a restored, fleshly leg. A perfectly ordinary right leg, knee poking through the fabric of my father's robe, thigh thrusting forward, keeping time with its left counterpart, walking through the sand.

Walking. In my dream, my dead father walked like everyone else. He didn't have to take a lurching step with his good leg, hitch the artificial one off the ground, swivel it forward, balance on it for half a second, then lurch onto the good leg again before the artificial knee could buckle under his weight. Kitchen floors and scatter rugs were treacherous for him in life. A single mile of sand like this would have exhausted him.

But he walked and walked, not at all tired by the heat or the ocean of sand. Sometimes he kicked the sand like spray. Sometimes he dug down with his feet and waded through it.

He smoked Export A's unfiltered, leaving a trail of butts behind him that the wind buried as quickly as it buried his footprints. He lit each cigarette inside a little cave he made of his hands. Both his hands. For his left hand had been restored too, like his right leg.

A stroke had paralysed his left side when he was sixty. His left hand lay in his lap for ten years until he died. It had to be lifted and poked into the sleeve of a shirt. It could wear a mitt but not a glove, for the fingers were frozen into a half-formed fist.

But now it waved a flame into smoke and flicked the blackened match away onto the sand. Then it reached down to adjust the rope sash that kept the robe lapped over his stomach. At last it strayed to his crotch and scratched there gently.

I waited for my mother's hissed, 'Bill! Stop that!' Subconsciously, I was expecting her to keep trying to neaten and tidy him and make him nice, even after his death. But my mother was not in the dream. Neither was I. Not yet. My father walked the desert alone.

Except for the camel.

In my father's right hand was a leather rein that he transferred to the crook of his elbow whenever he was lighting a cigarette. The rein led to a leather bridle, which the camel wore as it walked along behind my father, swaying like a big ambulatory plant. On either side of its hump was a tarp-covered load, professionally tied up, expertly strapped on.

Everything in my dream had that air about it that dreamed things do, of making perfect sense on their own terms. So no doubt my restored father would have loaded the back of the camel as matter-of-factly as he used to load the trunk of his car. 'Yeah, yeah, *tell* me about it,' he would have said around a cigarette when the animal groaned in token protest.

When they stopped at last for a rest, the camel lowered its belly to the sand, first its front end, then its back. My father sat down in the shadow it cast. He pulled off his burnoose, scrunched it like a baseball cap, swabbed his face and neck with it, then put it back on. He was clean-shaven, as in life, and his white hair was still brush-cut. His eyes were the ice blue I remembered, the pupils small dots of perfect black.

He looked out over the sand with a look I recognized. It was a look that saw what it saw and knew what it knew. His eyes shifted often and blinked seldom. I remember him looking that way at the surface of water. He would stand on his one leg on a beach, shoulders pushed high by his crutches, studying the lake as if his gaze could pierce its moving surface. He would hump-swing several yards into the water, throw his crutches like spears back onto shore, then dive. Once in the water, he was as free as a seal.

So I knew this look. And I recognized the way he now puckered his lips, and I heard before hearing it the cool thready whistle he breathed out. A single note, perhaps two. A phrase of a song known only to him. Long silences between notes. Then, after the longest silence, perhaps a lyric or two, more spoken than sung. Sometimes enough to allow the song to be identified. 'Flow Gently, Sweet Afton', or 'Surrey with a Fringe on Top', or 'Red Sails in the Sunset'.

The broken music-making ended at last, before the sun had quite set. In the colouring light, my father reached into a fold of his robe and brought forth the yellow vendor's copy of a purchase order. The carbon type was blurred, but legible.

*Go down, Moses*, the purchase order sang as soon as it was unfolded. *Way down to Egypt land. Tell old Pharaoh to let my people go.*

My father folded it back up, and abruptly the singing stopped.

'Sure,' he muttered around a cigarette, the last before sleep. 'You betcha.' He waved the flame into smoke. 'You just betcha.' He flicked the match away. Though his eyes followed its flight, in the growing darkness he could not see where it landed.

Egypt Land. The idea of Egypt. The thought of it. Even the word. The dream brought it all back.

'Eee-jipt,' I used to whisper to myself, hands cupped over ears to catch my own voice. 'Eee-jipt.' It was the most alien-sounding, most mysterious word I knew.

I felt responsible for Egypt. Knowing that the Sphinx's face was almost worn away by time, the Pyramids long emptied by adventurers and thieves, threw me into a kind of panic. I hated to think of the treasures scattered over the world, some trapped in glass cases, others traded and sold, changing hands until no one remembered what they really were. I tortured myself with crazy thoughts of Nefertiti's necklace lost in the beady clutter on top of my mother's dresser. Or, in a dark corner of my father's workbench, behind a jar of wing nuts, the golden mask of a god, jewelled eyes serene, patiently waiting to be worshipped again.

I wanted so much to find the lost treasures and return them to
Egypt. I ached to restore the face of the Sphinx.

'Can't they pick up the pieces that have fallen off and stick them
back on with something?' My mother always said my father could
fix anything.

'Nope. The wind's worn them away. They're spread all over the
place.'

'But are they still *there*? Couldn't somebody find them and pick
them up?'

'They're too small to recognize. They just look like sand.'

I would recognize them. I would know them from sand. 'But are
they *somewhere*? Do they —' I didn't know the word I wanted.

'Exist? Oh yeah. I guess so. Nothing ever stops existing.'

How could he know that the Sphinx's nose might be lying around
in plain sight, albeit changed, and feel no need to do something
about it?

I needed to save Egypt Land. I needed to find every particle of it,
however tiny, and put it back in its place. I saw myself travelling all
over the world, all my life, asking questions, following leads, finding,
taking, breaking into museums, haunting white elephant sales, stealing, liberating, restoring.

If I could bring all the pieces back together, I could bring Egypt
Land back to life. I could point the edges of the pyramids, curl the
lip of the Sphinx. I could make the wind carry the smell of incense
and sweet oils, the sound of pipes and drums. And through the very
heart of Egypt Land, I could make Pharaoh walk again.

It was my father who told me about Egypt in the first place. He gave
the impression of having discovered Egypt all by himself long ago,
long before me or my brother, long before my mother, before his leg
came off, before he was even born. There was something ageless
about my father, like the burnoose and sandals and camel he was
equipped with in my dream. Hymn-book phrases like 'the ancient of
days' used to make me think of him.

'Akhenaton wasn't your run-of-the-mill Pharaoh,' I remember
him telling me. 'For one thing, he'd made up his mind that there was
only one God, instead of half a dozen or so, and that he himself

wasn't it. That made him pretty damned strange for an Egyptian, and even stranger for a Pharaoh. That's how come he tacked 'aton' onto his name. It was the name of his God. Then along came Tut, and monotheism went to hell.'

Tutankhamun's tomb had been discovered early in my father's childhood. His whole growing-up world had been coloured by the Egyptomania raging for years after the discovery.

'Chances are, if Akhenaton had lived longer, just to give Tut a chance to grow up some, and learn something from him, Egypt might of been a different place. And all kinds of things around it and coming after it might of been different too.'

My father had once been a reader. I used to find his books in the house and put them on my own bookshelf in my bedroom. *Moby Dick*, *Morte d'Artur*, *The Odyssey*. Books he read before his leg came off and he had to quit school. The print was archaic, the pages faintly browned at the edges. They smelled of dust and damp rags. On the inside front cover of each, in ink-bottle ink, was my father's name, school and classroom number. I tried to imagine him in a cap and plus-fours, but couldn't. And all he ever read now was the sports section and the comics.

But he did once read about Egypt and the Pharaohs, the way he read about everything else. Voraciously until the age of fourteen, then not at all.

So what was he doing as Moses, Pharaoh's arch-enemy, in my dream?

When I was in Sunday school, I had a problem with Moses, for all that he was the good guy and Pharaoh the bad. I thought Moses had an unfair advantage, namely God.

'God hardened Pharaoh's heart,' Miss Urquhart would gasp at us in the basement of the church. 'He hardened his heart so he wouldn't let the Israelites go, not even when the plague of frogs came. Just imagine, children! A plague of frogs! Frogs hopping all over your plate at supper! Frogs hopping across your bed at night!'

Well, we thought a plague of frogs would be kind of neat, and besides we liked the way Miss Urquhart's face dropped like a stone whenever we laughed at stuff she thought was serious. Miss

Urquhart had the most unfortunate of Scots Presbyterian facial types, nose meeting chin, tiny lashless eyes close together. So we laughed and her face dropped and God hardened our hearts and we laughed some more.

Miss Urquhart illustrated her stories with paper cut-outs which she stuck onto a green felt board where they sometimes, miraculously, stayed. There was Moses, facing right, marching across the board to Egypt Land. There, in the middle, were the enslaved Israelites, all in a cut-out mass, crayoned brown. And there, aloof on the far right, was Pharaoh.

Actually, he was a pen-and-ink sketch of Tutankhamun's sarcophagus, but I didn't know that then. All I knew was that Pharaoh was beautiful. He was serene. He stared straight ahead, straight out from the green felt board, unmoved by the fuss being made by Moses and the Israelites and God and Miss Urquhart.

As an adult I finally saw the real Tutankhamun. That is, I saw his grave mask, through glass, from behind a velvet rope.

I wanted to touch his lips. Ridiculous thing to want to do, I knew, because Tutankhamun's lips had been made about as untouchable as anything could be. The whole Treasures of the Tomb exhibit was policed by uniformed guards who shouted, 'Please do not touch the glass! Keep your hands away from the glass!' every thirty seconds.

Maybe they had to do that because everybody felt the way I did about touching that smooth gold cheek, that sweet mouth. There is an irresistible boyish eagerness to Tutankhamun's face. For all its stillness and formality, there is something anticipatory in the expression. A kind of hope.

I have no pictures of my father as a boy. What that means, among other things, is that I have never seen even so much as a picture of his right leg.

When he was fourteen, he went picking berries. He spent the whole day on his knees, and when he tried to get up he could not straighten out his right leg. The next morning, he still could not straighten it out, and it had gone pure white, except for the faintest trace of green.

My father did not talk about losing his leg. I can remember him telling the story exactly once, and what I remember most vividly about the telling is my brother Ted's rage over the grim comedy of errors that led to the amputation. The combined ignorance and complacency that favoured folk remedies, salt baths and a good night's sleep over calling a doctor. By the time a doctor was reluctantly called, my father's toes had turned black.

His leg came off in stages as the gangrene advanced. First the foot, then the ankle, then the calf just below the knee, then the knee, then most of the thigh. The procedure took an entire year, during which time he did not leave the hospital. When he finally got out on crutches, the whole world had become the Depression. There was no more school for him, and no more reading.

Though I am able to imagine my father with a young face, there is an expression I cannot make it assume. The features have a basic rigidity in my memory, and they resist all my attempts to mould them.

The nurses kept him busy during that year in the hospital. Occupational therapy was still a thing of the future, but they taught him what they knew, knitting, rug-hooking, even embroidery. I have a baby dress that he trimmed in pink embroidery thread. One night, when my mother simply forgot how to do blanket stitch, he remembered.

But the nurses could not do anything about what was happening to his face. And neither can I now. I cannot remove from it the mask of resignation.

I'm told that nobody is ever miscast in a dream. But Moses? Moses the rebel? Moses the justice-seeker?

In the wake of my dream I reread the Book of Exodus. It seems that Moses was an unwilling liberator of the Israelites. He had been raised in the Egyptian royal household, after all, and Pharaoh was his adopted grandfather. So he protested to God that he couldn't possibly tell the old man to let the Israelites go because he was no good at public speaking. God got around that one by letting him take along his brother Aaron, who apparently had the gift of the gab.

Maybe that was why my father was restored in my dream. Maybe he protested to the issuer of the purchase order that he couldn't walk the desert with an artificial right leg, a paralysed left leg and a paralysed left arm. That he couldn't do it as the head, hand and torso he had become.

'Don't keep busted tools hanging around!'

It was summer, and I was sitting on the bottom basement step to read, because that was the coolest spot in the house. My father was at his workbench with his back to me when he said that about tools. He was lit by one hanging yellow bulb, his undershirt a white Y against his freckled back. He worked while he spoke, his arms reaching out to right and left. Bolts and hinges and screws. Bits and pieces, each, however small or dusty, compartmentalized in a dirty cardboard box according to specific use. Jars filled with nails in exact gradations. The smells of metal and sawdust. Paint, turpentine, varnish and oil.

'A busted tool is a piece of junk!'

He respected tools. He would tinker and mutter lovingly for hours over a broken tool. If it could be fixed. If it could not, he would throw it away without a moment's sentiment or regret.

It was the usefulness of tools he liked, their capacity for work. There was an air of rarefied contentment about him when he was doing a job. I recognized this in my dream. I saw it in the flare of his lit match, the creases of his knuckles, the still line of his mouth. He hadn't chosen to go down to Egypt Land, but it was a job. Work was work.

I never knew when he was going to come out with one of these life lessons. We could be together for hours, he puttering, I reading, without a single word being exchanged. Then all at once he would speak. It was as if he had suddenly remembered I was his child, and perhaps in need of wisdom.

'There're guys I know, haven't got the brains they were born with when it comes to busted tools. And their shops are full of junk. You ever get yourself something that won't work, don't fart around with it. Fix it or chuck it out.'

He lived for ten years after the stroke paralysed him. I only heard him protest once.

It was just a few weeks after it happened. My mother and I had been visiting him at night, and she was getting him settled down in his hospital bed. His left arm and leg had to be bolstered with pillows to keep him from rolling on them in the night. While she was doing that, I stepped out into the hall to give them some time alone.

The second I was out of sight, my father's voice rose in a long, cantorial wail. Wordless, higher and higher, thinner and thinner, it followed me down the hall into the elevator, found me even in the lobby, where I tried to hide from it.

The degree of my father's brokenness, the thing his life had become, terrified me. Any slip of the mask, any crack in his resignation, was an occasion for panic.

But the occasions were few. I never in fact heard him cry again. In time, the professionals deemed him 'completely adjusted' to his situation.

Maybe he was. Or maybe the Continuing Care wing wasn't as awful as I remember it.

It did have a disturbing smell. Not a bad smell, for it was kept very clean. The smell was delicate enough, but cloying. It was the smell of human flesh. Bathed and powdered. Animate. But inert.

Every morning of the ten years he was there, my father lay sandbagged by pillows, waiting for a nurse to come. The nurse would check the urine bag hanging out from under the bedclothes, then syringe the catheter tube that went up his penis into his bladder, to see if it was still drawing. She and another nurse would dress my father, pull him into a sitting position and slide him along a board into his wheelchair. There he would sit all day until it was time for him to go to bed again.

He lived in a room with three other men. One of these lay perpetually asleep on his back, eyelids purple, nose and chin jutting up from a sunken mouth that sucked and blew like an oyster hole. He finally died and was replaced by another sleeping man, whose sleep was like waves, rolling and mumbling.

My father was born down near the bay, in the east end of Hamilton.

He swam in the bay when he was a boy, and worked there as a life-guard when he was in his twenties. There is a photograph of him sit-ting up high on a lifeguard's lookout chair, staring out at the water with that look he gave the desert sand in my dream.

My brother asked him once how he could be a one-legged life-guard, and he said that if he spotted anybody in trouble, he would hop down off his perch, grab his crutches, run on them to the water's edge, then dive. 'I had three legs to the other guys' two,' he said. 'I could go like a spider.'

He pointed his old neighbourhood out to me once while we stood on the edge of the Hamilton escarpment. This is a rise of three hun-dred feet or so, just enough to make the lower city look small and old. Down there, he had been born into established poverty. My mother had been born on the 'mountain' into new wealth.

Two or three times a year, my father would come up the stairs to my room to tell me stories of the east end. I would hear his slow step, his good leg pulling the artificial one up, the clump of the wooden foot, then another step, then another pull. And I would hear my mother calling, 'Bill! She has homework to do!'

He would come into my room without saying anything to me, sometimes without looking at me. He would sit down heavily in my dresser chair and examine the walls for cracks, the ceiling for stains, the floor tiles for upraised corners. 'Got to fix that,' he would mutter when he spotted something.

Or his eye might lock onto something of mine, a pyramid of bristly curlers on my dresser, or a pink plastic hand whose splayed fingers were to hold rings. He would stare at it silently for several seconds. Then he would pick it up, turning it quarter-inch by quarter-inch, perhaps taking it apart and putting it back together. I never told him what these things were for. His investigation lent them a dignity far above the actual. To reveal that they were for curling hair or display-ing baubles would somehow have disappointed him.

And he was a disappointed enough man. He never talked about it, but I sensed his disappointment, as I might sense the lip of a hole just beyond my feet in the dark.

After a silence, he would light the first cigarette and begin, 'You know, when I was a boy down in the east end ...'

Aside from that bird's-eye view of his old neighbourhood from the escarpment, I had never seen the east end. It was as huge and as vague in my imagination as Troy or Xanadu. If I had ever been driven through it, I probably would have been shocked by the absence of horses clopping by, bobbing their heads in rhythm with their feet, like clumsy dancers.

It wasn't sentiment or nostalgia that brought my father to my room, though all his stories were of his first fourteen years. There was more a feeling of necessity about the telling, even of inevitability, as if something had finally come to the surface, something buried for centuries, that might explode in the air.

So I knew enough to listen silently as he told me about a woman whose self-appointed task was to gather old woollens from all the households in the neighbourhood, then unravel, dye and retwist the yarn. She would give it back to each mother according to need, so that the neighbourhood children would have warm clothes. 'One winter, we was all outfitted in green. The next year, kind of a tangerine colour. Depended on whatever dyestuffs she happened to have lyin' around. Nobody paid her. Nobody could of paid her. She just done it.'

Throughout the telling, my mother would listen loudly downstairs, sometimes rattling her newspaper, once or twice calling up that it was a school night, and that I had to get to bed soon.

My father hardly responded to her protests. His mouth might twist, or he might stub a cigarette out a little harder than usual, using the silver paper from the pack as an ad hoc ashtray.

I didn't want him to come to my room. I didn't want him not to. He was there. Talking for once, the way he almost never talked. So I listened.

Maybe he had once talked to my mother that way. Maybe she had once listened, silently, uncritically, the way I did. He would talk for half an hour or so, punctuating the talk with long silences. He hissed smoke out from between his teeth during these, staring straight ahead, snagged on a memory.

I listened on through the silences. I didn't question or probe or dig, but let the thing emerge as it would. I heard his diction and his grammar slipping farther back into the east end, and just let them.

And when the story was finished, I let the sound of it hang in the air like the smoke of his cigarette.

'Me an' Ernie ...' he began once, speaking of a boyhood chum who disappeared from his life about the time he lost his leg. 'We used t'go around together, an' the other kids used t'step out of the way when they seen us comin'. 'Cause anybody pick on one of us, he'd hafta deal with the other one too. We was fighters, Ernie an' me. We was on our way to being real street fighters. Kids used t'talk about the day me an' Ernie would fight each other. They used t'wait for it, like they'd wait for the day of a prize fight. But that day never come.'

He had no friends that I knew of. He went to work. He came home. I used to look at him and wonder if he loved my mother and Ted and me. If he loved anyone. Then I would try to love him, try to feel myself loving him. Maybe, I thought, there was something wrong with the way I was doing it. Maybe, if I really loved him, I would dig and dig at him the way my mother did. And his silence, his aloofness, would chafe me the way it did her.

'I shopped today, Bill,' she would try over supper, watching him while he ate. 'And I washed and ironed.' She would continue to watch, and he to eat. 'I got my hair done, too!' At last she would grab up her plate and clatter it into the sink. 'Not a word!' she would call to the air. 'No answer!'

If he said anything at all, it would be, 'You didn't ask a question, did you?'

I knew it must have been different between them once. I've seen a picture of them on their honeymoon. She's sitting on his lap and their faces look like they're hurting with smiles. But they never got used to each other. After decades in the same bed, there was still something unconsummated between them. A metaphorical virginity that would not give.

At some point, he stopped even trying to speak the language of the mountain. At the same time, she stopped even trying to tolerate the language of the east end.

'So I goes down to the shop –'

'I *go* down to the shop.'

'And I says –'

'And I *say*.'

'I says, look, fella, you gonna get off the pot an' close this deal or aintcha?'

My mother was a pretty woman, a fussy woman, uncomfortable with dirt and noise and vulgarity. Her country was the house, from the laundry tubs in the basement, up through the kitchen, into the farthest corners of the linen closet and up into my room, where she poked under my bed with her mop, dragging out grey tumbleweeds of dust.

Her country's boundaries extended out into the back yard, where she talked over the fence with Mrs Kiraja. Each woman stood with her laundry basket balanced on one hip, sometimes dabbing at the front of her hair in a token tidying gesture. They called each other 'Mrs' and spoke in hushed, courteous tones, looking directly into each other's wide eyes. Though they might shift their laundry baskets from one hip to the other, they would never put them down on the ground, for to do this would be to imply that they actually had the time to talk.

'A man he works from sun to sun,' my mother would sometimes recite, 'But a woman's work is never done.' She liked poems that rhymed, and she liked hymns, the older and more syrupy the better. Sometimes, in the middle of the day, in her housedress, with dust motes boiling up from the keys, she would play the piano and sing, 'And He *walks* with me and He *talks* with me, and He tells me I am his *own* …' Or 'Jerusalem,' or 'The Old Rugged Cross' or 'Onward Christian Soldiers,' all in her girlish soprano.

She came into her own on Sunday. She was the chooser of shirts, the straightener of ties, the whitener of shoes and the mender of gloves. In church, she bloomed while my father looked artificial.

My father's country, his world of work, was roughly male, utterly without ornament. He drove into gravelled lots behind machine shops. He hollered to men above the scream of machinery, and they yelled back.

I doubt that my mother ever went on a day-long sales trip with my father the way I sometimes did. I couldn't imagine her doing such a thing, or him asking her to.

I never knew what prompted him to ask me. Maybe he was just being fair, because he often took my brother along. The places we visited were identical islands of noise dotting long, silent miles of highway. Dusty offices flimsily attached to dustier shops. Screen doors that banged. Plants quietly browning in curtainless windows. Chipped Arborite counters with men behind them whose eyes widened when they saw my father, and who called him 'Bill!'

My father pushed his hat to the back of his head in these places, and leaned his elbows on the counter, his hips cocked at an angle. He talked loud, saying 'this here' and 'not nothin'.' His grin was fixed and fierce. He barked a laugh that would have made my mother look away and sniff.

'Got my sweetie with me!' he would say to explain my presence. Or, 'This here's my honey!' I would stare warm-faced at the floor while roars of 'Hey, hey, hey!' and 'Ain't she a cutie!' crashed like waves over my head.

I knew it was probably different when my brother came along with my father on these trips. 'This here's my boy,' he might say, or, 'Wantcha to meet my son.' *Son* had a ring to it. Shimmering, like the sound of cymbals meeting. Probably there were handshakes. Probably my brother stood beside my father, listening to the hard, spare talk. Learning.

But when I was there, a great to-do was made about what was to be done with me, where I was to be put, while business was conducted. 'She can sit right over there! Yeah! She'll be fine, wontcha, honey?' One of the behind-the-counter men once found me a dusty, cellophane-wrapped sucker.

Sometimes I was allowed to explore the concrete interiors of shops, the piled industrial barrels full of hardware. The floors of these places were dotted with pools of oil. The only natural light pushed through the grime of small, high windows. This was the world of my father's work. And I, for some reason, was being shown that world.

I didn't like going on those trips. They were boring, and the day felt long. My father was not good company. I had trouble thinking of anything to say to him as we drove along between shops, and whatever I did say was usually met with silence.

The silence was something that came from him, just as his stories came from him. It had the same feeling of necessity, of inevitability. So I let it be, and waited for him to break it. And when he didn't, I looked out the window and counted cows.

I tried not to think about my mother home all day alone. I still sometimes wonder if my father stopped speaking her language once I was born, once I began to hear, and see, and remember.

My father seldom touched me. I remember him holding me only once. It was when I was very small, and was trying to teach him to run.

'See? Watch me! You run like this!' I ran around him in a circle. 'And you jump like this!' I jumped and landed and fell over backwards. I got up and tugged at his belt. 'Come on and run!' I begged. 'Come on! I'll show you!'

He caught the back of my head and pressed my face into his stomach. He smelled of tobacco and sweat. Be still, the hand on my head said. Be silent, said the mingled scents.

'Oh, look what she's brought, Bill! Bill, look!'

We were sitting at a table in the Continuing Care coffee shop. We spent a lot of time there during visits to my father because it was one of the few spots that still allowed smoking.

'Oh, *look*, Bill!' My mother was turning the pages of the glossy Treasures of the Tomb brochure I had bought at the Royal Ontario Museum. She was leaning in toward my father so that he could see too.

'It's an incredible exhibit, Dad,' I said in the sitcom daughter-chirp I had adopted since his stroke. 'Really worth seeing.' I had also mentally installed an automatic editor that kept me from saying things like 'You should go and see it.' It was all part of the enforced good cheer that got me through these visits. I came once a month, armed with conversation pieces.

'Bill? *Look* at it, for heaven's sake! You should *look* at this when she's taken the trouble to bring it all the way from Toronto! Look at the mask, Bill!'

He did look at the mask of Tutankhamun, and I wondered,

fearfully, what he might be remembering. I imagined telling him about wanting to put my hand through the glass and touch those golden lips, about how moved I was by the expression on the face of the boy-king. But the automatic editor hardened my heart, and I was silent.

'They were a cruel people, the Egyptians,' my mother said, turning the page. 'They kept slaves and made them pull big rocks up the sides of the pyramids.' She turned another page to a photograph of a life-size golden cobra. 'Ugh!' she said, and turned again.

The cobra had been one of my favourite parts of the exhibit. I had stood in front of its glass case for ages, understanding how such a thing might be worshipped.

All at once my father said, 'They wasn't slaves, most of them.' We both looked at him.

'Yes, they *were*,' my mother said. I almost raised a hand to silence her. 'And they had to pull big rocks –'

'Most of 'em was indentured servants. They worked for so many years, then they could go anywhere they liked. Most of 'em stayed in Egypt. "Cause they liked it there.'

I hadn't heard him talk, really talk, for ages. Since the stroke his talk had been mostly monosyllabic answers to my mother's questions. Was he too hot, was he too cold, would he like some more coffee, did he want to play Scrabble again?

My mother had become a Continuing Care volunteer in a pink smock and photo ID name tag. She visited my father every day. She checked his laundry, filled out his menu plan, printed his name on every page of his newspaper, went with him on outings and special events.

I went along with them to only one of those, a barbecue that got rained out and ended up as a singsong in the hospital auditorium. Patients of every age and condition were wheeled into a circle and given a songbook. One of the requests was for 'Amazing Grace.' They sang it, those who were not catatonic, those who could focus their eyes, those who could form words. The hymn rose in a great ragged moan while I stood there, pressing my back flatter and flatter against the wall. I could not decently escape, though something in the back of my mind was shrieking at me to run.

For there, hunched in his wheelchair, head bent, eyes following my mother's pointing finger, was my father. Singing. '... once was lost, but now am found ...'

'What about the Israelites?' I said now. I wanted to keep him talking. 'What's the Book of Exodus all about if they weren't enslaved by the Egyptians?'

'The Israelites were originally under contract to make bricks. There was nothin' like slavery going on. Not for generations, anyway. They had no land and they had nothin' to eat, so they settled down in Egypt and went to work for Pharaoh. Simple as that.' He stubbed out his cigarette and began picking the cellophane off a fresh pack.

'Don't open that,' my mother said. 'You've smoked enough.'

My father ignored her. He would not speak again until his new cigarette was lit, and he would not accept help getting it out of the pack.

It was quite an operation, getting and lighting a cigarette with one hand. First he had to pick a hole in the cellophane, peel it off, open the lid of the pack and pull away the silver paper. Then he had to inch one cigarette out, using thumb and index finger, anchoring the pack on the table with the heel of his palm. It was the first thing he had learned in occupational therapy, and the first indication to the professionals that he was 'accepting' and 'adjusting'.

'You'll see,' my mother said, watching him. 'They're going to make this a no-smoking area too.'

'Then I'll go outside.'

'It's *cold* outside.'

'Then I'll freeze my butt.'

'Bill!'

'What about Moses?' I said quickly.

'What about him?'

'Why did he have such a tough time getting the Israelites out of Egypt, if nothing was holding them there?'

'Oh, by then somethin' was. They *was* slaves by the time Moses come along.'

'*Came* along. See? I said they were slaves. They had to pull big rocks up the sides of the —'

'Who made them slaves?' Couldn't she see that something was happening? That something was actually making the time move for a change?

'Pharaoh made 'em slaves. One of the last big Pharaohs. Just before everything started goin' to hell.'

'Bill, you don't have to shout.' My mother cut her eyes around the coffee shop, convinced as always that the chatting nurses and dozing patients were hanging on our every word.

'See, by the time Moses come along, Egypt was bein' chipped away at by everybody an' his brother. The Middle East was the same mess it is today.' There was a small spot of pink on each of my father's cheeks. His right fist was clenched. 'So Pharaoh hunkered down an' tried to hang on to what he had. An' what he had was this great big bunch of Hebes –'

'Bill!'

'– who'd been multiplying like hell for generations an' were as unified as all-get-out with their one God. He got scared they might side with his enemies an' attack him from the inside. So he done somethin' real dumb. Instead of makin' them his allies, he made them his slaves. Tried to work 'em to death.'

'And that was King Tut who did that, was it?' my mother said in the wrap-up tone she used to use for 'and they all lived happily ever after.'

'Nope. By Moses' time Tut had been dead a hundred years.'

'Well, then, what's so special about King Tut, for heaven's sake?' She was frowning at the price sticker on the brochure.

My father said nothing. He was looking off into middle distance with the look I would see again in my dream.

'Didn't Tutankhamun stamp out the monotheism that had just been introduced into Egypt?' I prompted.

He still said nothing. His cheeks were pale again, almost transparent. In the past weeks he had gotten very thin. The veins on his forehead could be seen to throb. And now he had simply stopped talking. As abruptly as he'd begun.

'Didn't that make Tut the most influential fifteen-year-old in history?' I was starting to sweat. It was *there*, damn it. I knew it was still there, if I could only dig down far enough. I could remember him spinning a whole alternative history of Egypt for me that started with Tutankhamun nurturing the radical new idea of one God, and ended with Moses and Pharaoh seeing eye to eye. No slavery, no bulrushes, no Exodus.

'Dad —?'

My mother put her hand on my forearm. Don't, her lips said. Don't. He can't.

I pulled my arm away. I hated her new solicitude, her regained powers. She would phone me sometimes and list all the things my father had been through in his life, and go on about what a shame it was, and how he'd done nothing to deserve any of it. I could hardly stand to listen, and I was jealous of her ability to say the words.

He was hers now. That time that he cried, she stayed in the room and I ran.

Sometimes I entertained a mad fantasy of renting a van, getting him into it somehow and taking him to a Canadian Tire store. Just so he could see something besides pastel uniforms and smell something besides talcum powder.

Maybe I could wheel him up and down the aisles, opening boxes for him. Letting him see again the precise gradations of nails and screws, feel again the oily smoothness of a brand new wrench. Or better still, maybe I could stay at the front near the cashiers and let him cruise the aisles alone.

I could see him pushing himself along in his wheelchair, stopping dead when something caught his eye. I could see him picking up whatever it was and cradling it for a moment in his palm, testing its weight. Then looking at its underside, its top, and each end in turn. At last laying it flat on his palm and bringing it level with his eye. Peering down its length. Checking it for straightness. For balance.

My father stubbed out his cigarette and reached for another one.

'Bill, that's your sixth since we've been sitting here!'

'Seventh,' he said, flicking his lighter.


I did not properly mourn my father's death. In time I worried that this neglected mourning might have form, might be a *thing* inside me that would surface someday, the way buried stones and relics will frost-heave to the surface of the earth.

My first reaction to his death was to wonder, perhaps absurdly, perhaps not, where he was. Where he had gone. I could not believe that he was nowhere, that he had simply stopped existing. Nothing ever stopped existing.

But I had never known him whole. A piece of him had always been missing. Over time, more and more pieces had gone missing. Over time, his words had become fewer, his silences longer. And now, here was this complete silence that might or might not be complete. I might or might not see and hear my father again.

He himself did have a God. That much I was sure of. It is possible that as a boy he prayed for the gangrene to halt its advance, or at least to spare him his knee. It is possible that as an old man he prayed for his left arm and leg to come back to life. And it is possible that when both prayers went unanswered, he prayed to die.

> *Oh, tell of His might, oh, sing of His grace,*
> *Whose robe is the light, whose canopy space ...*

The memorial service took place outside, on the edge of the escarpment. All through it, my mother held a small white cardboard box. I tried not to look at the box, but it drew my eye.

She had phoned me the night before, worried about the service, worried about whether the hymn she had picked out really had been my father's favourite, worried about which dress she should wear, worried about whether she should continue as a Continuing Care volunteer. She would stop and cry for a while into the phone, then blow her nose and start up again.

I let her go on and on, saying nothing. I had not, and would not for years, shed a tear. Tears would have been a comfort, and I did not deserve comfort.

To my brother had fallen the practical problems occasioned by a death. Contacting a minister. Getting the obituary into the paper. Answering the phone. Answering the door. To me fell the task of listening to my mother. It felt like a penance, and I welcomed it.

'They were very nice to me, the people at the crematorium,' she said into the phone. Then she hesitated. Her voice became small, the voice of a child confessing.

'They put it – you know – all in a nice white box. Very clean.'

No, I thought. Please.

'It's – the ashes – I opened the box – the ashes are white. All white, like talcum powder. Except –'

Please.

'– except they don't feel like talcum powder. They feel like sand.'

At the end of the service she scattered his ashes off the edge of the escarpment. She held the box out to Ted, who took some, then to me. I shook my head. How could I scatter him, disperse him, let him be more lost than he was?

She could. And when she had emptied the box, she held it for a moment upside down and tapped it gently. There was a wind. Hating my own sentimentality, I imagined it blowing some of the ashes toward the east end.

*His chariots of wrath the deep thunderclouds form,*
*And dark is His path on the wings of the storm.*

My father's God was the God who said to Moses, 'I shall be gracious to whom I shall be gracious, and I shall have compassion on whom I shall have compassion.' He was the God who hardened Pharaoh's heart for the express purpose of making things difficult.

My father knew this God in my dream, knew him long before my dream. Had heard his muttering and felt his tinkering from the age of fourteen.

'Come on now. Get down from there.' I knew in my dream that I wasn't really in trouble, even though my father had been called out of death, as out of retirement, to come all the way to Egypt Land to let me go.

'I said get down,' he repeated. He hardly ever told me to do anything. It felt strange when he did, like falling out of bed. But even then I knew he wasn't really mad. He sounded as if he'd caught me doing something more dumb than bad, and just didn't want to make an issue of it.

He was standing at the bottom of the dais, looking up at me. The camel peered over his shoulder. When it caught my eye, it groaned its token protest at me, as if it thought I might unpack its load.

I swung my feet for a little while longer. Pharaoh's throne was a high one. I had to stretch my arms straight out to reach the golden handrests. I was tired of playing Pharaoh, but it was hard to stop. Somebody had to tell me to.

Finally, when I figured my father might be getting mad for real, I slid down and landed with a thump. Then I came down the steps of the dais slowly, dawdling on each one.

'Go on home to your mother now,' he said. 'Nothin' keeping you here.' I dawdled some more, crouching and combing my fingers through the sand. 'I said go home!'

I asked him if I could keep the camel. He told me to go ask my mother. Then he pointed to the load. 'Tell her there's some stuff in there,' he said. 'Stuff that's hers. I've been meaning to let her have it.' I knew without being told that I wasn't supposed to peek inside.

So I started for home, leading the camel by the rein. I watched myself walk out of the dream. I was very small, and quite brown. My footsteps filled with sand the second I made them. The camel walked behind me, lilypad feet splayed, laden hump swaying out of sync with belly.

Once I was over a sand dune and out of sight, my father went up the steps to Pharaoh's throne. He picked up Pharaoh's sceptre, which was leaning beside it. He hefted it in his palm, balanced it on his index finger, hoisted it to his shoulder and squinted down its length. So preoccupied, he sat down.

He became Old Pharaoh, and the Sphinx and the pyramids. He became the wind and the sand and the pipes and the drums and the incense and the sweet oils. He became Egypt Land.

# Give Me Your Answer

*Mary Daisy Sangster McEwen is walking on water. Up the swells and down the troughs of the salt waves. Sometimes she stops to rest and shade her eyes with her hand. She stands this way for a long time, watching. At last, she smiles.*

*The cat is coming to meet her. In its own time. It stops to wash, pulling itself like taffy in all directions at once. Or it sleeps, curled into a perfect round. Then it wakes, stretches, yawns, and continues stepping along toward my grandmother. Its paws are as silent on water as on earth. Its fur is as black as the sea, and its eyes as green.*

◆ ◆ ◆

My hands are starting to look like my grandmother's. I recognize the square shape, the short, blunt fingers. Maybe the skin on the backs will get patchy the way hers did, too. Pink and brown maps. As a kid I could never decide whether the land was brown and the water pink, or the other way around.

My nails are also short like hers, and unpainted. She used to cut her nails with scissors, leaving just enough white to pick up a coin or separate the pages of a hymn book.

Strange that I should see my grandmother's hands, not my mother's, in my own. But I do, and it's not just a matter of appearance. Something besides shape and colour, something I can feel but not name, has skipped a generation.

◆ ◆ ◆

'She's a quiet one.'

'Yes, she is. She's happy with a book to read or a piece of paper to draw on.'

'You were the same way, June. Never any trouble.'

'Is that right, Mom?' My mother's voice goes little and high, the way it does when she phones my grandmother and tells her what housework she's done that day. But then it drops back down to her mother voice. 'Oh, this one can be trouble now and then,' she says. 'Make no mistake.'

I press harder with my pencil. I'm never trouble on purpose. The last time I was here, I opened a box I thought was full of clothes that used to belong to my mother and my Aunt Heather. All there was inside was a lamp, and my mother got mad at me for not asking first if I could open the box.

But I'm not supposed to ask for things when I'm here. Not even for the humbug my grandmother gives me, or the quarter I get from my grandfather. Or for this pad and pencil. I know I'm going to get them, but I still have to wait and not ask.

The pencil moves, and so does the line. I'm making the line and following it at the same time. And Ted says that no matter how hard I press, the line will never be black, just darker and darker grey.

'You know, I could fall asleep in this chair and stay in it forever,' my mother says now. She says that every time she's here. She calls it coming home, even though it's only a few blocks from our house. And when she's here her talk is like clouds, slow with spaces in between.

Upstairs there's a room that used to be hers and Aunt Heather's. I found some old books there once, on a shelf in the closet. *Chatterbox* and *Blackie's Girl's Annual.* Big thick books full of stories about girls with names like Maude and Fenella, who say *I say* and play hockey and catch spies.

'Stay on the pad, Daisy,' my mother says now. 'Don't just draw on a single sheet, or you'll mark Grandma's table.'

I know that. And I always stay on the pad. Grandma's table is mahogany, the most expensive wood there is. Everything here is expensive, except you're not supposed to say so. That's because my grandfather made a lot of money, except you're not supposed to say that either.

I'm not pressing with my pencil right now, anyway. I'm putting it on the side to make little shadows without outlines. The dog in the painting on the wall has speckles that are smudgy around the edges. Last year, to copy them, I would have drawn circles and filled them in, but this year I know better.

'Heather tells me Ian's decided on teacher's college,' my mother is saying. 'Imagine little Ian a high school teacher. I can hardly get used to him being a Bachelor of Arts.'

'He'll do well,' my grandmother says. 'There's good money in teaching.'

When she says good it rhymes with food. When I say it, it rhymes with stood. My mother's good is in between. Don't scuff those shoes. They're good leather.

'I'll never forget the way Heather shook when Ian went up to get his B.A.,' my mother says now. 'I was watching her, and she just shook.'

Is a Bachelor of Arts something you get or something you are? And why does *I was watching her* sound like my mother was waiting for Aunt Heather to faint, so she could give her artificial respiration? Ted learned artificial respiration last year in Scouts, and he demonstrated it on the living-room floor, with me as the drowned person.

There. The dog's head is done, speckles and all. I always start with the head, because I draw heads better than I draw anything else. Drawing is the most interesting thing I do. And interesting is the most interesting word I know. It's a word you go inside of, and then it's all curled around, like a snail.

I tried to tell Ted about interesting once, but he gave me that look that means he can't wait for me to grow up and stop thinking the way I think and start thinking the way he thinks. Ted's four years older than me, and always will be.

I'm drawing the dog's body now. It's easy, wide at the front and narrow at the back. But then there are all the legs, and they're all different.

McMaster was like a city, with all different streets and all different buildings. 'You'll both go here someday,' my mother said to Ted and me in the car on the way to Ian's graduation. Ted just looked out the window and nodded, as if he already knew which building to go into, and how to get a Bachelor of Arts. Or how to be one.

'Gus was saying he's going to put in strawberries this year,' my grandmother says. Sometimes she calls my grandfather Gus and sometimes she calls him Dad.

'Oh, that'll be *great*, Mom.'

'Well, they've gotten so dear down at the market, we might as well grow our own.'

The dog's legs are turning out harder to draw than I thought they'd be. I'm leaving one of the front ones till last. It's all curled up, and things that are curled up are the hardest things to draw. Even though they're the most interesting.

'You know, I seem to remember seeing a recipe for a strawberry pie in the paper not long ago, Mom. You talking about strawberries made me think of it.'

'I've never had strawberry pie.'

'Well, I saw a recipe for one. And do you know that Heather actually makes a grape pie? She puts Concord grapes in it.'

'I've never had grape pie either.'

Something's the matter. I wish they would stop talking so I could figure out what. When I just look at my drawing, it's sort of all right. But when I look back and forth from it to the painting, it's so bad I can't believe it.

'She gets her drawing from you, Mom,' my mother says now, watching me.

'No she doesn't. I can't even draw a stick man.'

'Sure you can. Or you could. You used to draw a cat. I remember you doing it. More than once.'

'That was a long time ago.'

'Even so, Mom, I remember.'

Shut up, shut up, shut up! Can't they tell something's wrong? I hate my drawing. I hate this piece of paper too, and I hate this pencil and I hate this table. Mahogany. Stupid, ugly word. I mouth it without making a sound, big and nasty, hating its shape. *Ma-hawg-a-n-ee.*

'What are you pulling faces for, Daisy?' my mother says.

'I'm not!'

'Oh, for heaven's sake! *Now* what's the matter?'

'My drawing's no good,' I manage to squeak out.

'Well, that's nothing to cry about, is it?'

'Nuh-no-o-o.'

'Come and show me your picture,' my grandmother says. 'Oh, now *look*,' she says when she sees. *Look* sounds like Luke in the

Bible. 'It is *so* good. Just look at the nose, and the tail, and the foot all curled up.' *Foot* sounds like *hoot*. Why can't she see how bad it is? Even upside down it's bad. 'And all the polka-dots all over. It's *nice*. It's *pretty*.'

'There now,' my mother says. 'Say "Thank you, Grandma".'

'Thang you, Gramba.'

'Here's a Kleenex,' my mother says. 'And just try to think about something else. Or go outside. You're inside too much.'

I don't want to go outside. And I can't think about something else. Nothing else is interesting.

My mother is talking again, this time about asphalt. After a while I open the pad to a clean sheet of paper. *Nice. Pretty.* My grandmother should have known better. I don't know what I mean by that. And I don't know why I'm so mad at her. But I am.

◆ ◆ ◆

'Do you remember the cat Grandma used to draw?'

'A cat?' My mother's eyes look bigger every time I visit her. Her hands are bundles of knobs on the armrests of her wheelchair.

I try again. The professionals have told us to keep stimulating her. Questions are good, especially questions about the past. 'Didn't Grandma used to draw a cat?'

'My mom?' I nod. She shakes her head. 'Oh, no. I don't think so. She had five kids. She wouldn't have had time to draw.'

'Well, she must have. Because I remember you once talking about it.'

'A cat.' The eyes are worried. She's eager to please now, like a child. Ted and I alternate our weekly visits to her, but she always forgets who's coming. One or the other of us will just appear in her doorway, a vaguely parental figure that makes her try to remember things.

She's smiling. Something must have come into focus. 'Remember Sammy?'

Oh God. Well, I did push the cat-memory button, didn't I? So we do five minutes of Sam, he of the unending etymology. At seven, I named him Sunny, for his colour. Ted was steeped in Indian lore at the time, and called him Sundance. Three years later, a bout of

Egyptomania made me rechristen him Sun-Ra and try to worship him. Somehow all this became Sam, or Sammy to my mother.

The cat himself answered to none of the above, though he would occasionally flick an ear when my father addressed him as Queen Mary. 'Well, Queen Mary, are you going to let me sit there? No? Fine. Don't move. I'll just find somewhere else to sit. It's not as if I pay for your food, after all.'

I try again. 'Grandma,' I say.

'My mom.'

'Yes. Grandma used to draw.'

'Draw? My mom? Oh no, I don't think so. She had five kids. She wouldn't have had the – oh, *listen*. It's my *song*.' She starts nodding her head to music and mouthing lyrics. 'Bill,' she whispers, naming my father. Then, 'Ted.'

My brother can never bring himself to sit through her song. He can do everything else. He has power of attorney. But whenever her song starts, he's on his feet, fishing for his keys. 'Gotta run, Mom,' he always says. 'I'll hear your song some other time.'

Sometimes it comes through her radio, or out of the communal TV in the lounge. We're in the garden today, so maybe she's hearing it over the nursing home's PA system. Or the birds could be singing it. I'm dying to know if it's a solo or choral rendition, but don't dare ask.

I feel her hand on my forearm, light and dry as a cat's paw. 'Are you listening?' she whispers. 'It's all about you now.'

◆ ◆ ◆

Pencil. It has to be an HB pencil, too, the lead soft and dark. H and F are too hard. They make a light scratchy line that would have driven my grandfather into one of his teapot tempests. 'Why would you even have such a thing in the *house*? It's not a pencil, it's a pin!' He had high blood pressure. He was a small man with too much blood in him. Everything, down to the lead in the pencils, had to be to his liking or he might explode.

So I find an HB pencil, then sharpen it the way she would have, with a kitchen knife. No need for a pencil sharpener when there's a decent knife to be had. Why spend good money when you can *make do*? When you can *cut corners* and *save* and *do without*? So that someday you'll be able to afford a mahogany table. There's good value in mahogany. Hardness. Strength. Good value for good money.

The wood of the pencil is scalloped and the tip square when I'm done. Now for something to draw on. Don't waste a new sheet of paper. Find something used. A flyer pushed under the door. No. Save that for a note to the milkman. The back of an envelope, then. Half of it. Save the other half for a grocery list.

There. Now sit and draw. Not at your desk. You don't have a desk. There's his desk, but it's his. Sit at the kitchen table, then. Snatch a bit of time before the kids come home from school. Before he comes home from work and stomps out into his garden to wing stones at any cat that dares come near his bird feeders.

Even so, there's one pair of round eyes too young for school, peering at you over the table edge. It's all right, dear. Mother's just – Go play. The eyes stay.

Oh well. You have your sharpened pencil and your half of the back of an envelope and your bit of time, if not privacy.

Now what do you do?

Draw a cat.

Why? Of all the things you could draw, why draw a cat? Why not draw your house, this room, your garden, your husband, this child still staring at you unblinking?

Because you want to draw a cat.

All right then, what kind of a cat do you draw? Is it sitting, standing, sleeping curled into a perfect circle or stretched like taffy in all directions at once?

Details aside, do you draw well? Do you have talent? Can you put that talent to work in these few minutes? Does your drawing tap into some universal cat-ness? Is it shaped and quickened by your memory of one cat in particular?

*Daisy, Daisy, give me your answer do.*

Mary Daisy Sangster McEwen has been dead for decades. In life, I never saw her so much as doodle in the margin of a church bulletin.

All I've got is that odd little memory, rattling around like a pebble in a sieve, of my mother saying what she said about her sometimes drawing a cat. And it is very odd, both the thing itself and my remembering it.

I suppose I could always ask Ted, the unofficial family archivist. Even as a kid Ted would sort through snapshots and put them in albums in chronological order. Whenever there was a picture showing grandparent, parent and child together, he would painstakingly print THREE GENERATIONS in silver pencil underneath it.

It would make sense to ask Ted about Grandma drawing a cat. And I would. If I wanted things to make sense. Which I don't.

I don't want to find out that she sometimes copied Felix the Cat out of what she called the funny papers. Not for her own amusement, but to humour some child who kept thrusting a pencil at her and whining, '*Draw* something!'

I don't want anything to polish down the oddness. I want my grandmother's drawing of a cat to be completely out of character. Furtive. Ungenerous. Lacking any redeeming usefulness. But hers. Without a doubt, hers alone.

◆ ◆ ◆

She gets up before I do, before anybody else in the cottage. I watch her, pretending to sleep.

She pulls her panties, which she pronounces *punties*, on under her nightgown, then steps into her blue slacks. They are the first pair of slacks she has ever owned, bought specially for this trip. It took widowhood to get her into pants. The wife of Angus McEwen wore a dress, always.

She hoists her nightgown and struggles out of it while holding her brassiere in place with one hand. Is she always this modest? I don't think she knows I'm watching her. Did my grandfather used to watch her? My mind shies from the thought. But he was a taut little man who would spring like a mousetrap at the slightest disturbance. Maybe that's how she learned this quietness, this deftness, this studied keeping of herself to herself.

She fastens her brassiere behind her back with difficulty. Her arms are withered, the skin loose and dry. She tries to hook the two panels of fabric together, but misses. Tries again. Misses again.

'I remember Grandma telling me once that when she was about your age she slept with her old granny.'

My mother said this while we were packing for the trip to Maine. It made the back of my neck itch.

My mother was getting more obtuse by the day. She was incapable of understanding the simplest question put to her, could not grasp the necessity of my most reasonable request. And yet she could still read my mind. At all the worst times.

I'd known for weeks that my grandmother and I would be sharing a motel room, and possibly a motel bed, en route to Maine. Then we'd share a bedroom for two weeks in a cottage by the sea before turning around and doing the motel thing all the way back again.

It was my mother's idea to invite my grandmother. 'I just can't stand the thought of her all alone in that house,' she said. 'Making her supper. Eating it all by herself. Going to her bed all alone. Night after night.'

What I couldn't stand was the way my vacation was being wrecked, my last summer vacation before starting high school. I only had a few weeks to figure out who I was, and then start being that person. Because I just couldn't start grade nine as plain old Daisy Chandler.

> *Daisy, Daisy, give me your answer do*
> *I'm half crazy over the love of you...*

I wasn't named for that song, but it had followed me all my life and I was sick of it. So I was going to be Di Chandler from then on. There. Di Chandler. Why couldn't they just get that through their stupid heads?

'Is that dye as in pigment, or die as in death?' my brother wanted to know.

'The name Daisy goes all through our family,' my mother said. As if I cared. 'It's not just yours and Grandma's name. There are all kinds of Daisys back in Scotland, aren't there, Mom? On gravestones.'

My grandmother, who was at our place for Sunday dinner, said something so softly that as usual we couldn't hear it. 'Quiet, all of you!' my mother yelled. Then, 'What was that, Mom?'

'It's the day's eye,' my grandmother repeated. We were all silent for once, waiting. Even my father, who was dozing off at the table, came awake in the sudden quiet. 'What's all this about somebody changing their name?'

'Shhhh!' we all said, focused on Grandma.

'It means the sun. The day's eye. The eye of the day. And if you look at the daisy, it's like a little sun.'

I loved it. I didn't want to love it, but I did. I didn't want to get my name from my grandmother, not just once but twice. But I had. I didn't want my grandmother to turn my name into something precious, something I'd keep safe, a secret, a treasure. But she had.

'Oh, that's lovely, isn't it Daisy?' my mother said, all fluttery the way she got when my grandmother was visiting us. 'I never knew what it meant. Don't you just love it when a name means something?'

'That should settle it,' my father said. 'Once and for all. All this fooling around changing your name is just a stage.'

'I'd like you to meet my sister, the day's eye,' Ted said, batting his eyelashes. 'This is my sister, the sun.'

I hated them. I hated them all, and I always would. If they would just shut up, if they would just stop for once, I could be the day's eye. The eye of the day. I could be the sun.

In the weeks before the trip to Maine, I would lie in bed at night and torture myself with comparisons. Sleeping with my grandmother, I decided, was worse than having to stand in front of my classmates at school and sing 'I'm a Little Teapot,' but not quite as bad as having to stand in front of them and sing 'Jesus Loves Me.'

The first night, in the first of our motel rooms, I scooted into the bathroom to change. Through the door I could hear my grandmother's running commentary on her own undressing. 'And now I'll just pull on my nightgown. And this is the kerchief I wear because my head gets cold.'

Finally we were safe, so I thought, with the lights out and a decent space between us in bed. But I had had chili for lunch and as I turned over let out an audible fart.

'That's the beans, dear.' My grandmother's voice was unbearably soothing in the dark. 'Every little bean must be heard as well as seen.' I bit a mouthful of sheet, silently screaming *die die die*.

My grandmother has finished dressing and is padding through the cottage toward the front door. This is the third morning in a row she's done this. Gotten up a good hour before anyone else, dressed and gone out. She probably just wants to sit in one of the wicker armchairs on the front porch. 'She gets tired of her bed toward morning, so she gets up and sits in her chair,' my mother has said more than once. 'The old don't sleep well. They can't get comfortable.'

Since my grandfather's death my mother has practically sung my grandmother's griefs and pains the way she would an opera aria. On this trip, she is treating her to a fussy, crooning attentiveness that makes me grind my teeth.

'Do you need your sweater, Mom? Sure? There's a cool breeze coming off the water. Let me get your sweater for you.'

'Try a little of my ginger ale, Mom. Just a sip. There. A little more. You'll be thirsty after that long walk.'

The *sweetness* of it, the very motherly-daughterliness of it, make my flesh creep. I couldn't stand getting that kind of attention from my mother. Can't imagine ever giving it to her.

I can't even imagine myself, as an adult, living within walking distance of my mother. Phoning her every other day to list the household chores I've done, or describe the soup I've made. Then walking a pot of that soup over to her for her lunch.

What I can imagine is a life so different and strange from the one I'm living now that sometimes wanting it to start can bring tears. This different life has no shape I can see or touch. It's more like a feeling, or an aroma, or a sound.

Sometimes I catch a whiff of it when I'm painting. I've brought my oil paints along with me to Maine. Maybe I'll be able to take hold of it, whatever it is, in this place that is strange and different, and far away from home.

'Now, if I could just do like Jesus, I could walk home.'

We had just arrived at the coast. My grandmother was standing in front of the cottage, looking out over the Atlantic. I was doing the same thing, trying, in my first glimpse of the sea, to think huge, oceanic thoughts. The homeliness of my grandmother's comment made me hunch my back. How could she stand to be so *ordinary*? All the way to Maine I'd had to listen to her and my mother talking about the price of tomatoes. During roadside picnic lunches, I'd had to endure her 'Put some lettuce in your sandwich. It's no good without lettuce.' *Nooo goood*.

'*Talk* to your grandmother, for heaven's sake,' my mother would say whenever she got me alone. 'You haven't said a single word to her all day.' So I would try, and then I would get, 'Don't show off how much you know when you talk to Grandma. Keep it simple. Keep it light.'

Tomatoes and lettuce, in other words. All I'd done was try to explain continental drift. My grandmother had commented that the wild roses of Maine were exactly like the wild roses she remembered from her girlhood in Scotland. So I informed her that they were indeed the very same roses, growing in the same soil, on the same rock, because everything was once stuck together before tectonic forces cracked it into pieces and pushed it apart.

'Oh?' she had said whenever I had paused for breath, and, 'I see,' and in the end, with a sigh, 'Thank you, dear.'

My grandmother has gone down the porch steps and is standing on the grass, looking out toward the sea. The morning fog is thick enough to smudge the horizon. The only solid thing I can make out, besides her, is the edge of the cliff that drops down a hundred feet to the beach.

When I heard the screen door open and close, I got up to go to the bathroom. On my way back I glanced out the living-room windows. I couldn't see my grandmother on the porch where I expected her to be, so I tiptoed to the door and looked out through the screen.

She is standing a few feet from the cliff edge. Waiting, I suppose, for the fog to lift so she can see the water. I am just about to turn and go back to bed when I see her take the first step.

I don't move. I can't move. She takes the second step. I can't make a sound. She steps a third time toward the edge of the cliff. I'm taking breath in, but I can't push any out. All I can do is watch her slowly bend double, as if preparing to dive.

All at once she takes three steps backward, not ordinary steps, but bouncing a little in rhythm. She claps her hands softly and hums to a cat, which follows her, purring. The cat is grey. It has stepped straight out of the fog. My grandmother turns in a circle, still clapping, still humming, and the cat follows her hands. She turns full circle the other way, and again the cat follows. Then she stands still. She stays bent over, stroking the cat's grey fur. It has the lithe energy of cats in the morning. It swirls like liquid under her hand, rears up to push its head into her palm.

I can see her breathing hard. Slowly, she gets to her knees, falling the last few inches to the grass. The cat rolls over onto its back and my grandmother begins an expert stroking. She knows how to stroke a cat, how to make it twist and writhe. She knows the secret places, the sacred places, of ear and chin and belly. She knows the sounds to make, the clickings and suckings, and the low throaty keening.

The cat sits up suddenly. It has seen something, heard something. It floats away back into the fog and is gone. My grandmother watches after it for a moment, then begins the process of getting to her feet.

I wait just long enough to make sure she can do it. She gets onto all fours, then brings one foot forward for leverage. When she begins to rise and find her balance, I turn and tiptoe quickly through the cottage back to bed.

The cliff must not be sheer, I tell myself. My feet are cold and my chest is thudding. There must be crevices and ledges all down the face of the cliff. That would explain where the cat came from. But that's all it would explain.

And then we all start seeing the cat. In the sunlight it's an ordinary grey tabby that seems to like my grandmother. 'Here's your cat, Mom,' my mother will say whenever the animal appears. We're sure it's not a stray, because it looks well fed and wears a flea collar.

When it comes near her my grandmother gives it a few perfunc-tory pats on the head, the same awkward up-and-down gesture she extends to Sam when she's at our house for Sunday dinner. Once, when it tries to get on her lap with muddy feet, she pushes it away and says, 'Scat!'

She is entirely predictable again, utterly ordinary. When my father brings home a lobster, she refuses to taste it. 'It's too indi-gestible,' she says, pronouncing it *indyejestible*. What she means is that it is too exotic, too far removed from the charred beef and mushed vegetables that have been good enough for her all her life.

I decide that I must have dreamed what I witnessed in the fog. And for a time, I forget even the dream.

'– then you said, "Oh, you're not going to put it into the boiling water *alive*, are you?" And then you ran out of the kitchen, because you just couldn't stand –'

'Mom, Dad *sent* me out of the kitchen because I kept trying to look into the lobster pot, and he was afraid I'd steam my face off.'

'– and then you wouldn't eat any of it afterwards, because you felt so sorry for the poor thing being boiled alive.'

'Mom, it was all leggy and spidery and it gave me the willies. I mean, I was morbid enough to want to watch a lobster being boiled alive, but not enough to want to eat it.'

My mother shakes her head, her eyes distant, fixed on the mem-ory of her own making. She has started rewriting my childhood. Recreating me in the image of the daughter she never had. I fully expect to hear that this phantom daughter married a nice doctor or lawyer and has two children who visit their grandmother regularly and write lovely thank-you notes.

'Mom, we were talking about the time we took Grandma to Maine with us.'

'Maine?'

'Yes. She was just recently widowed, and I was about thirteen, and Ted had to stay home because he had a summer job lifeguarding.'

'Maine. No. I've never been to Maine.'

'Yes, you have. You've been there lots of times, the first time with Grandma.'

'My mom.'

'Yes! Now. There was a cat that came out of nowhere on the island and seemed to be following Grandma around.'

'A cat.'

'A grey cat. And wherever Grandma was, the cat would show up, and just be there too. Remember? It was the strangest thing. Do you remember that? The cat in Maine?'

'Cat.' She puzzles for a minute. Then smiles. 'Remember Sammy?'

♦ ♦ ♦

I grew up in a time of dogs. The barking of dogs was as much a sound of summer as the jingle of ice cream trucks and the wheezing of push mowers. Sidewalks collected glistening mounds of dog dirt, which in turn collected footprints and flies.

But for all that, dogs were romanticized into noble creatures. We watched *Rin-Tin-Tin* and *Lassie* every week on TV, went to see *Old Yeller* and *Call of the Wild* at the show. Dogs were brave, intelligent, loyal and even patriotic. Dogs saved lives, led the blind and sniffed out Communist spy rings. Dogs were Disney's anthropomorphized Lady and the Tramp falling in love over a plate of spaghetti.

Cats, on the other hand, were selfish, sneaky, fickle and subversive. Cats were creatures of the night who befriended witches and ate baby birds. Cats were Disney's Si and Am, sinisterly alike, their slanting eyes and sing-song voices aimed at the prejudices of a postwar audience.

But I didn't know any of that when I asked for a kitten.

I remember my mother's typical, 'But none of us has ever had a cat!' She herself had grown up with a Boston bull terrier, a tiny pop-eyed creature named Janet. And in our extended family there were a dachshund, two boxers, a golden cocker, three beagles and a border collie. But not a single cat.

My Grandfather McEwen's influence in this was paramount. His hatred of cats was on a par with his hatred of Catholics, and his children would no more have acquired one of the former than they would have married one of the latter.

Until I asked for one. A cat, that is. Which I must have done with considerable authority.

My mother told my grandmother about Sam's advent, but left it up to her to break the news to my grandfather. 'I never thought I'd have a cat in the house,' she was still saying, weeks after he took up residence. She couldn't get comfortable with him, she said. She was a *dog* person, she said. 'He's a nice pet for Daisy,' was all she would concede. 'After all, Daisy *asked* for him.'

'Did I just hear you offer the cat a bowl of Cheerios?' I'm half asleep, and think I may have dreamed it. I'm in the high school play, and have to get to school two hours early in the mornings for rehearsal.

'Well,' my mother says, 'one morning I came into the kitchen after I'd set out the breakfast. Your father was in the bathroom shaving, and Sammy was perched up in his chair, eating his Cheerios. So now I just give him his own bowl, and he leaves your father's alone.'

My mother slides a bowl of cereal under Sam's nose, then goes and gets a quart of milk from the fridge. Sam waits regally while she bends and pours. 'He likes it with a little milk,' she says, 'but he doesn't take any sugar on it.'

'Well, at least he's letting Dad back into the bathroom to shave,' I say, listening to Sam crunch his breakfast.

'Yes, he's a good boy again.'

Sam has just gone through one of his stages. This one consisted of curling up in the bathroom sink at the precise moment my father was about to start shaving.

'Oh, let me go and get the camera!' my mother said the first time he did it. My father ended up in the kitchen, shaving among the breakfast dishes with the aid of a hand mirror, while my mother used up a roll of film on Sam and told him what a naughty boy he was, not to let his Daddy use the sink.

This stage lasted two weeks, during which time Sam went around with a sopping wet head. He liked to catch the drips from the tap between his ears, in a kind of prolonged auto-baptism.

'Let's just hope he doesn't fall in love with the toilet next,' my father was heard to remark when the two weeks were up.

Sam's colour was a mixture of canary yellow and cadmium orange according to my paintbox. But although he would condescend to be photographed, he would not suffer himself to be painted. Even in his sleep, he could hear my paintbox open, would flick an ear, open an eye, stretch and be gone. My portraits of Sam were not so much unfinished as barely begun. Ghostly outlines in watery white paint. Hastily pencilled eyes. Shapeless splashes of orange.

At seventeen years of age, arthritic, incontinent and with the cartilage in his ears collapsing, he still refused to die, necessitating the only house call his vet ever made in a career spanning a quarter century. My mother detailed Sam's final hours in an eight-page letter that assured me he died at peace and in no pain, surrounded by family. It also managed to hint that I might, in all decency, have made an effort to be home at such a time.

I was home. I was in my new home, on the other side of the country. Sitting in my rocking chair with my new cat on my lap.

I have since come to believe that we only ever have one cat, a feline totem that pads in and out of our lives in assorted shapes and colours. It takes fur and dwells among us as many times as we are fated to enjoy the illusion of owning a cat.

By the time Sam died, I was twenty-four, had finished at Guelph and had started a graduate degree in creative writing at UBC. As I rocked, swaying between resentment and guilt brought on by my mother's elegy, I thought for some reason of my grandmother. She had been dead by then for about three years. What came to mind was something else that I had heard my mother say about her, besides the fact that she sometimes drew a cat. The something else was that she had always wanted to go to Vancouver.

She never did. When she was raising her children there was neither time nor money for such a trip. In retirement, my grandfather preferred to vacation in places like Bermuda and Nassau. He would never have let my grandmother travel anywhere, much less across the country, without him. And once he was gone, she was too frail to travel alone.

As I sat in my Kitsilano apartment with the warm weight of my cat on my lap, it occurred to me that I didn't know what I was doing at UBC. Oh, I could list the reasons I had come, both personal and academic, and they all made sense. But the impulse, the need to go as far away as I could, was all at once a mystery.

As much a mystery as the need, at the age of seven, for a cat. Or for this cat, rhythmically pressing my thigh, her soft pads offering the barest hint of claw.

◆ ◆ ◆

My grandmother took the mug of tea from me with both hands. The mug was the only clean one I could find in the lounge kitchen. It was plastic, its rim gnawed. It imparted, I knew, a distinct plastic flavour to any liquid, hot or cold. I had pulled out my desk chair so she could sit down. My mother sat beside me on the bed, and my father stood.

This was my room in residence, with red brick walls, grey carpet and a tiny window like a slit in a fortress. My bed was a slab of foam on a wooden platform, and my desk had a scarred Arborite surface.

I was eighteen. Every morning when I woke up, I saw the posters I'd put on the walls of this room, the books stacked on the bracketed shelves, the bulletin board frantic with coloured notices, all the reminders of my astonishing new life.

My grandmother sipped her plastic tea and looked around my room while my parents and I talked. It was a Sunday afternoon in October. They had picked her up from the nursing home and taken her for a drive to see the colours. Then, since they were in the Guelph area, they had stopped in at the university on the chance that I might be in.

I was, and I was glad. My first weeks away from home had brought on a short-lived flush of clannishness. I kept glancing at my grandmother. I wanted to ask her what she thought of everything, my marvellous closet, my wonderful orange metal waste paper basket, my exquisitely ugly high-tech desk lamp.

One of my glances caught her eye. The look she gave me was naked. Stripped for once of whatever it was that made her my grandmother, and me her granddaughter.

'– and her teacher came to her house, came on his bicycle, and begged her father to let her stay in school. Because she was so bright, and such a good student.'

My mother's stories of my grandmother's early life are polished as smooth as the parables of Jesus. She can recite them perfectly even now, when it's beyond her to remember what day it is.

'But her father, and all she would ever say about him was that he was a hard man, her father said, No, her brothers had to go out to work, so she'll go out to work too. So she was hired out as a skivvy in the kitchen of an inn, miles from her village. And the cook made her scrub the pots in scalding hot water. My poor hands, was all she would say. My poor hands.

'And then after three weeks she was allowed a day off, and she came home and begged her mother to let her stay. But her father, and all she would ever say about him was that he was a hard man, her father said, No, if you let her stay home this time, she'll never be good for anything. So back I went. That's all she would ever say. Back I went.'

At fourteen, the age she was when she was forced out to work, I came to view my grandmother as an anthropological specimen. A bit of living history. I had a tape recorder I had gotten for my birthday and one Sunday night when she was at our house for supper I thrust the microphone at her and grilled her about her schooling.

Her soft, hesitant voice barely recorded. 'Well,' she said, 'the boys was on one side, and the girls was on the other. And we had to do the Latin.' She was silent for a moment, but the microphone didn't go away. She sighed. 'And once a week, we did the barbells.' She raised her arms up and down, demonstrating.

'Here, see, here she is when she worked at the inn.' My mother is holding one of the framed photographs I grew up with. Looking at pictures that are so familiar I can't see them any more is part of the ritual of visiting my mother. The walls of her room, the tops of her dresser and night table are a family gallery. We're all there, over and over, my father and Ted and me. And there are at least a dozen studies of Sam in various poses and attitudes.

My mother wipes dust with her sleeve from the one she is showing me, then tries to tilt it out of the glare of the window so I can see. No need. I have this particular photograph memorized. It formed the basis of the first short story I ever tried to write.

I still can't finish it. It's not really a story, just two fragments, a beginning and an end. I can't even decide which is which. In one, my grandmother is a young girl working in the scullery of an inn. The other is a kind of dream sequence in which, as an old woman, she walks upon the sea. Both fragments feature a cat that seems to play some kind of doppelgänger role. Beyond that, I can't find the link between the two. I can't write the guts of the story.

But I can't abandon it either, the way I've abandoned so many others, more than I've published. The fragments actually embarrass me. They're flowery and romanticized and young. I've thrown them away I don't know how many times, then retrieved them and put them back in their file. God knows why.

Maybe because they're my first bit of writing. I wrote them shortly after my grandmother died, when I was experiencing what I can only describe as heartbreak.

So I know this particular photograph very well. It is a formally posed portrait of the service staff of the inn where my grandmother worked. By the time it was taken, she had risen through the ranks from kitchen skivvy to upstairs maid.

She is dressed in starched white, her waist cinched small under a square-bibbed apron. As befits the grown woman she has become, her hair is turned up and pinned under her maid's cap. She does not smile. Her expression is that mix of diffidence and duty I would see in later photographs, and in life. She is sixteen years old.

I wonder now if she ever gave a thought or a glance to the tall footman in the greatcoat and top hat, the one with the Charles Dana Gibson chin. I wonder if she envied the downstairs maids their lace collars and their prettiness. Did she get along with the housekeeper, the serious one seated importantly in the middle with what looks like a Bible or maybe a black bonnet on her lap? Or was the mere sight of the woman her own personal cross?

## Daisy, Daisy

What I was hoping to hear when I held the microphone to my grandmother's mouth was the story she had never told. I wanted to hear what happened after her father said no, and her teacher left on his bicycle.

Did she plead, at least? Were there tears? Was her voice raised in protest for the first time? Was a blow struck to silence it? Then, was there one sleepless night of rage, just one, before that relentless good behaviour, that utterly uninspired practicality, set in for life?

*give me your answer do*

I didn't know how to ask. And she didn't know how to tell. The tape turned on silence.

♦ ♦ ♦

My grandmother's hands are lapped one over the other. They have that floating, suspended appearance embalmed hands have, as if the one on top does not quite touch the one underneath, and neither is actually resting on the body.

I am standing beside her coffin to pay my respects. (*Casket*, I can hear my mother insisting.) My feet hurt. I got new shoes yesterday to go with my one remaining dress, a little navy and white thing with a sailor collar. 'Oh, you look *nice*,' my mother said when she and my father picked me up from the bus station this morning. Her obvious relief that I hadn't shown up in sandals and jeans made me wish I had and glad I hadn't.

How long is paying your respects supposed to take? And what are you supposed to do? Pray? I can't. I've stopped believing in God.

It was very sudden. A clunk, like falling out of bed. I'd toyed with atheism since starting university. All my friends had achieved it. They could completely discredit a professor with, 'He's an *Anglican*,' or, 'She goes to *church*.'

My vestigial faith didn't consist of much, just a sentimental attachment to Jesus, as to a balding teddy bear. And then one morning I woke up with even that gone.

It was strange at first. Still is, at times like this. As if I've committed a crime all alone and unseen. No one knows but me and God, Who doesn't exist any more. I wish sometimes that He still did, so I could wave my unbelief in His face and get some kind of reaction.

Well. I suppose if there's no God, there's no afterlife, so that's it for my grandmother. Over and done with. All gone.

Except there she is in the coffin. *Casket*. It's the coffin they carry you off in, Daisy.

I concentrate on her hands. It's easier to look at them than at her face. She's wearing a blue dress, with blue lace at the wrists. Most likely a Better Dress from Eaton's. I remember my mother telling me, in that hushed tone she reserved for talking about her parents, that Grandma always went straight to the 'Better Dresses' section of Eaton's ladies' wear. It was a matter of value. If money was to be spent, it was to be spent wisely. A Better Dress was cut more generously, from better stuff. Sterner stuff. The seams were finished so as not to give way under stress. The hems ravelled not, nor did the buttons hang by a thread.

And blue was her favourite colour. Or was it my grandfather's favourite colour? Probably his, knowing her.

Knowing her. What do I know? What do I feel? When Ted phoned on Sunday night to say, 'Grandma passed away,' all I felt at first was relieved that the funeral would be in the middle of the week, and I could use the next day's classes as an excuse to rush back to Guelph.

Then I curled up on the residence lounge couch, afraid. I didn't know what of. It felt like being in trouble, a cold tickly spot just under my breastbone. As if I was somehow to blame for her death, which everybody had been waiting for for months and everybody had been saying would be a blessing when it came.

'I never thought I'd hear language like that coming from my mother,' my own mother said one weekend last winter when I was home. She has never gotten over my rejecting McMaster for the wilds of Guelph and a bed not my own. But lately, especially when she confides in me or asks me questions that have obviously piqued her for years, it is as if distance has turned me into a safe, neutral stranger. Our conversations now include short lectures from me on what is in the Dead Sea Scrolls, how something like yogurt can be alive, and what exactly homosexuals do with each other.

'Everybody has a submerged personality,' I said when she told me about my grandmother's latest outburst. 'A kind of shadow side. And when a person's defences are down, it shows.'

But she wouldn't have any of that. 'Not my mother,' she kept saying, shaking her head. 'My mother never even knew the words that are coming out of her mouth now.'

The incident that had brought this on was my grandmother's eighty-eighth birthday. In the middle of the small celebration in the nursing home, she had told her five assembled offspring that they could all just grow up and start wiping their own asses for a change, because she was sick of them and sick of their shit.

My explanation sounded pretty lame, even to me. The truth was, my grandmother's outburst had left me with a feeling of déjà vu. There was something *familiar* about it, something eerily authentic. I felt as if I had just glimpsed the dim outline, through wallpaper, of a door that had always been there.

'Heather and I still go to see her. The boys can't bring themselves to. They don't want to see their mother the way she is now. But Heather and I just tell ourselves it's not Mom saying those things. It's not Mom.'

Then who's that in the coffin? *Casket.* I don't know. So I'm back to square one. And if those are my respects, I've paid them.

I turn away and go over to my mother, who is whispering damply to my Aunt Heather. 'Just *ridiculous* what they've done,' I hear her say as I get near. She turns to me. 'Did you see those glasses perched on Grandma's nose, Daisy?' she says. 'They've gone and put her *glasses* on her. Have you ever seen anything *sillier?'*

Aunt Heather chimes in, 'It makes her look like she's fallen asleep in her *chair!'*

Both sisters blow their noses, then tuck the used Kleenexes into their already full purses. As one, they pull forth clean tissues, ready for the next blow.

'Well,' I say carefully, 'why don't you just ask the funeral director to take the glasses off her?'

I should have known better. That frozen look I've seen all my life comes over both faces. Seek not, lest, God forbid, ye find. Then there are the quick shakes of the head, and the declarations that no, no, we wouldn't *ask*. We would never *ask*.

'And don't you go asking either, Daisy,' my mother pleads. '*Please.*'

'I *won't.*'

She and her sister blow their noses in unison again, then take a turn around the chapel, reading the cards on the floral tributes. I watch them go, half expecting them to hold hands like the orphans they suddenly are.

Their three brothers, uniformly paunched and balding, are standing in a tight circle in the middle of the floor. I can't hear them, but I can guess that they're conferring about where to park and who will drive whom to the cemetery. They've left the tears and flowers to their sisters. They may have wept in private for their mother, but here they will *hold in*. They will *show some backbone*. Or if, God forbid, they do *break down* or *go to pieces*, they'll waste no time in *pulling themselves together*.

Every now and then one of them catches my eye and gives me a vague avuncular smile. *We're not sure what to do with you any more*, the smile says. *You're not like our own daughters, married and settled and safe, thank God*.

Two of their settled and safe daughters are off in a corner together, the bobbing of their chins practically synchronized. It amazes me that Sheila and Jean can find so much to say, given that they live within walking distance of each other and talk on the phone almost daily, according to my mother.

But they've always been more like sisters than cousins. I remember them sitting side by side on our grandmother's couch, stitching away at scraps of cloth she'd given them. Funny. I haven't thought about that in years. How Grandma would give them threaded needles and bits of cloth to sew together, but a sharpened pencil and pad of paper to me.

This afternoon when we greeted each other we pretended the usual frantic interest in each other's lives. 'So you're in *third* year now!' Sheila all but screamed at me. 'And next year you'll *graduate!* That's *terrific!*'

'And just look at *you!*' I roared back at Jean. This time it's Jean who's pregnant. One or the other of them always is. 'When are you *due?* I bet you're hoping for a little sister for the boys!'

We don't care. We don't know each other. We never give each other a second thought. But here we are. Together in this room for an hour. The children of the children of the dead woman in the coffin.

*Casket*. And it's not a woman, it's *Grandma*, and she isn't dead. She has *passed away* and is *at rest*. Soon she will join our grandfather, who has been resting for years at Mount Hamilton Memorial Gardens, where he is treated to *Perpetual Care*. That is, for a price the grass around his resting place is cut and the dandelions pulled. Well, he always insisted on a neat lawn.

My face is aching now, in rhythm with my throbbing feet. The pain comes of maintaining a smile that is called seraphic, I remember from Art History 110, and is in fact obsolete. Human beings just don't wear that expression on their faces any more. If they ever did.

But we do. We are all seraphs here today. Inhaling the scented air and contorting our features into masks of sublime, sweet sadness.

I've got to get off these shoes. I go and take a seat beside my father in the row of chairs second from the front. The front row is reserved for my mother, my aunt and my three uncles, the primary mourners. We, I suppose, are considered secondary, those behind us tertiary, and so on.

My father is fidgeting the way he does when he needs a smoke. His hand snakes under the lapel of his jacket, fingers the pack of cigarettes in his shirt pocket, then remembers where it is and falls back out onto his lap where it drums its fingers for a minute or so before starting the whole thing over again.

My father and I often end up together at McEwen gatherings. I don't know what would happen to us at Chandler gatherings, because there aren't any. When I first heard about the Big Bang, I was reminded of my father's family. The Chandlers are like those exploded particles, forever putting more and more distance between them.

But from my parents' house in Hamilton I can still walk to the homes of any of the McEwen siblings. They never got over sharing beds as children. Breathing one another's breath.

My father leans over suddenly and says to me, 'You didn't get a return ticket, did you?' His breath smells of hot metal.

'Yes, I did.'

'Well, save the other half of it. I'll drive you back to Guelph after this.' He waves vaguely at the surroundings. 'We'll take your mother out to dinner. Then I'll take you back.' His hand travels under his lapel to his cigarettes again, then remembers again and comes back out empty.

'Thanks,' I say awkwardly. Small ceremonies, like thanking, are wasted on my father. My mother sets huge store by them, will count the days between sending a wedding present and receiving a thank-you note from the bride. But my father appears not to expect gratitude, for things large or small.

'Now let me get this straight,' he said to me when I was digging my heels in about going away to school instead of staying home the way Ted did. 'If you go away, you have to spend money on room and board.'

I nodded, my throat dry.

'And that's money you could save if you stayed home.'

I nodded again.

He was silent for a minute, hissing smoke out from between his teeth. Then he said, 'Well, it's not what I would do.'

I waited for more. There wasn't any more. No criticism, nothing like my mother's tearful demanding to know *why* I would want to go away, when there was a perfectly good university right in Hamilton, good enough for my brother, just a bus ride away, and I could leave every morning with a brown bag lunch, then come home every night to a decent, nourishing supper and my *own bed*. From my father, there was nothing like that. Just this flat statement of difference. I felt at once grateful and bereft.

Things are about to start. The primary mourners have taken their places. The funeral director has drawn a curtain around the coff – *casket*, I guess to close it. Ted has taken a seat off to one side, along with five other grandsons. They range in age from eighteen to thirty-two, and they're everything from ponytailed to bald. Yet they are eerily alike in their dark suits and funeral faces.

'Get ready,' I overheard my mother say to Ted a few weekends ago when I was home. My grandmother was, in family parlance, *low*. 'It'll probably be her grandsons who'll be pallbearers.' Don't go to pieces, in other words. Don't break down.

I can more easily imagine Ted spontaneously combusting than breaking down. The last time I saw him in tears was when he was eight years old and had caught a sunfish that was too small to keep. I remember being amazed to see my big brother, who could bait his own hook, start to squeak and blubber when his fish went back into the lake.

Now I watch him grin at something our cousin Ian has just whispered, and I know that, in a way, he's enjoying himself. Ted appreciates any excuse, even a funeral, to get together with family.

*Grandma passed away.* His words to me over the phone had the ring of this clan, practically the smell of it. And he himself looks more like a McEwen all the time. It's not just a physical resemblance, either. It's an attitude. An assumption. A very deliberate shouldering of – what? Connectedness? Belonging? I don't know. I'm beginning to think I never will.

An unseen organ is playing a syrupy rendition of the twenty-third psalm. It's a version I once had to sing in a school choir, and my memory unwillingly pulls up the lyrics.

> *The Lord's my shepherd, I'll not want;*
> *He makes me down to lie-ie*
> *In pastures green; He leadeth me*
> *The quiet waters by-y-y …*

Reverend Culver has taken his place at the lectern. It's been years since I've seen him. He has led this little flock of aging Presbyterians for decades, and hasn't so much changed as become more like himself. Always a tired-looking man, he now appears to be on the brink of exhaustion.

'Let us pray,' he intones, and as one, we hunch forward.

There is something foetal about the attitude of prayer, I decide, as the pastor drones on about the resurrection and the life. Here we all are, curled up, heads bowed, eyes shut. Back to the womb *en masse*.

> *If I should die before I wake*
> *I pray the Lord my soul to take*

I suppose I'll never forget those words. I was made to say them every night from the time I repeated them after my mother or father until I could be trusted to say them silently to myself. *Now I lay me down to sleep.* The babyish sing-song used to embarrass me. Still does. But I had to say my prayers. Even though they weren't mine. And Ted had to say them before me, even though they weren't his either. And probably my mother said them to my grandmother.

Did my grandmother say them too, when she was a child? The Man Upstairs was how she referred to God. 'I'll ask the Man Upstairs,' she would say, if somebody in the family wanted to get married or get pregnant or get a job.

I wonder if she ever asked for anything for herself. And if she did, what was it?

'Amen,' says Earl Culver, and we all sit up, backs and chairs creaking.

'Mary Daisy Sangster McEwen,' the minister begins, 'built her life on a firm foundation whose four cornerstones were her husband, her children, her home and her church. Her husband, Angus McEwen, was sustained in his work and anchored in his prosperity by her loyalty and faith in him. Her children were nourished both by her love and by her example. Her home was a place of peace and plenty, remembered not only by the grandchildren but even by some of the great-grandchildren here present. And as long as she was able, her church was graced by her presence, her support and her service.'

She was a saint, in other words. Well, what did I expect him to say? She *was* a saint. One of a whole generation of martyrs named Mrs. I still see them sometimes, stepping along the treacherous pavement. They travel in pairs, clinging to each other, keeping an eye on each other's feet. Careful. Careful. Break a hip and you're in a home. They still have those skinny ankles and big, rattling, Minnie Mouse shoes. They still wear navy silk with white polka dots. Their hair is still done in tight white curls that let pink scalp show through. And they're all the widow of, the mother of, the grandmother of.

Not me, I've always thought, when I've seen them. No way. Never. As if I've escaped, just barely, with my life.

I've had the same thoughts when I've seen Sheila and Jean, with their contrapuntally swelling stomachs and their talk of saving up for a coffee table. Have you *seen* the price of coffee tables these days?

Not me. No way. Never.

'When I last visited Mrs McEwen in the senior citizens' home,' Reverend Culver is saying, 'I was pleased to find her alert and in good spirits, as she was not always able to be, as you know, toward the end. Before partaking of Communion, we gave thanks together for her bountiful life.'

Bountiful. Nice word. Makes me think of a cornucopia. Something full. Overflowing. My cup runneth over.

'As we prayed,' the minister goes on, 'she named each of her children in turn, and, with very little prompting, was able to name every one of her many grandchildren.'

Was I one of the ones she had to be prompted over, I wonder. Stupid question. The bottom line is, she named me. I was there, in her memory. Part of the bounty. Something she could name. Something she could point to.

'And then, after Mrs McEwen and I had partaken of Communion, I read aloud the Twenty-Third Psalm. Though she was silent, I saw her lips form the words as I said them.'

I can't point at anything. Not even at painting. Not any more. I used to. I used to say, there. That's what I am. That's what my life is.

But in the last media course I took, the professor stood watching my tortured, self-defeating brushwork and then put her hand on my wrist. Stopped me mid-stroke. 'It's *painting* you're supposed to be doing here,' she said. 'Not *writing*.'

I didn't know what she meant. I still don't. And now there's nothing I can point to. All I know is what I'm not, what I don't want to be, what I can't be. All I know is the *no way*. The *not me*. The *never*.

I can't say to myself, *At least* I will do this. Raise this child. Tend this garden. Help this man. Worship this God. All the things my grandmother must have said to herself when she couldn't have whatever it was she wanted, and continued to want, all her life. *At least.*

I have no *at least*. Nothing to keep me from disappearing. Nothing to keep the still waters from closing over my head.

'Yea, though I walk through the valley of the shadow of death,' Earl Culver is reciting, 'I will fear no evil: for thou art with me; thy rod and thy staff they comfort me.'

Oh, shit. Now I'm in trouble. My throat's closing up and my nose is starting to itch. A movement off to the side catches my eye. A piper in full regalia is arranging his pipes, fitting his mouthpiece. Jesus Christ, where did *he* come from? Whose idea was it to have a fucking piper pipe her out? What are they trying to do to me?

Ted and the other grandsons have risen and stepped forward. I have to try to find some kind of control. Is there an art to pallbearing, my mind jabbers at itself, frantic for cynicism. Did the six of them decide beforehand who was going to be front, middle and back? Have they agreed to hoist on a count of three?

The piper skirls the first notes of 'Amazing Grace.'

The coffin lifts.

I go to pieces. Break down completely.

I'm not the only one, but I might as well be. Heads turn, my brother's among them. Eyes are on me. My mother's. My aunt's. My uncles'. My cousins Sheila and Jean both manage wobbly smiles in my direction.

I feel my father's hand close over my own. His other hand fumbles for something. Not his smokes, for once. For a handkerchief. It is folded into a square, its edges sharp. My God, my father still uses cloth handkerchiefs, I think stupidly. My mother still irons them piping hot and flat as paper.

I blow my nose into it and give it back to him. He tucks it, full of his daughter's snot, back inside his lapel.

His other hand is still closed over mine. The eyes are still turned on me. My mother, my cousins, my uncles, my aunt. The eyes are kind, and the hand a comfort. But I wish my father would let go, and I wish the rest of them would leave me alone.

And slowly, as I begin to pull myself together, they do. Too slowly. Will they *never* let go and leave me alone? My whole head feels as if it's on fire. Will they please never let go and leave me alone?

♦ ♦ ♦

My grandmother comes up behind me and says she'll keep me company. *I don't want company*, I could almost scream at her. *I want to be an artist.*

I've set my easel up on the stony beach. The wind keeps blowing seaweed and sandflies onto my canvas, where they stick in the wet paint. I never expected the waves to stand still, but I wish they would at least do the same thing twice.

My grandmother has brought a yellow plastic chair with her from the porch. She goes a few steps in front of me, settles the chair smack in the middle of my seascape, and sits down.

I try to paint around her. I try to paint through her. There's no getting away from that yellow plastic chair. With the white orthopaedic shoes sticking out to either side. And the blue sun hat poking up above. And the pink and brown hand on the armrest.

So I scrape my canvas and turp my brushes. Maybe tomorrow. Except tomorrow's our last day. After tomorrow, I'll have to leave the ocean and start grade nine. I don't know why that scares me so much. I keep thinking that if I can just do one decent seascape and bring it back with me, if I can just have one painting that I did of the ocean, then it all won't be so bad.

I glance at my grandmother while I'm folding my easel. From the angle of her head, I can tell that she's fallen asleep. I'm tired too. Neither of us slept well last night.

She hadn't meant to wake me up. She was standing by the open window of our bedroom, trying to be quiet. But I heard the ragged edge of her breathing, and the wet blowing of her nose.

The sounds scared me. I wished I hadn't heard them. They were too raw and too wet. For some reason I wanted her to be dry, to be healed over, with all her hurts, the ones I knew about and the ones I didn't, just a memory.

*If I could do like Jesus, I could walk home.*

Did she really miss Scotland all that much? She had never been back. My grandfather would never take her, and he wouldn't let her go on her own either. He hated Britain. He used to say somebody should pull the plug and sink it.

Maybe it was my grandfather himself that she missed. Well. Somebody had to love him.

I finish cleaning my brushes. She's still asleep in her chair. I'm down on my knees, looking for the cap from my tube of cerulean blue, when I freeze.

I do this now and then. I don't know why. Spook myself. Scare myself silly. Think thoughts that are like a stranger's voice whispering in my ear.

*Your grandmother's gone*, the voice says. *She's not there because she was never there. You won't even see an empty chair if you look now. Because the chair was never there. Because she never put it there. Because whoever she was, she was never your grandmother.*

I'm breathing loudly, almost whimpering. With a little yelp I make myself stand up and turn and look.

◆ ◆ ◆

'Would you like to have that picture of Grandma at the inn, Daisy?'

'No, thanks, Mom. You keep it.'

'You can have it, you know. I've got plenty.'

'No, I'll get them all someday. You keep it for now.'

But she needs to give us things. She's forever pressing photographs, sweaters, her watch, money from her purse, on us both. Ted just takes whatever she offers him, then puts it back when she's not looking. I, for some reason, still put up a fight.

She has wheeled herself over to the dresser and is taking the pictures off it one by one and putting them in her lap. Oh God. I start toward her to stop her, pausing to put the one I'm holding back on its hook on the wall.

The shadow of my head falls squarely across the glass, and I see something I have never seen before. Or have been seeing all my life.

'Mom!'

She turns, her eyes questioning.

'Mom, can I have this photograph after all? Please?'

She wheels over and looks. 'Oh. That one. You want that one, do you?' She's forgotten she offered it to me.

'Please. I'd really like to have it.'

'Well, you know you'll get them all someday, don't you?'

Ted would just take the damned thing. What I'll do is wait until she offers it to me again. Which could be ten minutes from now. Then, for once, I'll say yes.

It's not a Bible in the housekeeper's lap. It's not a bonnet either.

It's a cat. A black cat. The creature stares directly into the camera, across an ocean, across an age, with that self-possession peculiar to cats. That air of secret knowledge.

♦ ♦ ♦

*Every morning the cat comes out of the shadows to sit on the kitchen hearth while the young girl lights the fire. The girl is always the first one up. After starting the fire she has to fill the great kettle and hang it over the flames, to boil water for the servants' morning tea.*

*The cat has learned that it might get a bit of leftover salmon from this girl, or perhaps a saucer of cream. From the cook, it gets milk but no food, to keep it keen for mousing.*

*The girl has ten minutes before the arrival of the cook, who will greet her with, 'Look more cheerful over there. I'll not have a sullen face in my kitchen.' In those ten minutes, the girl talks to the cat.*

*She talks soundlessly, stroking the black fur, telling the animal about the strange and different life she is going to live. Someday. Somewhere far away. She can barely find words for this life, for it has no shape that she can see or touch. It is more like a feeling or an aroma or a sound.*

*The cat blinks and purrs, lifting one forepaw then the other in a slow dance of joy.*

# Half in Love

'YOU SHOULDN'T HAVE LET ANY OF this happen, Daisy,' Trevor said. He lay on his back beside me in my university residence bed, one forearm across his eyes and both feet sticking out from under the top sheet. Trevor was tall and very thin. His body looked like a stalk, and whenever he bent his thick-haired blond head down to me, he reminded me of a sunflower.

Just then, the sight of his bare feet sticking out from under the sheet was reminding me of something else, but I wasn't sure what. I knew it would come to me, and I had a feeling it was probably the last thing on earth I should be thinking about at that particular moment.

'You know that nothing can come of this, Daisy,' Trevor went on in slightly ringing tones, as if we were on stage. 'You know I can never marry you. *Never*.'

Well, of course he couldn't. He was already married to Geraldine, who was a Catholic, and whom I felt I knew, because he talked about her so much. Just then his feet fell a little apart, and I realized what they were putting me in mind of. Toe tags. Those identification tags they slip over the big toes of corpses in a morgue. I was right. It was the last thing on earth I should be thinking about.

Trevor rolled over and started touching me gently under my eyes. 'Are you all right?' he asked, as sadly and anxiously as if I were an accident victim. I suspected I had just missed my cue to burst into tears.

I did have odd little accidents the whole time I was with Trevor Cleverly. I fell off my shoes once when he spun around on the sidewalk and jostled me. He spun around because he thought a group of children walking single file toward us was his daughters' class at school, out on some excursion, and he was afraid the girls might see him with me. My shoes were high and wobbly, with those inch-thick soles and stacked heels that were popular in the early seventies. 'You should wear something more sensible on your feet,' Trevor said, helping me up.

Another time, in my room in residence, he nose-dived so sharply to kiss me that the backs of my knees caught the edge of my bed and buckled, making me sit down on my favourite LP, *Bridge over Troubled Water*. 'You should never leave records on your bed,' he said, examining the two neat halves.

And then there was the time we were parked in his car at dusk, having a milkshake. Trevor drank a lot of milkshakes, because he suffered from what he called an inchoate ulcer. He had finished his, but I was still slurping mine when he suddenly slammed the car into reverse and careered backwards around a corner. My milkshake, strawberry, went all over me. 'I saw a woman coming toward us,' he explained. 'An old friend of Geraldine's. She would have recognized me, and seen you. Everything would have been ruined.' Then, while he was helping me mop my chest with paper napkins, he said, 'You should have drunk this up more quickly.'

Trevor kept telling me I shouldn't love him, that he couldn't possibly make me happy, that we had no future together, that our situation was hopeless. I couldn't have agreed with him more. When he said, 'Everything would have been ruined,' I was quite aware that he didn't mean me, or the two of us. He meant his twelve-year marriage to Geraldine, their century stone house on Oxford Street and their twin daughters, Rosalind and Imogen, who went to Montessori school. But that wasn't what kept me from loving him, any more than his *you shoulds* and *you shouldn'ts*, which I decided were kind of sweet and fatherly. He was thirty-four, after all.

In not loving Trevor, I wasn't being sensible or sophisticated. I wasn't being anything. I would have welcomed a bit of passion, actually. It might have lent some meaning to all my falling down, breaking and spilling things. But since the start of my third year at Guelph, I had felt half asleep. Or half awake. Nothing was real. Nothing mattered. Trevor Cleverly might as well have been somebody sitting down beside me on the bus.

'Do you think it might just be the weather?'

Rowena Matheson lived in the same residence as me. Her room

was one up from the lounge, mine one down, and we met in the morning to boil water for instant coffee in the communal kettle.

'I'm serious, Daisy. Don't rule out a lack of sunshine. It affects animals, and that's all we are. I mean, we had a crappy, rainy October, and November so far has been nothing but grey. There isn't even any snow to brighten things up.'

Rowena was studying veterinary medicine, specializing in large animals. She had crinkly orange hair, a Dennis the Menace nose and a slow, deft way of moving that I imagined would be soothing to some frightened creature in a barn.

'Get yourself a sunlamp. Look in the yellow pages. You can probably rent one from somewhere. No kidding. Ten minutes a day under one of those things and you'll perk right up.'

It was true that we had had a practically colourless autumn. Under the pelting rain the leaves had fallen as soon as they had changed, and the ivy on the older campus buildings had gone from green to brown with barely a week of red in between.

But there had to be more to whatever was bothering me than a lack of vitamin D. And I couldn't let a sentimental attachment to colour undermine my Advanced Media 312 project.

For two years, I had been looking forward to third year. Fourth year was all about finishing the degree. But third year was a chance to show what you could do with all the theory and history and technique you had absorbed. And what I had decided to do with it was throw it away.

For my project, I was going to divest myself of an artist's traditional tools. I was going to do a series of portraits of people I knew well – relatives, old friends, teachers I had had. I was going to draw them in simple black on white, because I had banished colour from my palette. And here, I believed, was the truly heroic part. I was going to permit myself neither models nor photographs, just notes I had jotted down in a series of scribblers. In other words, I was going to do portraits *from memory*.

Well, it had all seemed heroic when I thought it up in September. But now I was beginning to wonder if it wasn't just weird.

All I knew was that whenever I clipped my pad of paper to my easel and picked up my charcoal pencil, I froze. Who did I think I was? How could I have ever believed for a minute that I would do amazing things that would be shown on slides to generations of art history students? That I might be the subject of essays and exam questions for centuries after my death?

I envied Rowena her down-to-earth ambitions, her tucked-in future. Rowena had decided to be a vet when she was nine, had gotten engaged at eighteen to a dairy farmer named Pete, and now went home to Drumbo every weekend to sleep with her fiancé and go to church with her parents. 'It'll work,' I had heard her say more than once. 'I'll have a country practice, and I'll keep our own stock healthy on the side.'

I didn't have a future any more, tucked-in or otherwise. I was twenty-one, and it was all over for me. Every morning when I woke up, hopelessness and pointlessness sat like weights on my chest. *My heart aches*, I would recite silently to the bathroom mirror while Rowena sang in the shower. *And a drowsy numbness pains my sense.*

'You shouldn't have piled them so high.'

That was the first thing Trevor Cleverly ever said to me, seconds after backing into my desk at the start of an Early English Romantic Poets 310 lecture and knocking all my books to the floor.

He was auditing the course, the way he audited all his courses. 'I've already done a degree,' he told me after class that day. 'A Bachelor of Commerce, if you can imagine. I've done the essays, the midterms, the sweating for marks. Now, I just want to sit back and listen and learn.' And not have to come to classes, apparently, because he missed as many as he attended.

'I was working,' he would tell me, to explain his absences. It took me a while to realize that *working* meant writing poetry. 'At least, I was trying to work. The twins were up all night with diarrhoea, and then Geraldine went off and left them with me all day.' Another thing it took me a while to realize was that when Trevor said Geraldine *went off*, it meant she went to do a secretarial job she had gotten in a real estate office, shortly after he quit his job at the bank.

He sat beside me through that first lecture, doodling and whispering comments that undermined what the professor was saying. After class, he drove me to the Dairy Queen, got milkshakes for us both, then parked the car under a tree beside the Speed River.

'I was in banking,' he gasped between enormous draws on his straw. He said it the way he might say, 'I was on Devil's Island.' I gave the soft, sympathetic groan I sensed was expected of me while he sucked again on his straw. *Gasp.* 'I actually rose to the position of assistant manager.' *Suck.* I clicked my teeth and shook my head. *Gasp.* 'And then one day, in the middle of a staff meeting, the manager excused himself, got up and left. Half an hour later, I sent one of the male tellers into the men's room to see what was keeping him. And two days after that, the same teller and I were helping hoist his coffin.' *Suck.* I made another concerned noise in the back of my throat, trying not to imagine what the manager had been doing when he died. 'I needed half a bottle of Milk of Magnesia to get through that funeral,' Trevor went on. 'And when I came home afterwards, I looked in the mirror and said aloud, Today your stomach lining. Tomorrow your soul.' *Suckrattle.* 'So,' he ended briskly, crumpling his container and stuffing it into the plastic bag hanging under the glove compartment, 'I quit. Just packed it all in to be a poet.' A half second late, I lifted my milkshake to him in a toast.

Trevor never hesitated to call himself a poet, though he had yet to publish, submit for publication, or in many cases write down his poems. Those that were written down tended to be full of capitalized nouns:

*Bring the Boy to the Sea!*
*Print his protean Feet*
*In dark and giving Sand ...*

When he recited his poetry, which he did in a loud, declamatory sing-song, I could see what he was hoping to be. A *bard*. He wanted the word *bard* to be whispered in his wake. He was growing his hair out, and each time I saw him he had learned to do something else to make himself more *bardic*, like unbuttoning his shirt halfway, or, when it started to get cold, throwing a long silk scarf around his neck so that the ends trailed down his back. He always came to class a little late, all in a flurry as if fresh from creative chaos, his face pointing the way like the prow of a ship.

'Geraldine didn't *have* to run right out and take the very first job that came along,' he said that day in the car beside the Speed River. I could see the word *bitterly*, as if in parentheses, accompanying his speech. 'She doesn't *have* to serve Kraft Dinner and tuna casserole to us night after night. And she doesn't *have* to upset the girls by telling them they'll be going to public school next year.' The word in parentheses changed to *woundedly*. 'These things are all *gestures* on her part. Gratuitous slaps in my face. Statements to the whole world of what a bad husband and father I am.'

Being with Trevor was like watching a play in which the dialogue sounded as if a dozen well-known scripts had been put through a blender together, and the acting was just sufficiently off to be perversely fascinating. Starting with our first conversation, I found myself trying to guess the adverbial stage directions that informed just about everything he said or did.

(*intensely*) 'When I saw you in class today, I knew I had to speak to you. I can't explain it. Something about you just seemed to call to me.' (*wistfully*) 'I do need someone to talk to. I'm not simply selfish, though my actions may make me appear so. Or if I am selfish, it is only in the best sense of needing to be myself, to at least find out who that person is, before it's too late.' (*stoically*) 'Still, I know that in the eyes of the world I am almost criminally irresponsible. Mayhap even ridiculous.' (*nakedly*) 'But my pain is real, Daisy. I hurt. I hurt terribly.' (*heroically*) 'And there is nothing ridiculous in that.'

He (*abruptly*) turned away and (*hastily*) ran a hand over his eyes. Then he stayed turned away, his other hand (*desperately?* No, *torturously*) clenching and unclenching on the steering wheel. I counted eleven clenchings before he lurched back around, threw himself on me and pinned me against the passenger door. Literally pinned me. A pin I was wearing came out of its clasp and stabbed me just under my collar bone.

'Trvrr,' I tried to say around his mouth. 'Trvrrr!' Finally I shoved him off me and pulled out the pin.

(*strickenly*) 'I've hurt you.'

'No, it's okay. It didn't go all that far in.'

'Let me see,' he said, so I handed him the pin. 'That's not' (*meaningfully*) 'what I mean.' He (*tenderly*) undid the top buttons of my shirt and (*chastely*) kissed the wound, while I kept a lookout for passers-by. Then, after (*gallantly*) detaching himself from me, he looked at the pin and said, 'You shouldn't wear things that won't stay done up.'

> *Darkling I listen; and, for many a time*
> *I have been half in love with easeful Death ...*
> *Call'd him soft names —*

Oh, God. The Cryer in the Carrels was starting in again. I looked up from my Early English Romantic Poets 310 textbook and stared at each of the white walls of my study carrel in turn, trying to guess the direction of the sound. The library carrels were clustered, forming an acoustical maze. The crying, a breathy, muffled sobbing, could be coming from the carrel next to mine, or from all the way across the room. I couldn't remember when I first heard the Cryer, but now I was hearing him at least once a week. Or her. Most of the time the crying was so subdued that I couldn't tell if it was male or female. Tonight it sounded a bit more like a man.

There was a sharp intake of breath, practically at my ear, then a soft, wet spluttering. The Cryer could just about paralyse me when he got going. As long as he kept it up, I couldn't read, couldn't write, couldn't think.

I could always go back to my room in residence, but I was trying to avoid talking to Trevor. We only met once a week for an hour of hurried sex while Geraldine was at her real estate course and the twins were at Brownies, but he still managed to call me almost every night. Sometimes he called from a phone booth downtown, but more often he would whisper to me from the phone in his den.

'Daisy? Are you all right?'

*I'm as all right as someone can be when they don't give a sweet flying fuck at the full moon about anything at all including you, Trevor.* 'Yes.'

'I can't take much more of this.'

'Of what?'

'*Geraldine.* Tonight, while I was trying to eat my supper, it was just money, money, money. That woman is more bound up with money than I ever was when I worked at the bank. She cannot *conceive* of life except in terms of cash flow.'

*Is the mortgage payment due? Do two growing girls need clothes? Is Christmas coming?* 'That's too bad.'

'She has no sympathy for my situation whatsoever. She has not so much as tried to imagine what it is like to wake up one morning and realize you are almost thirty-five years old and have not got a single thing to show for it that you really want.'

*What does Geraldine really want?* 'That's too bad too.'

Sometimes, after one of these conversations, or while remaking the bed once he had left, I would ask myself seriously why I had anything to do with Trevor Cleverly. The best answer I could come up with was, because he was there. He was in my life. Maybe he was even part of my fate, the way a car that had hit me might have been. Or a brick that had fallen on my head.

Trevor was my second lover. The first had been Calvin Kirst, a minister's son from Kitchener, who was doing a combined honours in Latin and geography, and whom I met in a climatology lab I was taking as my first year science credit. Calvin used to remain standing until I had sat down, and would not so much as kiss my cheek in public. The contrast between his public manners and his fierce, private lovemaking, under the covers in my locked and darkened room, aroused me to heights that seemed to alarm him. By midterm, if he so much as reached for me in bed, I would moan or twitch or squeak, and he would snatch his hand back as if burned. Just before finals, I managed a resounding orgasm that must have frightened Calvin, because I never saw him again. That summer, he wrote to me to explain that he had confessed what we had been doing to his father, who had informed the Holy Ghost. The Holy Ghost had gotten back to Reverend Kirst to recommend that Calvin transfer immediately from Guelph to Waterloo Lutheran.

Trevor, untroubled by the Holy Ghost but with an eye on the time, was an adventurous lover. 'I've never done this before,' he would gasp, raising his head from between my thighs or pressing me down on him while he lay on his back. He implied that Geraldine was unwilling to try anything new or different in bed. I wondered if she was just tired, as completely unmoved by his onanistic pumping as I was.

The Cryer in the Carrels was still at it, hitting his stride. Then, all of a sudden, he stopped. In the silence, empty except for the hum of fluorescent light, I could tell that everybody else had been listening with me. Slowly, the silence began to fill up again with the sounds of pens scraping, pages turning, the occasional cough.

> *Now more than ever seems it rich to die,*
> *To cease upon the midnight with no pain ...*

My Keats essay was due next week. And I should have had my Advanced Media 312 project proposal more together by now. And semester finals were less than a month away. And minutes ago, I had had a pretty good insight into 'Ode to a Nightingale', but I had lost it when the Cryer started up. What was it? Come on, *what was it?*

Maybe the Cryer in the Carrels was affecting every one of us in exactly the same way. I pictured the white cubicles as if from above, all the heads bent over 'Ode to a Nightingale', trying to remember the wonderful insights they had had just minutes ago for their essays on Keats. And then I began to think of all the generations of students who had already written Keats essays, then all the generations still to be, with their Keats essays yet unwritten.

A break. Coffee. I got up, went to one of the common areas, put a quarter in a machine and got a paper cup of brown liquid I knew would taste of nothing but heat. I sat down with it at an empty table, where somebody had left a copy of the campus newspaper. I picked the issue up and thumbed through it, stopping at the headline, WATCH FOR CEDRIC.

*Be on the alert for Cedric,* the article began. *He usually appears in late November or early December, if he's going to show up at all. Since his death in 1927, Cedric Ellington has been seen by no fewer than twelve Guelph students. He tends to appear late at night near Massey Hall, where he died.*

Massey Hall, I thought, taking a sip of hot brown nothing. Massey was one of the oldest buildings on campus, octagonal in shape, with windows like portholes and a rooster weather vane. I had heard that it was a gymnasium years ago.

*Cedric is naked when he appears, and he puts out his hand in a gesture that has been variously described as beckoning, threatening or pleading for help.*

I glanced at the bottom of the page, where an old photograph was reproduced. It showed a group of muscular, serious-eyed young men in trunks and tank tops. The caption read, *The 1927 swim team. Cedric Ellington, aged twenty-one, is second from the left in the middle row. Weeks after this picture was taken, he was found in the early morning, naked and floating face down in the swimming pool in the basement of Massey Hall. A star athlete and a scholarship student, Cedric apparently went swimming alone one night and drowned.*

I studied the young man second from the left in the middle row. He was the only one looking away from the camera, his eyes cast down and to his right. He was the only one with a smile on his face too, a small bemused smile that gave him a dreamy look.

*What happened,* I thought at the small grey figure. *How could you possibly drown? You were a trained swimmer. And you must have known better than to go swimming alone.*

Was it shyness that made him look away from the camera and brought that smile to his mouth, I wondered. It was a sweet mouth. I ran my finger lightly back and forth over the grainy lips, then stopped for fear of smudging the newsprint.

*Were you half in love with easeful death, Cedric? Was that it? Did you cease upon the midnight with no pain?*

'*How small my craft,*' Trevor chanted while I held the phone receiver a little away from my ear.

> '*How tall the Wave!*
> *Waits Crest,*
> *Or Trough,*
> *Or watery Grave?*

Silence. That was the end of the poem, I guessed. 'Well,' I started, hoping I would think of something to say, 'it's very –'

'It's a haiku! I have actually written a haiku! I've compressed the whole of the artist's conundrum into seventeen syllables!'

'Oh. Well,' I began again. 'That's really –'

'I'm proud of it. I don't mind saying so. And it's the *compression* I'm particularly proud of, Daisy. The double meaning of *craft*. The ignominy of *trough*, with its hint of things porcine. That *is* there. Isn't it? I'm not just reading it in? The hint of things porcine?'

'Oh. Yeah. Sure. It's there, all right.'

'And of course, the ultimate ignominy, that of oblivion, which I believe I capture in *watery grave*. With its evocation of salt tears, of course.'

'Of course.'

'I'm experimenting with form, Daisy. I have to find my one true shape, so to speak. So today was haiku. Tomorrow, I'm going to produce a sonnet. Alexandrines on Thursday·...'

*Save heroic epic for a long weekend, Trevor.*

After I hung up the phone I went and stood again in front of my easel. The square pad of charcoal paper clipped to it was still empty, the page still blank.

I had decided to start with a portrait of my brother Ted. I had gone through the notebook where I had scribbled down Ted memories and Ted anecdotes and words or phrases that somehow evoked Ted. Then, hearing his voice in my mind, I had picked up my charcoal pencil.

Nothing. I couldn't move. It was as if I was afraid to put a mark on that perfect white sheet. And then the phone rang, and it was Trevor with his poem of the day.

I had never told Trevor what I thought of his poetry, and I hoped he would never come right out and ask me. It was not so much bad, I felt, as just not quite good. And that was somehow worse.

But who was I to talk? I was beginning to suspect the exact same thing of my own drawing and painting.

I put my charcoal pencil down without having drawn a single line. Then, as I was doing more and more at times like this, I reached into my jeans pocket and pulled out the photograph of Cedric that I had clipped out of the campus newspaper.

I carried it with me all the time now. One day when I forgot it, I skipped a class to come back to the residence to get it. At night when I undressed, I took it out of my pocket, unfolded it, kissed Cedric's face, then folded it again and put it in my dresser drawer under my underwear. I was terrified of accidentally putting it through the wash. Cedric's face was starting to blur anyway, from my lips and fingers.

I sat down and spread the photograph smooth on my knee. There was something about the fuzzy, grainy image of the boy forever looking away that I *needed*, somehow. That *fed* me.

When I finally looked up, the sky was black and it was long past the time I usually went to bed.

Rowena had delivered twin lambs that day. 'You look in,' she said laughing, 'and you see these two little noses. Both trying to come out first. So you stick your hand in to help one of them, and they both start sucking on your fingers. It feels like two little wet vacuum cleaners.'

I laughed along with everybody else in the lounge. But I was paying as much attention to the dirty light coming through the window, to the heat of the mug of coffee against my palms, as I was to Rowena's story.

I had done something remarkable that day too. But I didn't think I could tell anybody about it. I had skipped the afternoon's classes and had gone instead to the university archives in the Admin Building. Once I was there, I went through the microfilm library and found the original photograph of the 1927 swim team.

I loaded the cassette and brought the photograph into focus on the screen. What I saw made me breathe in a quiet *Oh!* Cedric wasn't fuzzy and grainy any more. He was sharp and real. I could make out a mole on his cheek. Hairs on his chest.

*Look at me*, I thought to the dead boy, over and over, half expecting his lids to flutter, his eyes to look up and find mine.

How could I tell anybody that I sat in front of the microfilm monitor for two hours? That I unzipped my jeans and caressed myself where I was swollen and wet the way I hadn't been for months? How could I tell anybody about that?

'So finally I get one of the lambs out,' Rowena was saying, 'and it goes, *Baaa!* And so help me Hanna, there's this answering *Baaa!* from inside the sheep!'

Someone had left a crumpled green gum wrapper in the study carrel. I picked it up and smoothed it out and sniffed its peppermint smell. Then I folded it into tiny pleats and fanned my nose with it.

My Keats essay was going to be late. I'd get an automatic B for that. And final exams were like a storm I could now see gathering.

My Early English Romantic Poets 310 textbook was in front of me again, open this time to 'I Wandered Lonely as a Cloud'. I had had an interview that afternoon with my Advanced Media 312 project adviser. When I explained my idea of doing portraits from memory, letting distance and reflection enhance the original impression, she accused me of reinventing Wordsworth.

Well, so what if I was? Had he taken out a patent on emotion recollected in tranquillity? I looked at the poem, whose words I knew too well. I supposed I could relate to *in vacant or in pensive mood*. But my heart hadn't danced with anything all semester, much less daffodils.

No. That wasn't true. What about the slow, rhythmic dances I did almost every day now in front of a microfilm monitor with Cedric Ellington?

'Daisy, please tell me what the point is of doing a portrait from *memory*,' my project adviser had said. 'I have no problem at all with you drawing purely from imagination, without a model in front of you. But if you're going to call something a *portrait*, then surely it needs that immediacy, that electric *thing* that happens between a particular model and a particular artist. Doesn't it? I'm sorry. I'm talking too much. Please. You.'

I sat looking at her. I couldn't remember any of the complicated aesthetic arguments I'd come up with to support my project proposal. I couldn't remember anything. Couldn't think of a single thing to say. My mind was blank, save for an image of Cedric.

'Daisy, I'm sorry if I sounded discouraging. I don't mean to discourage you. What I'm trying to do is —'

*Cedric.*

'Maybe a portrait's immediacy doesn't have to depend on the model being in the room,' I interrupted. 'Maybe a memory, or a dream, can be every bit as powerful as so-called reality.'

Last night I had dreamed about Cedric. Except for being naked, he was exactly as he was in the photograph, small enough for me to hold in the palm of my hand. He still looked down. Still smiled. Still would not meet my eyes. But I could feel his small heart beating under my thumb, and the soft give of his nipples and the pointed bud of his sex that sharpened as I caressed it.

'Daisy? Daisy? Yoohoo!' My project adviser was waving at me. 'Lost you there for a minute. Okay. Okay. You may be right. And it could be interesting to see how an impression is filtered through your memory and through time. So go ahead. Show me. I *want* to be convinced. One thing, though. This is an *advanced* media course, and I wish you'd consider being a little more adventurous when it comes to execution. I mean, flat black on white. It almost sounds as if you'd rather be *writing* than –'

'I'll be doing white on black too. Sometimes.' I knew I sounded gruff, defensive. This was not going well. She probably couldn't stand me, would talk about me later in the faculty lounge and roll her eyes back.

'Fine. Fine. It's your project. But take a look at some of the other proposals. They're really exciting this year. People are working with taped sound. Film, even. One guy wants to include a live goat in his collage, and we *are* trying to discourage that! But who knows? He might be on to something.'

*On to something.* I could add that to the list of all the things I was never going to do or be. I was never going to be *on to something.*

I crossed my arms on my textbook and put my head down on them. This was becoming a habit. Come to the library to avoid Trevor's nightly phone call. Stare into space. Put my head down on my arms. Sometimes even fall asleep. I had no business falling asleep. Except for dreaming, I slept like the dead. But every morning when I woke up the blankets felt heavier, and the cool air of my room was more of a shock when I finally pushed them back.

I kept waiting for something to change, for the clouds dulling my mind to lift, for some of my old energy to come back. Because if I went on like this, just drifting along until finals hit me in a deluge, I was going to fail. And I'd never failed. Not once. At anything. I couldn't even imagine it. What would it be like? Would it be like dying?

Cedric would know. If I could just talk to Cedric. If he could just be here with me, and listen to me. He was the only one I could possibly tell any of this to.

I put my face into the crook of my elbow. Took a mouthful of sweater. *Hey, everybody! Guess what! I've found out who the Cryer in the Carrels is. It's me. For tonight, anyway. But don't despair. Tomorrow, or next week, or next semester, it could be you!*

'Jesus, Daisy,' Rowena said, looking at my bottle full of morning-after pills. 'These things are going to turn you inside out.'

'I think that's the idea.'

'So what happened? Clever Trevor forget his rubbers?'

'Not exactly.'

'Oh, my God,' Trevor had gasped, looking down at himself seconds after withdrawing from me. 'Where *is* it?'

*Where would it be, Trevor?*

'You should have been on the pill! Or using a diaphragm! Or something! You should have realized that these things break, or come off inside, or —'

'Trevor. Calm down. It's probably all right. But just in case it isn't, I'll go to the campus clinic and get a prescription for a morning-after pill.'

'*Will* you? Will you go right away? Will you promise me?'

The campus clinic doctor, a genial Father Christmas type, looked disappointed when I told him what I needed. Writing out the prescription, he explained that a morning-after pill was in fact twenty-five pills, that I would have to take one every four hours around the clock for five days, and that even if I had just finished a period, I would have another one. That is, I would if the pills worked. There was no guarantee.

'Did Trevor even go with you to the clinic?'

'No, he had to drive Geraldine and the twins to —'

'Jesus Christ, Daisy! You're going to be in hormone hell for a whole week, taking these things! You're going to lose sleep, you'll be a nervous wreck, you'll probably be nauseated on top of everything else, and you tell me that that big dumb *fuck* couldn't even force himself to —'

'That big dumb fuck is the man I love, Rowena.'

No, he wasn't. No, I didn't. But it seemed like the thing to say. To justify what was happening. To make it all a little less ridiculous. Less pathetic.

'Oh,' Rowena said. 'I see. Well. That's up to you. But I'll tell you one thing. Pete would never put me through any of this shit. Not in a million –'

'Great. Say hello to Saint Peter for me.'

'Look, if you had any respect for yourself at all –'

'And thanks for the medical advice. *Doctor.*'

I turned and walked away from the sudden, wet hurt in Rowena's eyes.

*I'm in the archives again, sitting in front of the microfilm monitor. I bring the photograph of the 1927 swim team into focus for the hundredth time. Look. Look again. Then search, frantically. Cedric isn't there.*

*I check the caption. Yes, this is the right photograph. But at the end of the list of names are the words: 'Absent: Cedric Ellington.'*

*Just then I look up and see him at the end of the big room in the basement of Admin where the archives are stored. He still looks down and away from me, but he puts out his hand in that ambiguous gesture I have never seen but know so well. Then he turns and goes up the stairs.*

*I get up and follow. At the foot of the stairs I see the door just swinging shut behind him. I follow him out of Admin onto the campus. It is night, the black sky bright with stars. Cedric is heading across the court, onto the grass, straight for Massey Hall. I have to catch him. I have to stop him before midnight. Before he ceases upon the midnight with no –*

My alarm was ringing. It must be midnight. No. Morning. Except it was dark. I hit the button on the clock three times before I realized it was the phone that was ringing.

'Hello?'

'Please come to me. I'm all alone. And I need someone.'

'Who is this?'

(*petulantly*) 'Trevor.'

The clock said seven. I had lain down that afternoon and fallen asleep. 'Where are you?'

'At home. Please come. I'd pick you up or send a cab, but –'

'What about Geraldine?'

He told me that, three days ago, Geraldine had been laid off from her real estate job. Now she, Rosalind and Imogen were all in England, with her mother. The day she had been laid off, she had come home, given Trevor an ultimatum, gotten the twins out of school, taken them with her to a friend's house, then waited to catch a standby flight overseas. They would be back, she had said, when and if Trevor got a job.

'Please. I'll cook dinner for you. And you can spend the night.' (*brokenly*) 'The house is just so huge with them gone. And so empty.'

I could go, I supposed. There was no point in going to the library. I'd just fall asleep again. And Rowena and I weren't speaking. We were stiffly polite when we met in the lounge in the morning, where waiting for the kettle to boil had become an ordeal.

I would have liked to make up, to let her know that everything she had said about the effects of morning-after pills was absolutely true. After four and a half days of taking them round the clock, I was so tired I felt as if I had an anvil on my head. My hands shook, I jumped at the slightest noise, and I kept seeing dark insect shapes out of the corner of my eye that scuttled into invisibility when I turned to look at them. Eating was a labour, the sight of the butter pats stuck to the cafeteria ceiling enough to send me lurching outside for air.

I wanted to confess all this to Rowena, humbly, contritely. But her closed face and cool eyes reminded me every time of the unforgivable truth she had spoken. So even being with Trevor would be better than being alone with my shakes, my nausea and my imaginary bugs.

*'My Flesh has wings of feathered Bone,'* Trevor chanted, pressing my face to his shirt front with one hand and kneading my buttocks with the other. *'Not so my Soul, still as a Stone ...'*

We were in the kitchen of his house, where I had found him crumbling dried chili peppers into a hissing mess of ground meat and canned beans. When I asked if spicy foods weren't bad for his inchoate ulcer, he shrugged (*hopelessly*) and said that all he knew how to make was chili and omelettes, and he was all out of eggs. He stood (*bleakly*) staring into the bubbling pot for several seconds, then swung round, grabbed me and held me against him.

*'My Body throbs with warming Blood....'* His erection was pressing into my navel. His chin was digging into the top of my head, one dig per syllable. He had fumbled my jeans open and was working his fingers under the crotch of my underwear. *'While Spirit's Cold and Lost and Lone....'*

I began to feel a warm tingling, such as I had never felt with Trevor. The tingling got warmer as he caressed me, then hot, then started to burn. *'Half-buried in Life's viscous....'*

'Trevor! Your hands! There's something on your fingers!' I pulled away from him and grabbed my crotch. The burning didn't stop. I saw the jar of dried chili peppers on the counter, and remembered him crumbling them into the meat. 'Trevor, I'm going to have to take a bath,' I said, hopping around the kitchen. 'Now!'

Upstairs in the bathroom I couldn't wait for him to finish running the water, just threw off my clothes, got in the tub and started swishing waves between my legs. When the tub was full Trevor bent to turn off the taps, saying, 'Well, you shouldn't have –'

He stopped. We looked at each other. I shouldn't have what? Shouldn't have let him feel me up? Shouldn't have had a vagina that chili would burn the way it burns a mouth? Shouldn't have been there? Maybe shouldn't even exist?

It was a dangerous few seconds. We both saw everything, all at once. The odd little accidents he made happen, then blamed me for. The stupid sneaking around. The complete and utter waste of time this whole thing had been. In the next breath, we might have screamed invective at each other and parted enemies. Or we might have laughed together and become friends.

But Trevor straightened up suddenly, said, 'Something's burning,' and raced out of the bathroom and down the stairs. I heard 'Oh, *no*!' then pots banging in the kitchen and water running. In a minute he called up the stairs that the chili was burnt, he was going out to get some eggs to make an omelette, and he would be back in a little while.

I sat in the warm water, staring at a bottle of bubble bath shaped like Disney's Snow White. *Someday my prince will come*, I kept expecting it to sing, in that trilling falsetto. Finally I got out of the tub, got dressed and explored the house.

It was one of those tall, narrow brick structures with dark wood trim and many small rooms on each floor. Upstairs, Trevor and Geraldine had the smaller of the two bedrooms, which the bed just about filled. It was a very feminine room, with ruffles on everything – the curtains, the pillow shams, the bed skirt. On the walls were framed wedding photographs. Trevor with the comically short hair and horn-rimmed glasses of 1960. Geraldine a traditional bride in white. Her smile looked kind of like mine. No. It looked a lot like mine.

Downstairs in the living room there was a fireplace with more framed photographs crowding the mantel. A winter scene in one. Trevor and Geraldine and the twins against a backdrop of snow. Probably taken last winter, to judge from Trevor's hair length – short enough for an assistant bank manager, but longer than in his wedding pictures. The girls in matching yellow parkas, carrying balloons on sticks, one red one blue. Their parents standing behind them, leaning into each other easily, familiarly. Geraldine a small, dark, pretty enough woman in her early thirties. Looking, I realized, much the way I would in a few years.

Back in the kitchen I pulled open drawers and looked at silverware. I stared at a jumble of cooking utensils, some old, some still shiny, standing in a narrow crockery jar. There was a messy bundle of coupons and opened letters tucked between a cookie jar and a flour canister. I went through them, not reading them, just shuffling them and glancing at the envelopes. *Mr and Mrs Cleverly. Trevor and Geraldine Cleverly. The Cleverlys.*

*Marriage*, I thought. It's so cluttered, crowded with so many *things*. Things stacked on each other. Propped up against each other. Even the word was a mouthful, layered and toothsome. *Marriage.*

I had to leave. Now. Before Trevor came back. I looked for something to write on, then thought, no. It's enough that he'll see my coat gone. That he'll find me gone. Odd thought. To *find* someone *gone. Begone*, the house seemed to be saying to me, as if I were a ghost haunting it. *Be gone.*

Outside it was much colder than it had been when I walked down from the campus, and it was starting to snow. I didn't have money for a cab, so I headed off Oxford to Norfolk, then on to Quebec Street to catch a bus at Wyndham. By the time I reached the bus stop, the snow was falling thickly, big wet clumps that flew straight into my face. The street lamps glowed fuzzily through it. The traffic lights were frosted pink and watery yellow and pale green.

I was just wearing my short coat and running shoes, and I had no gloves. After ten minutes of hugging myself beside the bus stop, I decided to walk back up to the campus. The movement would keep me warm, the wind would be at my back, and I would stick to the bus route so that if one finally came along I could catch it.

It was even colder now, and the snow wasn't fluffy any more. It was sharp and driving, like needles. By the time I turned off Wellington onto Gordon Street, the sidewalk was starting to ice up. I wondered if Trevor might be cruising around, looking for me. The thought made me bend my back and walk faster. *Be gone. Be gone.*

I slipped twice going up the Gordon Street hill toward College. Each time, the stumble brought me back to myself, pulled me down from a high place where I had seemed to be floating, watching my own small figure struggle through the freezing rain.

Once on the campus, all I had to guide me were the distant lights of the court in front of Admin. I couldn't feel my feet any more, and the edges of my pockets hurt my hands. For whole minutes at a time I would forget where I had been, or where I was going. All I would remember was that I had to keep walking.

I was floating high up again, watching myself pass the dim shape of Massey Hall, then the library. I could see the residence from where I was, and was just wondering if my small, grounded self could see it too, when I fell.

The steps beside the library were iced over. I slid to the bottom on my stomach in a smooth dive which must have been lovely to watch from above. I couldn't tell any more, because the fall brought me back down to earth.

At the bottom of the steps I lay still, thinking about how easy falling had been. I wasn't hurt at all. I was very comfortable, in fact. Strangely warm. It was a relief to stop moving. Maybe I could just curl up and stay where I was for a little while. Rest. Sleep. Would that be all right?

'Yes. That would be all right. Wouldn't it?' I said drowsily to the pair of bare feet standing just inches from my face.

In a dim, faraway part of my mind I knew that it was odd to see bare feet on a night like this. But all I could think about was how beautifully drawn they were. They looked as if they had been sketched by one of the Old Masters in white chalk on black slate. They were perfect in every detail, the jutting ankle bones, the ridged and faceted toenails, even the hints of callus and cuticle. They were so perfect that it didn't surprise me at all to see one of them lift itself to scratch the back of the other's ankle with a toenail, then settle back down on the icy ground.

I raised my eyes slowly, taking in the muscular calves, shinbones and thighs, all drawn in perfect white-on-black chiaroscuro. The genitals were perfect too, the penis bent a little to the left, the testicles pouched and heavy-looking, the pubic hair a crown of dense, springy curls.

As I watched, a Michelangelo drawing of a hand lowered itself, palm up, to the level of my eyes. It was a square, muscular hand. I could see creases on the palms, and the whorled prints of each fingertip.

The fingers crooked, beckoning. Crooked again. And again. *Look at* me, they said. *Look up. Look into my eyes.*

'Look into my eyes, Daisy. Look straight into my eyes.' Rowena's face was so close I could see the pale little moustache hairs at the corners of her mouth.

'Okay. I don't *think* you're concussed. But you fell, didn't you? You're sopping wet, and you've ripped a knee out of your jeans. Am I right, Daisy? Please try to answer me. Did you fall down?'

After a long moment, I nodded. Yes. I fell down. I could remember falling. But not getting up.

'Did you hit your head? Try to stay with me, okay? Did you hit your head when you fell?'

I thought this over for a minute, then shook my head. Why couldn't I remember how I got back to the residence?

'Okay. Okay. I think you're in a slight state of shock. That can happen when you fall down. Did you know that? It's because your blood sugar takes a sudden dip. Did you know that? Daisy?'

Rowena was staring at me so intently that I thought I had better answer, even though I had already forgotten the question. I shook my head no again, hoping that was right.

'Can you talk at all? Can you tell me what you were doing out there? Because nobody else is. The buses aren't even running. It's the ice storm of the decade.'

I did get up. Yes. After I fell. I could remember that much now. I got up and I ran and ran toward the residence, the cold air aching in my lungs. But what was I running from? I looked at Rowena. Opened my mouth. Shut it again. Shrugged.

'That's okay. I'm used to my patients not talking to me. And you'll talk when you're ready. So. What do we know? We know that you fell down. And we know that you're half frozen. Okay. Let's make some hot tea, and put some sugar in it, and meanwhile check out your extremities.'

She put the kettle on, sat down beside me on the lounge couch and took my hands in hers. She looked at my fingers, then pulled off my shoes and socks and looked at my toes. 'Well, by some miracle, nothing's frostbitten. I'd put you in a hot tub, but you should probably warm up slowly. So let's get you to bed while the kettle boils.'

In my room she hung my wet clothes up while I changed into my pyjamas. She pulled the covers up over me once I was in bed, then went away for a few minutes and came back with some sugary tea, which she fed me with a spoon, because she didn't want me to put my hands on the hot mug.

I was still trying to piece together what had happened. I could remember leaving Trevor's house, walking to the campus, falling, getting up again and running to the residence. But that was all.

Spooning a dribble from the side of my mouth, Rowena said, 'Did anybody hurt you out there? Chase you, or anything like that?'

I thought, then shook my head.

'Because we can call the campus police if you want.'

I shook my head again and smiled. The thought of calling the police was funny, but I didn't know why.

'Well, okay. But I thought I should ask, Daisy, because to tell you the truth, you came tearing in here looking like you'd seen a gho –'

The rest of the mug of tea went all over her. Luckily, it wasn't too hot any more.

And then I could talk. I told her everything all at once, about seeing Cedric in the campus newspaper, and dreaming of him, and searching for him in the archives, and carrying his picture around with me all the time. 'It's in my jeans pocket. It really is. You can look at it if you want.'

'No, that's okay,' Rowena said. 'I believe you.'

'Do you?'

'Yes.'

'Do you believe I saw him tonight?'

A hesitation. Then a nod.

There was another question I wanted, and feared, to ask. Rowena must have sensed it coming, because she said briskly, 'You should sleep now. We can talk again in the morning.' Then she pulled my blankets up and turned off my light.

The morning sun was searing my eyelids. I got out of bed, went to my balcony window and looked out on a world of glass. Every twig of every branch of every tree was coated with ice just starting to melt. I could imagine it all chiming in the wind like thousands of bells.

I felt a familiar ache and checked the crotch of my pyjamas. The blood was an amazing bright red. I looked at it and looked at it, as if seeing the colour red for the first time. Then I looked out again at the sparkling day. The sky was the purest cerulean blue possible. And there were the subtler shades of winter, too, the burnt umber of the trees, the yellow ochre of the fields. I recognized and named each one proudly, like a child learning her colours.

For the first time in a week, I had slept through the night. And for the first time in many weeks, I had not dreamed of Cedric.

I went to my closet and reached into the pocket of my still-damp jeans. The folded newspaper photograph was a pulpy wad, impossible to smooth out. I started to throw it into my wastepaper basket, then walked over instead and set it in gently.

I suspected I would never dream of Cedric again. When I

searched that strange, dark place he had occupied within me, I found him gone.

In the lounge I plugged in the kettle to make coffee and wait for Rowena to come down from her room. I grinned, imagining how Rowena would answer the question I was no longer afraid to ask.

'You want to know if I think Cedric was really *there*? Okay. Here's what I think. I think that if I'd had a week of sleep deprivation from pumping heavy-duty drugs into my system round the clock, and *then*, if I'd half frozen to death in an ice storm, and *then*, if I'd fallen head first down a flight of stone steps, well, *sure*. Cedric would have been really there waiting for me at the bottom. Hell, Daisy. Santa Claus, the Easter Bunny and the Tooth Fairy would have been really there too, waiting with him.'

It didn't matter, I thought, still grinning, pouring hot water into my mug and hearing the jangle of coat hangers coming from the closet in Rowena's room. As far as I was concerned, I was the thirteenth Guelph student to see the ghost of Cedric Ellington.

Maybe I could make that the subject of my Advanced Media 312 project. Do it as a huge, three-dimensional collage. A dozen or so life-sized cut-outs of Cedric. Strategically placed trays of ice cubes to represent the storm. Wordsworth off to one side, recollecting daffodils in tranquillity. Keats in another corner, forever ceasing upon the midnight with no pain. Trevor the Big Dumb Fuck in between them, declaiming his lousy poetry. Continuous tapes of a nightingale singing and the Cryer in the Carrels crying. And in the middle of it all, standing in for Rowena and the entire Faculty of Veterinary Medicine, a live goat.

I was laughing out loud by the time Rowena came down the stairs. I couldn't stop right away, had to wait to tell her how right she had been about vitamin D. I looked forward to telling her. In fact, I couldn't remember looking forward to anything so much in my life.

# Beastie

THREE IN THE MORNING. Two forty-five, last time I looked. Who called these the wee small hours? And why? And who cares? Not me. I don't even want to think about it. I don't want to think about anything. I'd like to take my head off and lay it beside me on the pillow.

His pillow.

Where his own head should be.

He's coming home, Daisy. He's on his way. Any minute now there'll be the sound of his key in the door.

So go to sleep.

Sleep.

Sleep.

Sleep.

It's five after three.

Jesus Christ, Brian, what could possibly keep you at a party for – when did the show let out? Ten o'clock? For *five hours?* I mean, what's the attraction? How can you stand to be in a room full of smoking, shrieking actors for more than five minutes? Don't your muscles tense up? Doesn't your face start to ache from the phoney smile you're trying to maintain? Don't you get fucking, screaming *bored?*

Obviously not.

I sit up. Punch my pillow. Punch his harder. Lie back down.

I should have gone with him. I should be there now. At least I'd be asleep. I always fall asleep at cast parties. Even lying on the coats piled on somebody's bed would be better than lying here, hating the way these sheets feel, hating the smell of this pillow.

No, it wouldn't.

Not after last time.

Beastie. That little chirp she makes as she hops onto the mattress and aims her face into mine. Stealing my breath, as people used to think.

'Where's Daddy?' Her green eyes become slits as I smooth her ears back. 'Daddy's not home where he should be, is he? Daddy should be here, patting his lovely kitty and telling her what a pretty girl she is.'

Actually, Beastie is neither lovely nor pretty. She wasn't even a cute kitten. When we first got her, I remember saying to Brian, 'Is there, um, something kind of *spidery* about her?' She froze in the middle of washing, just as if she had understood, and gave me that look cats give anything that moves. *Should I eat you?*

'She *is* kind of spidery,' Brian said. 'She's a long-legged beastie.'

Now she's lanky and vaguely malevolent, like the cat in that art-nouveau poster, *Chat Noir*. But for some reason we preserve the illusion that she's cute and fluffy.

'Such a pretty lady Beastie is,' I say now, lying through my teeth. 'And Daddy's going to come home soon to his nice wee girl. Yes, he is.'

Cats are so handy for projecting feelings onto. Whatever it is, they just take it in and process it back out when they purr. Interesting thought. That whatever you're going through, however tragic you think it is at the time, all it will ever come down to is a cat's purr.

It's three-fifteen.

He's never been out this late before. Not when I was with him, anyway.

So did I always cramp his style? At all the other parties, that is? Not just the last one, when I turned into a crying drunk?

*A crying drunk*, part of my mind kept saying. *I'm a crying drunk.* As if it was an achievement.

He kept asking me what was wrong. We were outside, walking up and down the dark street, trying to sober me up.

'It was that woman,' I kept saying. 'That actress.'

'Which one? The place is full of actresses, Daisy.'

'And they're all the same! And they're all doing the same thing! And I can't do what they're doing! I can't be that way!'

'Daisy, for Christ's sake, will you settle down and tell me what you're talking about?'

We were at the corner of the street. I was digging my fists into my eyes like a little kid, and my bare toes were curled over the curb. I must have kicked my sandals off at the party.

'I can't –' I started to cry again. He waited. 'I can't do what those women, all those women, at all the parties, do all the time.'

'What do they do?'

'They, they, they kind of ricochet around the room. And smash into each other. Like bats, or something.'

'Bats?'

I knew I wasn't making any sense. In a part of my brain that wasn't drunk or crying, I knew that bats didn't smash into each other. That was the thing about bats, in fact. The point of bats.

'It's theatre people,' I said at last. 'I just can't stand them. No. Wait a minute. I don't mean *you* –'

'I know,' he said, moving a strand of hair off my forehead. His body was starting to twist away a little, his elbow pointing back toward the house with the party in it. But he would stay out here with me as long as I needed him. He would even take me home, if I asked him to.

Except I wouldn't ask, because I didn't deserve to be taken home. Or comforted. Had everybody seen me start to cry? Had they all watched us leave, me stumbling and sobbing under his arm?

'Tell me,' he said. 'What got you so upset in there? Did somebody say something to you?'

'No-o-o.'

'Was it me, then? Something I did?'

*Hang in, babe*, he had told me as usual. *I'm off to see the wizard.* Then I had watched the way I always did, from the edge of the crowd, while he moved through it. Gracefully. Strategically. Tapping energy, gaining momentum with every encounter.

It was what always happened at these gatherings. And I knew it was just part of being an actor. So there was no reason for me to bite the edge of my third glass of wine. Cram it into my mouth, trying to keep my face still.

I didn't want Brian to be anything except what he was. I loved seeing him on stage, himself and yet not himself. I loved saying casually, 'He's an actor,' when people asked me what he did, then watching their faces change. An *actor*, I still sometimes said to myself. Not an accountant. Not a salesman. Not a truck driver. An *actor*.

I even loved our poverty, the stretches when he was without work making the odd bursts of tiny wealth all the richer. I loved our shabby Kitsilano apartment. Our brick-and-board bookshelves. The card table we sat at to eat. The second-hand chairs we sat on. Our Indian bedspread curtains. Our Indian bedspread bedspread.

*I'm living with an actor,* I would tell myself, hardly able to believe it was my own story. *It's 1974, I'm a creative writing student, I'm on the west coast, my hair is down to my waist, I wear flowered skirts, and I'm living with an actor.*

Sometimes I would deliberately scare myself, imagining what my life would be like if I hadn't met Brian. If I hadn't just happened to take that playwriting workshop where he had been hired to assist the professor.

I would still be living on campus, in residence. With my four housemates. Bonnie Sue, Brenda Sue, Suzannah and Susan. They called people like Brian hippies, even though the real hippies had stopped calling themselves that. And they put signs everywhere. In the kitchen: PLEASE DO YOUR DISHES AND PUT THEM AWAY. In the bathroom: PLEASE REMOVE HAIRS FROM THE SINK. And wrapped around the receiver of the phone: PLEASE LIMIT CALLS TO TEN MINUTES OR (PREFERABLY!) LESS.

'Honey, I have got to get you out of here,' Brian murmured to me the first time he came to visit. He was sprawled on the couch in the lounge just off the kitchen. Wearing his fringed leather jacket and that grey felt Stetson he had when I first met him. I remember the little smudge of goatee he had then too, the long moustache and the Wild Bill Hickock hair.

I looked at him that day and thought, I've come west. This is west.

Bonnie Sue was taking her turn cooking supper, wearing the apron we were expected to fold neatly and put back in the designated drawer. She turned all at once and looked at Brian too, not because she had heard what he said about getting me out of there, but as if she were suddenly scenting an enemy.

There was something unencumbered about Brian. He wore the past, the present and the future as lightly as he wore his hat. When we walked together, I half expected him to hop over fences, spring across intersections. With me, slave to gravity, scurrying along behind.

'You are a writer,' he would sometimes say to me very distinctly, as if teaching me a new language.

'I'm a creative writing *student*, Brian.'

'You are a writer.'

'But I'm not *published*.'

'Look, am I only an actor when I'm under contract? Will you stop making up all these goddamned *rules*?'

What Bonnie Sue and I both scented that day in the residence lounge was the difference between what was and what could be. It scared me, but not the way it scared Bonnie Sue. It scared me because I wanted it. I wanted to get there from here.

So I had. I was there. Or as close to it as I would ever get.

'When actors are together in bunches,' I tried to explain to Brian that night on the sidewalk, 'they're all glittery and loud. And I get the feeling that for all the kissing and the sweet talk, they really hate each other. They want to eat each other.'

But not me. They didn't want to eat me. Because I wasn't even there, as far as they were concerned. Or if I was, I was like a sparrow among peacocks. But I couldn't say that to Brian.

'Daisy, all they're doing in there is what they have to do. It's just the biz. You know that. These parties are just part of the biz. You have to show up everywhere and talk to everybody all the time, whether you want to or not. Or else you'll be forgotten. You can be forgotten over night.'

It's three twenty-two.

Beastie has fallen asleep. She's making that high-pitched sighing sound that passes for a snore with cats. What must it be like to nap, and wake, and nap again, as easily as breathing? To have no wants or needs beyond this bit of food, this warm place to sleep?

Brian tries to live that way. Be that way. Succeeds, most of the time. In spite of me. I'll tell him with my waking breath that we don't have the rent money, and he'll stretch and say, yeah, but the sun's out for once, so let's go to the beach.

I don't know how he does that. Just puts something like the phone being cut off right out of his mind. Forgets it completely and goes to the beach. I can't. For me, it's like carrying a cannon ball around. And even if I do go to the beach, I'll just be there on the sand with my cannon ball.

Three twenty-five.

Go to sleep, Daisy. Stop thinking. Stop worrying. Go. To. Sleep.

Where do we *go*, when we *go to sleep*? And why don't we *come from sleep*? Because it is like a place. A place we can't remember. We know we've been there, but we haven't a clue what we did or what happened. And time is compressed there. A whole night passes in what feels like a minute. What's that line, from a psalm or a hymn? *A thousand ages in Thy sight are like an evening gone.*

Must be nice.

Beastie sits up abruptly. Washes her belly furiously for ten seconds. Drops back down in a ball against my thigh.

What a life. Sleep. Eat. Wash. No worries. No responsibilities. No yesterday. No tomorrow.

If I lived that way, I would be asleep now. If I lived that way, I'd be a totally different person. Or I might not *be* at all. I think sometimes that I *am* my worries. That my what-ifs and my should-haves and my might-bes are what I consist of. And they're all about him. Brian. Because there is nothing more nerve-racking that living with a relaxed person.

Even when we're grocery shopping, I'll suddenly look around and he'll be gone. So I'll careen with the cart up and down the aisles until I find him. And there he'll be, reading the label on a jar of caviar or something else that isn't on the list and never will be on the list.

'What do you mean, where was I?' he'll say. 'I was right here. I knew where *you* were.'

There. That's it. That's why I can't sleep. He knows where I am, but I haven't a clue where he is. And I won't relax until I do. Until I hear his footsteps. His whistle. The chime of his keys in the door. I need that hit of joy, that rush of relief.

Jesus Christ. Listen to me. Where's my pride? Where's my self-respect?

Where's my man?

*Don't say that. Don't say 'my man'.*

Oh, my God. My mother's list of *don'ts*. I'll probably never stop hearing them in my head. *Don't point. It's vulgar. Don't stare. It's rude. Don't swing your purse. Prostitutes swing their purses. Don't say 'my man'. It's cheap.*

It was okay to say *my husband*, but not *my man*. Maybe it was the nakedness of *man* that bothered my mother. *Husband* was clothed. Respectable. Domesticated.

*Your father's a good husband*, she would sometimes say. It would come out of the blue, like the beginning of a story. Except I never heard the rest of it. I did hear a comma after *husband*, followed by thoughts I could only guess at. *Even though he's not at all demonstrative. Even though he hardly talks to me. Even though I can count on the fingers of one hand the times he's said 'I love you'.*

Three twenty-seven.

Well. At least he came home at the end of the day. I always knew when it was exactly quarter after six, because my mother was putting supper on the table and my father was pulling into the driveway.

What's that? That noise? Beastie hears it too. Jerks out of sleep to listen. Footsteps? Coming up to the downstairs door?

No. Just somebody out on the street. The steps fade. Beastie settles her head back down on her paws. In a second she's snoring again.

*A good husband.* Dependable. Sober. Employed. Yes, my father was all of those things.

But I can't imagine my mother shuddering and screaming under him. Grabbing his buttocks and pressing him hard into her, saying, *Fuck me, fuck me, fuck me!* Taking him into her mouth afterwards, tasting herself and him together.

And how many fingers would I need to count the times Brian has said *I love you?* I'd have to use the hairs of my head. He touches me all the time, too, not just when we're having sex. Strokes my cheek with his thumb when we talk, pulls me over to lean against him on the couch, curves like a crescent moon against me in bed.

'Is all this touchy-feely stuff going to end once we're living together?' I asked him early on.

'Nope,' he answered into my mouth.

And it hasn't. And it won't. And it'll start up again, just as soon as he's home. Which he will be. Any minute now.

Three-thirty.

Couldn't he at least phone? The phone is hooked up again, after all. Though God knows how long it'll stay that way, now that his show has closed. But couldn't he call, just to say that he was okay, or that he was just leaving, or that he would just be a little while longer? I would. I would have called at midnight. No, I would have been *home* at midnight.

But that's the difference between him and me. And differences are good things, aren't they? Oh my yes. Necessary things, too. Why, allowing for each other's differences keeps a relationship alive and healthy, doesn't it? And blah and blah and blah.

My parents didn't have a *relationship*. They had a *marriage*. Lying together in that same room, that same bed, night after night, year after year. Real professionals. They may have lain sleepless and rigid at times with rage, but by God they lay *together*.

Still do.

Beastie wakes again. Stretches in a tall U. Steps off the mattress onto the floor and leaves on some nightly cat business. In a minute I hear her crunching kibble out of her bowl. When she's finished she'll bathe every inch of herself, then go back to sleep. Being a cat means being unconditionally in love with yourself. No wonder they were gods in ancient Egypt.

Beastie doesn't need Brian or me. Yes, we fill her bowl, empty her litter pan. But if we didn't somebody else would. And she knows it. That's why we worship her. Tell her she's beautiful when we know she isn't. Buy her treats when we can't afford shoes. Get up in the middle of the night to let her on or off the balcony, even though we need our sleep. We worship her because she worships herself. We love her because she loves herself.

There's probably a lesson in that. But I'm not sure I want to know what it is.

Three thirty-three.

What time would it be for my parents right now? I can never remember if Vancouver is three hours ahead of Hamilton or three hours behind. Either way, I'd be phoning at an odd time. If I did

phone, that is. Which I won't. Because no matter how
breezy I kept it, my mother would sense that something v
And I can just imagine what she'd say if I wailed that it wa
three in the morning, and Brian wasn't home. Well, she'd ͜͜ ͜ ͜ ,, ͜ ͜ ͜ ͜ ͜
did you expect? You didn't get married, did you? You didn't hold
out for marriage. Insist on it. Not give an inch until you had that
ring on your finger. You didn't respect yourself then, so what makes
you think he's going to respect you now?

And I would lecture back at her that Brian and I have risen above
the sexual repression and superstitious fears of her generation. That
we do not need to shackle each other with legal papers and religious
vows. That we wear no rings. Have no illusions about the future.
Live one day at a time.

Like hell we do.

I hate this.

Hate, hate, hate.

I flop onto my stomach. Pound the pillow with my forehead, hating it. Then flop onto my back, staring at the ceiling. Such a cliché,
to stare at the ceiling. But I do it. Even though I hate the ceiling as
much as I hate the pillow. The sheets. This mattress. My life.

'Brian,' I say out loud, 'get your ass home right now and ask me to
marry you. Then get a normal, steady job and buy me a house in the
suburbs. I want Tupperware and garden gnomes and two point
seven children.'

Who am I trying to kid? But maybe that's my problem. I want all
the wrong things. Because there are still women who do want that
whole suburban trip. Demand it. Get it, too. Women like Bonnie
Sue, Brenda Sue, Suzannah and Susan. They're out there right now,
driving hard bargains. Not giving an inch.

Not *that* inch, anyway.

Hey, that's good. I'll have to remember and tell it to Brian. He'll
love it. *Not that inch, anyway.*

The first time he and I went to bed, he reached down and put his
thumb right smack on my clit. No fumbling. No groping around and
missing it by a mile. And I didn't have to hike my legs and *show* him
either, the way I did for my second lover who said, 'Really? That far
north?'

'How could you find me so easily?' I asked Brian afterwards.

'I knew where to look, babe,' he said. 'I knew where to look.'

Three forty-five. Quarter to four. In the morning.

It will be daylight soon. I can hear the birds waking up. I should get up too. Stupid to lie here, when it's obvious I'm not going to sleep. I am a morning person, after all.

That's another thing about us. I like the day new and untouched. He likes it grubby. Used. Funky. He avoids the morning, if he can. Sleeps as late as possible. Cheers up visibly as the day ages. Is all ready to go dancing just when I'm thinking about going to bed.

So what on earth are we doing with each other?

Well, at the moment, nothing. Because he'd rather be there than here. He'd rather be with them, the cast and crew, than with me. Not to mention all the hangers-on that drift from one theatre party to another. Most of them women.

No.

That's not what this is about. It's not.

Why isn't it, Daisy?

Because it isn't.

But *why*?

Because I don't want it to be.

Right.

I turn onto my stomach again and put my face in the pillow. Breathe a warm tunnel through its layers.

Why shouldn't he be with somebody else? We didn't take any vows, did we? We didn't sign any papers. And we never said the words *forsaking all others*.

I flop onto my back and stare again at the ceiling. It's not quite as dark now. I can make out our round rice-paper lampshade.

*Don't wait up, hon.*

Yes, he did say that.

*You know what closing night parties are like.*

Yes, I do, Brian. I've spent all kinds of them sleeping on coats.

*Don't worry.*

Me? Worry? Don't be ridiculous.

*Just go to sleep.*

I am asleep, Brian. Can't you tell? I always sleep with my eyes wide open and my fists clenched.

Maybe a hot bath would help. Except, if he comes home while I'm in the tub, he'll know I lay awake all night worrying. And I don't want to give him the satisfaction. Christ, that sounds wifely. *I don't want to give him the satisfaction.* But I don't. Well, maybe I should just get up and walk around, then. That might make me drowsy.

There's a bit of a smudge to the sky now, and the birds are getting louder. I've never done this before, walked around the apartment naked before dawn. The shelves and furniture have a strange, half-alive look, as if they might be quietly breathing.

I go to the balcony door and look out. The moon is still up, and the streetlamps still on. If I went and stood out there, I could see Brian come down the street from the bus stop. Except the buses won't start running for another hour. All right then, I could see him step out of a cab. No. He doesn't have the money for a cab. Okay, I could see him step out of somebody's car, then. Somebody who's giving him a ride home from the party.

And then what would I do? Wave and call yoo-hoo? He'd love it if I did. He loves stunts, especially when they're out of character.

And that certainly would be, for me. If I was going to do it. Which I'm not. I'm not even going to go out onto the balcony, in fact. There's no point. Because all I would do is stand there and stand there, with the rosy-fingered dawn twiddling my nipples. Watching the street fill up with everybody on earth. Everybody except him.

Because he's not coming home.

Beastie hears me. Comes and sidewinds in and out my legs until I pick her up so she can lick my face. She loves the taste of tears and snot. Has since she was a kitten.

When she's finished I blot my cheeks on her fur and hold her the way she likes to be held, her forepaws on my shoulder, her face Janus-profile to mine. I walk her slowly around the apartment, turning my back to the shelves to let her sniff a brass incense holder here, a dribbly candle stuck in a wine bottle there. She likes to nuzzle the thumbtacks at the corners of posters. And she always sniffs all the way round the frame of our one piece of real art, a pen-and-ink sketch of black skeletal trees in winter.

We almost didn't buy it. If it had been up to me, we wouldn't have. It was going to cost more than a week's groceries, and Brian was out of work again, and we had to pay our B.C. Med premiums, and, and.

'Can't you just forget all that shit for once, Daisy? There's this thing here in front of us, right now, and it's perfect, and we love it, and it's ours if we just say yes.'

'But –'

'There you go. You're a knee-jerk nay-sayer.'

'I just –'

'Say yes. Come on. For once. Just say yes.'

'I would, Brian, if you'd say no now and then.'

He went all quiet and hurt when I said that. I bought the sketch for him as an apology.

And the very next day, there was a big residual cheque for him in the mail. A movie he had had a small part in years ago was being sold to television. 'You see, babe?' he sang, dancing me around the apartment while Beastie scrambled away from us and hid under the couch. 'You see?'

The sun's coming up. Colour is bleeding into things through the grey. It's morning. No question about it. No avoiding it any more. It's morning, and he's been out all night.

I put Beastie down and stand in the middle of the living room floor, my hands cupping my elbows. I don't know what this is. Is it anything? It would be if I did it. But I'm not him. I know I wouldn't do this to him, and I know why. But I haven't a clue why he's gone and done it to me.

I don't know what to think. What to do. How to feel. My mother would have been on the phone all night, calling hospitals, alerting the RCMP. And then God help my father when he finally walked through the door.

But I'm not my mother. And Brian's not my father. And I'm not Brian. And I have to handle this. All alone. I, myself and me, as we used to say.

All at once I'm cold. I start to walk around, chafing my arms with my hands. The apartment is suddenly too big. All our furniture and books and records seem strange, as if they belong to someone else.

Well, maybe they do. Or will soon. Maybe 'our' has no meaning any more. Maybe there is no 'our' or 'us' or 'we' any more.

I don't know.

I don't know.

I don't know.

I walk around from thing to thing, looking, touching, making little whimpering sounds. Beastie paws my leg, chirping, her way of telling me to pick her up. In my arms she sniffs under my eyes and licks my cheek hopefully, purring all the while.

I oblige her with tears as I visit the couch, the shelves, the old travelling trunk we use as a coffee table. Mourning each object in advance. Who will get what? Where will it all go? Where will Brian go? And where will I go? And where –

Steps.

Whistle.

It's him.

He's home.

He's going to find me here.

Naked.

Crying into the cat.

I can hear him fumbling for his keys. I put Beastie down. Open the hall closet door. Duck in and pull the door shut just as he puts his key in the lock.

It's dark, and I can hardly hear for the sound of my own heart in my ears. 'Hey, little mama,' he whispers to Beastie just outside the closet door. He's keeping his voice down because he assumes I'm asleep in the bedroom. 'How's Papa's pretty lady? Oh, she wants her belly rubbed, does she? Yeah, she does. There. That good? Huh? That – Ow! Leggo! Let go! Beastie! Beastie, Daddy would like his pretty pussycat to pull in her claws. Please. Thank you. That's a very good girl.' Then, as he walks past the closet door, he mutters, 'Fucking cat.'

I hear him put his shoulder bag down. Unzip it and take something out. He starts to move around the living room, back and forth, rhythmically, as if doing some kind of dance step. Then he goes into the bathroom and shuts the door. I hear him open the medicine chest. Probably looking for something to put on his scratches.

I sneak out of the hall closet and tiptoe into the living room, keeping an ear cocked toward the bathroom door.

The living room is full of colour. He's liberated part of the set, a long canvas streamer painted all different colours. There were hundreds of them hung together from the flies to represent a forest in autumn. This one snakes along the floor, loops around the lamp, doubles back over the couch and coffee table. Reds and yellows and oranges, going on forever.

He always brings something home from any show he's in. We have boxes full of trophies in our storage closet. Candlesticks. Scarves. Gloves. Fans. A block of painted wood. A brown paper bag filled with crumpled newspaper, tied at the neck and labelled *Ambrose*.

I used to be able to remember what show each trophy was from. I used to be able to remember what he told me about each of them too, the in-joke, the bit of business or dialogue that made them precious.

There's too many of them now. We should probably go through them. Throw some of them out.

But not the first one. Not the black-painted cane with the gold-painted top. Because I'll never forget the way Brian handed it to me on closing night. As if he was presenting me with a ceremonial sword. It was the flourish that I loved. The extravagance. The pure gesture.

There's the medicine cabinet closing. And the sound of him peeing.

Quick. Quick. I haven't much time. I gather up the streamer, running on tiptoe, wrapping it around one hand like a muff.

The toilet flushes. The tap turns on.

I put one end of the streamer outside the bathroom door, then unravel the rest along the floor, back into the living room. It's just long enough to reach to the balcony door. I open the door, step out onto the balcony and close it again. Beastie scoots through it at the last minute. She chirps and paws my leg while I position myself as close to the door as I can so as not to be seen. I pick her up and hold her, waiting.

The bathroom door opens. Then there's a silence. I imagine Brian looking down at the streamer, wondering how it got there.

I have no idea what I'm going to do when he opens the balcony door. Yell 'Kill!' and throw the cat at him? Smile and say hello? Scream at him for being out all night? Announce calmly that I'm leaving him? Put the cat down and just as calmly unzip his fly?

The rising sun is warm on my bare skin. There are traffic noises now, sounds of the city waking up. I imagine someone down below spotting me. People starting to look up and point. A crowd gathering.

Brian's coming. I can hear him. Laughing softly as he follows the streamer to the balcony door.

Beastie's whiskers are tickling my eyebrow.

The doorknob is turning.

Beastie is purring like an engine in my ear.

# Sparrow Colours

I WISH BRIAN WOULDN'T JIGGLE the table. Does he have to chop up his eggs and sausages and potato pancakes all at once? Now he's buttering his toast. More jiggling. Will he ever stop worrying his food and just eat?

I shake open my napkin and settle it on my lap, wondering why the jiggling table bothers me so much. Then when Brian starts spreading sour cream all over his potato pancakes, I know.

The other night I woke up and found him with the light still on, studying a script. It must have been the jiggling of the bed that woke me. *I could climb aboard*, I thought, when I saw what he was doing. *Or at least lend a hand*. But I didn't even let him know I was awake. There was something sad about the small geyser of semen when it came. The thickness and whiteness of it. Even the sound it made lubricating his hand, *snick-snack, snick-snack*. When I went back to sleep I had dreams about dry plants I had forgotten to water, starving cats I had neglected to feed.

Feed. Food. Eat. We did come here to eat, didn't we? Breakfast, specifically. I pick up my fork and look down at my plate. Did I order this? *A medley of fresh seasonal fruits nestled round a generous scoop of frozen strawberry yogurt.* My yogurt is becoming a pink lake. The cubes, crescents and triangles of fruit remind me of educational toys.

When I look up, Brian is watching me. He watches me a lot these days. Practically follows me around, like a little boy afraid of losing his mother.

'Not hungry, dear?'

I put my fork down and shake my head.

'Not feeling well?'

'No. Yes, I mean. I'm fine, really.'

'Because we can go home. If you want to.'

'No. I'm okay. Just not hungry. That's all.'

'We don't have to do this. If you're not up to it. Not today, anyway. We can always –'

'Brian.'

I don't often call him that. He doesn't often call me Daisy. We call each other honey, hon, sweetie, sweetum, sweetheart, sweet stuff, boo boo, boo bum, bumble, boopsie, stink. ('Do you two fuck while you're doing the dishes?' somebody once asked us.) Pooh, Pooh-Bear, noodle, strudel, doodle. (One of our running jokes is that we in fact never exchanged names, and are now too embarrassed to ask.) Baby, babe, Daddy, Mommy, Papa, Mama.

'Brian. I feel fine. I'm just not hungry. And I don't want to go home. Okay?'

'You're sure? Because –'

I lean across the table and kiss him. To shut him up. We've always been a very kissy pair. We can have whole conversations practically eating each other's faces. This kiss is brief. Efficient. There is coffee on his breath. His moustache is wet, as if we've just made love. I go to wipe my lips with my napkin, but catch myself just in time. Then I put my chin on my hand and look out the window. Under my elbow, the table starts to jiggle again.

How many times has he lain awake and jerked off in the last three weeks? That's how long it's been. For the first two, we had no choice. It was even in writing, in the pamphlet they gave me at the clinic. *You must refrain from sexual intercourse ...* But this last week, it's been up to me. It's been my call. And Brian has been so good about waiting. Staying on his side of the bed. Kissing me closed-mouthed or on the forehead. I know he'll never hint or manipulate. I know he'll wait for me to come to him.

I just wish I knew what I was waiting for.

There isn't much to look at out the window. Grey sky. Brown sidewalk. White patches of snow speckled black with grit. It was a strange winter for Vancouver, snowy and cold. And now spring is taking its time.

'The colours of March are sparrow colours,' I announce, hating the chirpiness of my tone but glad of anything to break the silence.

'You're right!' Actor that he is, Brian invests so much enthusiasm in those two words that I think I might cry. 'If we want to check if a poster or a frame is going to blend in, all we have to do is look out at the day.'

Sparrow colours. Grey, beige, charcoal and white. I'm the one who named them, once we had finished shuffling paint chips. We're going to do the whole new apartment in those four shades, starting right from scratch.

'It'll be strange to have all new stuff,' I say, turning away from the window.

'It'll be *great* to have all new stuff.' And I can see that for him, it will be. He has a talent for novelty. He likes a clean break. It irritates him to see that big, pale new place dotted with our dark, shabby old things.

'I hate this crap,' he kept saying while we were packing. 'I hate forks that don't match and I hate brick-and-board bookshelves and I hate Indian bedspread curtains. And I'm sick of sleeping on a damned mattress on the floor. I want a *bed*. A decent, proper *bed*.'

'You'll have it,' I kept telling him. 'We just need this stuff for a little while longer. After that, you can have whatever you want.' When he let me know how much he was making for the TV series pilot, all I could say was, 'Are you sure?' Then I started packing the dishes we would end up giving to the Sally Ann.

Our quarry today is posters to frame and hang on the walls. Next month, it could be a couch and coffee table, or maybe bedroom furniture. But today, it's posters. We have so much more wall space now, what with the second bedroom. *You need a study*, Brian kept saying when we were apartment hunting. *And now I can afford for you to have one.* 'A room of her own!' one of our friends trumpeted, helping us move in last weekend.

Which sparrow colour should go on the walls of my room, I wonder, and which on the trim? Because there's no question of doing it in orange or purple. Not that I would. But for all it's mine, it's still ours. And from now on, everything, the posters we get today, any furniture or fabrics we pick out after today, will have to blend with grey, beige, white and charcoal.

Good thing for us that we're somewhere between beige and white. Good thing for Beastie that she's black.

'I wonder if Beastie will ever settle in,' I say, putting a bit of cream in my coffee. Brian has persuaded me to have coffee, at least, even if I'm not going to eat.

'She has to. She's got no choice. But sweetheart, as long as you fuss over her, she'll sulk.'

It's hard not to fuss over Beastie, given her stage presence. These days she manages to eat, wash, even sleep with the air of a dispossessed monarch. 'It's all the same stuff,' I tell her again and again. 'The same couch you used to sharpen your claws on. The same corners where you rubbed your chin.' But all I get is the green glare. As if she knows the truth. That her old world will in fact disappear bit by bit until she has only her bowl, her litter pan and the two of us for continuity. Well, another of our running jokes is that we stay together for the sake of the cat.

'Yeah, you're right,' I say briskly. 'She's getting too used to prowling around on top of those boxes, too. I should unpack them.'

'Only when you feel like it, hon. There's no rush.'

'You know, if we got our new shelves, I could do the books and records, at least. They're what's taking up most of the room.'

'Okay, babe. But be careful not to overdo it.'

'I'm *fine*, Brian.'

Honestly, what does he see when he looks at me? Something pale and Pre-Raphaelite? I'm as much a Brueghelian milkmaid as ever. Less than an hour after coming out of the anaesthetic, I was striding down the hall of the clinic, with Brian running after me to take my arm.

But I still haven't unpacked those boxes. I should. I don't know why I haven't. Their labels, in my printing, rebuke me at every turn. BOOKS, AUTHORS D TO F. MEDICINE CABINET AND SPICE RACK. RECORDS, ARTISTS M TO P. WIND CHIMES AND CANDLE HOLDERS.

I discovered I had a talent for packing. Could work obsessively at it for hours without saying a word. There was something about wrapping fragile things in paper, dovetailing them in a box with other fragile things, then sealing and labelling the box, that absorbed me.

'Are you okay?' Brian asked me more than once in the week before we moved.

'Yes. I'm okay.'

'Do you want to talk? We can. You can tell me about it, if that would help.'

I waited until I had finished wrapping a cup. I wasn't used to this kind of attention. Usually I was the one who worried about him. Felt his forehead if he had a cold. Asked him what was wrong if he was quiet. Spun panicky scenarios if he was late. *He's been killed. He's been seduced.*

'There's nothing to tell,' I said at last. 'I went to sleep. Half an hour later, I woke up. It didn't hurt. And I don't remember a thing.'

'Was anybody mean to you? I've heard that they can be.'

'No. Everybody was incredibly nice.'

'You don't – feel bad about it, do you?'

'What, guilty? Do you think I should?'

'No! I'm just a bit worried, that's all. You're kind of off in your own world.'

'There's a lot to do.' It was true, if not quite the truth. But I wasn't sure what the truth was. What if I had had to push through a crowd of demonstrators? What if just one person had been less than incredibly nice? Or if I had stayed awake? Had a local instead of a general? Would I have had some hurt, then, to bring home and cry about in Brian's arms? And would that have made a difference?

Maybe. Maybe not. I fitted the wrapped cup into a box of wrapped cups, then picked up another.

Now Brian reaches across the table for my hand and holds it, stroking the back of it with his thumb. 'Look, doll, I know that whenever we do something new, I always jump in with both feet while you're still trying to weigh the pros and cons. But all this stuff that's been happening. The good stuff, I mean. It's happening for you too. Because it's all just so much crap if I can't give it to you. And I want to give you things, now that I can. I want to give you time. And freedom. To write. Just write. I don't want you to take shitty day-jobs any more.'

The friction of his thumb is making a warm spot on the back of my hand. I don't want to hurt his feelings by pulling away.

'And listen,' he says. 'We both know that I'm not doing anything for you that you wouldn't do for me. If you suddenly wrote a best-seller or something. Right?'

I have to smile. I have yet to publish a single word. My thesis novel, *Dame Julian to Her Cat*, is a monologue spoken by an anchorite walled up for life in a whitewashed room.

'I love you, honey.'

'I love you too.' The warm spot on the back of my hand is getting positively hot. There was a time, just three weeks ago, when I would have turned my hand over to get his stroking on my palm. Then leaned close to whisper, 'Fuck the posters. Let's go home.'

Now all I can do is try to keep from pulling my hand away and wonder how, exactly, someone falls out of love. Funny phrase. Fall out of love. It feels more as if love has fallen out of me. Because I honestly don't know where it's gone. I had it. Now I don't. It's not something I would throw away. Or pack away in a box. And it couldn't be surgically removed, either. Scraped free, then suctioned out. So where is it?

'Everything okay here?' The waiter.

On cue, still holding hands, we smile and say, 'Terrific!'

◆ ◆ ◆

'How do you feel about the test results?'

The question sounded practised, the voice professionally neutral. Her nameplate said Doctor Zareen Dotiwalla. A friend had recommended her as *absolutely non-judgemental*. She was waiting for directions. From me. Answer A would set one chain of events in motion. Answer B, another.

I wanted to go home. I wanted not to have to sit in this office, have this conversation, make this decision. I wanted to be as young as I felt. But I couldn't be. Because I was *in trouble*. One of those oddly formal phrases, like *juvenile delinquent*, that had dotted adult conversation when I was growing up. I was, potentially at least, an *unwed mother*.

The doctor pushed a box of Kleenex toward me. Her voice warmed up a little. 'Is there someone you would like to talk it over with, Daisy?'

'I – we already have talked it over.'

'And what did the two of you decide?'

'He said it was up to me.'

The doctor was silent. Her face maintained the studied neutrality of a banker's face, a policeman's face.

'That makes him sound like he's copping out,' I said into the silence. 'He's not. He just thinks he has no right – He thinks that since it would have such an impact on my body and my life, I should decide.'

It had sounded wonderful when Brian said it. I wished he could be here with me now to say it again, but he had an audition. 'I'll cancel it and come with you,' he had offered. 'If you want me to. Just say the word.'

'So your partner has no preference, one way or the other,' the doctor said. 'And you tell me this is not at all convenient, and that you were taking steps to prevent it.'

I nodded, remembering my crunchy-granola objections to the pill. Remembering sitting in the bathtub with Brian, saying 'Balloop!' then winkling out my diaphragm and twirling it on one finger. Jesus Christ.

Dr Dotiwalla sighed. 'Well. What is done is done. The important thing is to help you do whatever you want to do.' She waited, face, posture, manner once again entirely neutral.

I looked at her desk. At the framed diplomas on her office walls. Then back at her. She was still waiting. When I finally spoke, my voice sounded as young as I felt. The words were whispery, full of breath.

Slowly, expression blank, the doctor nodded. It was an oddly liturgical gesture.

Then she told me she would be right back, that there was a form she had to get from her receptionist, but in the meantime she would like me to review the proper use of the diaphragm, and to at least reconsider going on the pill, once all this was over. She handed me what looked like a viewmaster and told me to look through the lens and turn the crank. I did. It was a colour video of a woman inserting a diaphragm. She was dressed in a short white lab coat and nothing else. She put one foot up on a chair, spread her labia and inserted a diaphragm into her vagina.

All I could think was, my God, is she an out-of-work actress? Does Brian know her? Did they pay her union scale? Did her agent phone her up and say, *I've got a job for you. It's a little different…?*

Then I discovered that I could speed the film up by turning the crank faster, or slow it down, or make it go backwards, or forwards and backwards. Foot up, foot down. Labia spread, labia closed. Diaphragm in, diaphragm out.

I began to giggle soundlessly, turning the crank. I was all loose and jangly inside from crying, and the laughter came out in scraps and shards of breath.

Dr Dotiwalla smiled when she came back in, carrying a printed form. 'A bit surreal, isn't it?' she said. Her manner had relaxed, warmed. I wondered if she approved of my decision, or if she would have acted the same way no matter what I had decided.

She sat down at her desk and wrote something on the form. Then she leaned on her elbows and looked at me. 'Now, Daisy, what happens is this. I write to my hospital board, saying that continuing in your present condition would cause you physical and psychological hardship. It is just a formality. They will not ask for proof, and no one is ever turned down. Then, once they approve my recommendation, we make an appointment for the procedure to be carried out.'

'How much is it going to cost?'

Till now, living poor with Brian had been an adventure, funky and bohemian. But three words, *It was positive*, had shrunk my life down, had made it grubby and desperate. I was still a student, working part time shelving books in the UBC library. Brian was unemployed. His last stage job had ended a week ago when the show he was in folded. His audition today was for a part in a series of root beer commercials. We both knew it was a shot in the dark. Too big a job for an unknown to get.

'B.C. Medical will cover everything,' Dr Dotiwalla said, 'except for a nominal sum. About seventeen dollars. Is that all right, Daisy?'

I nodded. It would have to be. And we always managed somehow. Always found enough for the rent. And for Beastie's food and litter. Now we would find seventeen dollars.

'So,' the doctor was saying, 'If all goes well, and I assure you it will, I will be in touch with you in a week or so about your appointment.'

'And then, do I come back here?'

'Here? No, I should not have to see you afterwards.'

'No, I mean, for the – Where does it happen?'

'In one of the out-patient clinics. Doctor Bernstrom will give you the address when he sees you.'

'Doctor Bernstrom? Who's he?'

'He is the – I am sorry. I should have been clearer. I am a GP. I do not actually do these things.' She grimaced very slightly, just a flicker, then her face smoothed. 'You see, once the hospital board has approved my recommendation, I will make an appointment for you to see Dr Bernstrom. He is a gynaecologist. And he is the one who will actually carry out the procedure.' She smiled sympathetically. 'This must seem like a great many hoops to jump through.'

It didn't, actually. I looked again at her desktop. Once more at the framed diplomas on her wall. Finally back at her.

'Something else you want to ask?' she said, when our eyes met.

'This is –' I began, then stopped.

'Yes, Daisy?'

By some bizarre chance, had I wandered into the wrong office? Was she the wrong Doctor Dotiwalla? Had we been talking all this time about my teeth?

'This is an *abortion* I'm having, right?'

The tiny grimace again. 'The medically correct term is dilation and curettage. D and C. It is minor surgery. And Daisy, I would like to suggest that you think of it that way. As minor surgery.'

◆ ◆ ◆

'What are you thinking about?' Brian asks me, once the waiter has topped up our coffee, taken my untouched plate and left.

'I'm remembering something.'

'Well,' he says helpfully, 'what are you remembering?'

'Something from when I was a kid. I don't know how old I was. Not too old. Eight or nine. I was in the back yard looking over the fence at the man who lived in the house behind us. He was cutting his back lawn. Ordinary man. Ordinary house. Family just like ours. But all of a sudden I noticed how *square* everything was. The house was square, the yard was square, even the man was kind of square and beefy. He had started on the outside and was moving round and round into the centre, in smaller and smaller squares.

'And I remember thinking, *He should have started in the centre, so he could end up on the outside. That way, he could escape. Just leave the lawnmower where it is, and go. Run away. Someplace where he could be all by himself.* Because I was convinced that that was exactly what the man wanted to do, deep down. But the squares he was cutting in the lawn were somehow keeping him from doing it.

'And it was as if a door or something had opened up in my head, because I started looking at everybody that way. I suddenly didn't know why people had anything to do with each other. Why friends were friends, or why families were families. I didn't know why my father came home every day, or why we all ate supper together, or why my parents visited my school on parents' night, or anything.

'It wasn't that I hated other people. Or that I thought they hated me. I just needed to understand what kept them together. I needed to know what that human glue was.

'I asked my mother, and she said, *It's because we love each other.* So I asked her what that meant, to love somebody. She said, *Well, I love you and I love your brother and I love your father and Grandma loves us all, and so does Grandpa, and so does Aunt Heather....*

'She went on and on, naming just about everybody I knew, but she never said what love *was*. And she must have seen the look on my face, because she said, *You love us too, Daisy. Don't you?*

'Well, I think I came out with something like, *Do I have to?* I wasn't being a smartass. I really wanted to know. But my mother got all flustered and said, *What kind of question is that? Of course we have to love each other! Because if we don't – Well, how would you like it if we all went for a trip in the car someplace? Port Dover or Port Maitland. And at the end of the day, when we were coming home, we just got in the car and drove away and left you there? How would you like that?*

'I thought about it for a minute. And then, I said, *Why don't you?'*

I stop talking and just sit looking out the window. Brian doesn't say anything. He doesn't say anything for a long time. So long that I have to turn and look at him. And when I do, I know what's going to happen.

He didn't plan it. He didn't bring me here to do it. But I can see it in his face, his hands, the slant of his body. 'Daisy,' he says, then stops. I know what he's going to say. He opens his mouth again, then closes it again. He's going to say he's tired. Of waiting. Of staying on his side of the bed, in more ways than one. Because it's not just sex. It's everything. He can see right inside me, to the empty spaces where my feelings used to be. And he's decided they're never going to come back. So he wants someone new to go with his new apartment and new life. Someone who can share his joy.

'Daisy —'

Or maybe it's something very simple. Maybe he just didn't like my childhood reminiscence. Does there have to be a reason? I'm a fine one to ask.

Here it comes. I do feel afraid. A little. And sad. A little. And something else. I feel —

'Will you marry me?'

— free.

♦ ♦ ♦

In the weeks between Doctors Dotiwalla and Bernstrom, I kept waking up in the middle of the night, going into the kitchen and making myself a cup of chamomile tea. Then, once I had drunk it, I would go back to bed and most often be asleep while Brian was getting ready to leave for the day's shooting.

The first cheque had already arrived. *Pay to the order of Brian Beagle*, followed by an amount that, even after his agent's cut, was more money than we had ever had.

The root beer commercials, twelve of them, were being shot all over Vancouver, and would be released nationally, one every month, for a year. In the meantime, Brian's agent was pushing him for a part in a TV series pilot. 'It's starting, babe,' he said to me more than once, his voice whispery with excitement. 'I've paid my dues, and it's starting to happen.'

It was. And there was no reason that it shouldn't. Brian's bearded, rubbery face was perfect for the part, a mad scientist trying to duplicate the client's root beer formula. And being an unknown had actually worked in his favour. He was fresh. He carried no typecast baggage. He was a find.

So there was no reason for me to keep imagining him sneaking into movie theatres, sitting all day in the dark, then coming home and telling me lies about filming a commercial. Or to worry that we had gotten somebody else's luck through clerical error, and when some bureaucrat found out, we'd have to give it back.

I wondered if it might be his name. *Brian Beagle* just didn't sound like a celebrity, however minor. But there it was on the cheque. So it was happening. It was real.

The mornings he was shooting, I would wake up to find his place in bed empty and cool beside me. We had always started the day together, and I missed that. But when I apologized for not being awake to see him off, he shook his head and said simply, 'You're pregnant.'

It became an all-purpose excuse, an automatic absolution. Tired? You're pregnant. Bitchy? You're pregnant. Don't want sex? Then wake him up two hours later because you've changed your mind? You're pregnant. Can't eat? Eat everything in sight? Can't sleep? Sleep half the day? Constipated? Paranoid?

You're pregnant.

I wished that *pregnant* was something Brian and I could both see. Touch. Walk around and examine from all sides, like a mushroom growing up through a crack in the floor. But it wasn't. Pregnant was inside me. No. It *was* me. Pregnant was what I had become.

I had always wondered whether, if I did conceive, some primal maternal instinct would finally kick in. Some fierce, earthy joy that would come up out of nowhere to buoy me through the nine months till delivery. It hadn't. All I felt was invaded. Inhabited. Occupied. I couldn't love the thing that had attached itself inside me. I didn't hate it either. I just wished it would go away. And it would, soon enough. But in the meantime, I was pregnant.

I began to hate the word. Such a fat pink pig of a word. And from there, I went on to hate maternity clothes. Not that I would ever have to wear them. I just hated them on principle. Their pastel cuteness. All that beribboned fuss at collar and sleeve, designed to draw the eye away from the stomach.

And the world was suddenly full of stomachs. I couldn't go into a supermarket without seeing at least half a dozen. Women like oceans walking. Swollen, bulging, stretched to bursting with something not themselves. Something that elbowed their organs, siphoned their blood, leached their bones and teeth.

And kept them awake at night.

Beastie used to visit me in the kitchen while I was making my cup of chamomile. She had always been a prickly, catty cat. But these nights she was strangely kittenish, s-curving through my legs, then kneading my lap while I sat at the table waiting for my tea to cool.

I wondered if she knew something was up, the way she knew about earthquakes. Beastie was a living seismograph that registered tremors neither of us could feel. She would flatten her ears, brace her legs, freeze into what Brian called her Norma Desmond pose, then streak under the couch. There she would stay for hours, while we called to her to stop being such a silly girl, that nothing was happening, that everything was okay.

But then, over the next few days, we would find knick-knacks that had sidestepped their dust circles by half an inch. Hairline cracks in the plaster that had widened or lengthened. And once when I opened a cupboard, a juice glass creeping forward to lean against the door leapt like a live thing into my hand.

That's when we would remember Beastie going strange, and promise to take her more seriously next time. But we never did, and she remained our resident Cassandra.

Those nights in the kitchen, she took to sniffing my breasts, licking a nipple if she could get at one, the way she used to do when she was a kitten. I wondered if she could smell the onset of milk. I didn't know if it was too early for that to be happening. I didn't know anything about being pregnant. And I was perversely proud of my ignorance. Something else I'd started hating was the pregnancy and childbirth sections of bookstores. Was it my imagination, or were they all moving closer to the front? The glossy covers caught my eye the minute I opened the door. *Countdown To Motherhood. Labour of Love. Taking Control of Your Pregnancy.* And always a picture of a woman, smugly exultant or serenely madonnaesque.

How simple to be an animal, I would think, while Beastie stood up on my lap, stretched into a tall U, then settled back down in a ball. How simple to have no choice. None now because she's been fixed. And none a couple of years ago, because we'd only had her for a few months, and she was so tiny that her going into heat took us by surprise. Her too. The only one who wasn't a total innocent was the long-haired tortoiseshell tom we named Pretty Boy Floyd.

Beastie, for all her seismographical acuity, never twigged to what was going on in her own belly. No matter how lumpen she got, she would try to jump up on the kitchen counter as usual, then slide back down, dragging scratches in the Formica. Or she would wriggle into one of her favourite nooks, get stuck and have to back out while we tried not to laugh.

Then one night Brian and I woke to a wetness at our feet and an impossibly tiny mewing. Very gently, we lifted the two-headed creature out onto the rug. There, while Beastie purred and blinked, the miniature head protruding from her rear grew two reaching paws. Tiny claws gripped the rug as the shrieking creature pulled itself out. It lay exhausted for a moment, then began the long blind journey to the nipple, dragging its parachute of afterbirth behind it.

In the morning, when all the kittens were born, Beastie jumped with no trouble at all onto a chair back. From its height she surveyed the squealing, bloody bundle she had left on the rug. She was a different cat. There was a new arch to her neck, a huge self-approval in the slitting of her eyes. She could have posed for the cover photo of one of those pregnancy books.

Except, once they started to grow, she didn't like her kittens much. Would look at them, then glare accusingly at us. Would separate them one from the other and leave them in odd places, behind books, in low kitchen cupboards, under laundry, as if hoping to lose them.

She did all the mother cat things, but she did them hatefully. Sometimes while she was washing one of her kittens a manic look would come into her eyes and she would start chewing on its neck, only stopping when it began to strangle. And when it was time to wean them she put a back foot on each one's face in turn and simply shoved.

Mother love.

I had never even played with dolls. The rocking and feeding and dressing and undressing that other little girls inflicted on their pink plastic babies had mystified me. It still did. I saw mothers on the street now and wondered how they could have let this happen to them. The trapped look in their eyes as they pushed one child in a stroller and pulled another by the hand. Their inability to finish a sentence. The impression they gave of having misplaced themselves. Along with the piano, the easel, the manuscript they were going to get back to, just as soon as the kids were in school, out of school, married, gone.

Gone.

Mine would be gone soon.

Mine.

How could something be mine when I couldn't see it, couldn't feel it, didn't want it? How could it be Brian's?

While the cat purred on my lap I would sip my cooling tea and listen to Brian snoring in the next room. He needed his sleep. The day's shooting started early. But I used to wish he would wake up and come and find me and sit with me. Just sit. Not say anything. There was nothing to say. Or nothing he hadn't said before.

*I will respect your decision, whatever it is.*

*Of course I have feelings in the matter. But that's not the same as having rights.*

*I won't leave you if you decide to have this baby.*

That last one had jarred me. Why did he think he had to say it? I knew he wouldn't just disappear, like Pretty Boy Floyd. Or did I?

People never guessed that Brian was an actor. He didn't glitter or talk loud or suck up all the attention in the room the way other actors did. But at theatre parties I would stand by myself and watch him work the crowd. He was so good at it. He fit so easily into that world. He did try to include me. Would introduce me to somebody who would gush that it was just *wonderful* that I *wrote*. That I was finishing a *master's*. In creative *writing*. And where was I *published?* Oh, but I *would* be! I *would!* And they just couldn't *wait* to read my *work*.

What if that was what Brian was really like, underneath? And he was restraining himself for my sake? How long could he keep it up? How long would he stay with me?

Why *did* he stay with me, anyway? And why did I stay with him? Because we loved each other. But what did that mean? What was it that had made us fall in love? Strange phrase. *Fall in love.* Like falling into a vat of something sticky.

I had never thought it would happen to me. Didn't think I was capable of it. But I was. It had. I could even remember exactly when. Brian and I had just gotten off a bus together, him out the front door, me out the back. We hadn't spotted each other during the ride, but we collided on the sidewalk. We were already friends. We had met in a playwriting course I was taking as part of my master's at UBC. Brian and some other actors had been hired by the creative writing department to help the class workshop their scripts. Mine was so bad, so essentially unplayable, that for ages after I started meeting him for coffee, I assumed he was befriending me out of pity.

But we made each other laugh. And when we bumped into each other outside the bus, we started to laugh again, and couldn't stop. We ended up just holding on to each other, laughing and kissing.

*I won't leave you if you decide to have this baby.*

Not much danger of that. I didn't even like children. Hadn't liked being one. I was one of those owlish, elderly types whose intelligence in the classroom rendered them stupid on the playground. I could never speak the language of children, or crack their social codes.

But now I laughed and cried so easily in Brian's arms. Talked baby talk and played games. Called him Daddy and Papa. Felt small and cherished, worthy to be held close.

Had he ever noticed how children shied from me? As if they sensed that I had never really been one of them? I was ashamed of my childhood. The awkwardness and loneliness were my dirty little secret.

Would a child of my own see through me? And help its father to see?

*I won't leave you —*

Oh, there was no point in thinking these thoughts, worrying these worries. It was all academic. The thing that had barely started was soon going to end. The thing that hardly existed would soon not exist at all. As if it had never been.

It. Foetus. Embryo. Infant.

Infanticide.

Infanticide sounded like something out of a Noel Coward play.

*There's a whiff of infanticide in the air this evening, my dear. Do you smell it?*

Did Beastie smell it? Would she hiss at me when I came home from the clinic? Or would she give me one of her rare, barbed kisses?

The morning that Brian was out shooting the sixth in the series of commercials, Dr Dotiwalla phoned. As expected, she said, the hospital board had approved her recommendation. Should she go ahead and make an appointment for me with Dr Bernstrom?

It was a sunny morning. Rare for Vancouver in March. Rare for Vancouver anytime. I could see dust motes moving in the air. I could hear the clock ticking from the bedroom.

One word. The doctor was waiting for one word from me.

*Very well*, she answered when I finally said it. Her voice was again carefully neutral. I pictured her once more giving that slow benedictory nod.

♦ ♦ ♦

'Don't answer. Don't say a word. Not yet. Just listen to me. Please.'

He looks so young. Chock-full of whatever is so very important, right this minute. 'I –' he begins, then stops. 'You – Oh, fuck!'

I pull a Kleenex out of my pocket. For a second I picture myself holding it to his nose and ordering, *Blow*.

'Sorry,' he says, dabbing at his eyes. 'I've just been so worried. And so scared. I know you're mad as hell at me. I don't blame you. I've been having all the fun, and you've been taking all the shit. If it was me, I'd be pissed off too.'

*Mad as hell? Pissed off?* All I can think to say is, 'Why did you ask me to marry you? I mean, why now?'

'To get your attention.'

'*What?*'

'No! Yes. Partly. I did need to get through to you, Daisy. For weeks now, it's been as if you don't know I'm in the room. And I'm not just talking about sex. Believe me. That's the least of it. Living with you right now is like watching a movie about somebody who lives alone. Eats all her meals alone. Sleeps alone. And I've started to wonder if what I'm seeing is what you want.' He stops, his eyes, his face, his whole body a question.

I look down at my cold coffee. Two weeks ago, while Brian was signing the lease for our new apartment and writing the cheque for first and last month's rent, I stepped into the smaller bedroom and shut the door. I stood all by myself in the middle of the bare floor and breathed. *Oh*, my breath said, going in. And coming out, it said, *yes*.

But then I opened the door back up. I went quickly and found Brian, and put my signature on the lease under his.

For just a moment, I had envisioned staying in that room alone forever, like an anchorite. Never opening the door again.

Dame Julian did it. Survived the plague that killed her husband and child, then spent the rest of her life in a white room without a door, transcribing the visions she had had while hovering between life and death.

She had her meals passed in to her and her slops taken out through a single window. And she had the company of a cat who was there to keep the rats down. Not a bad existence for a medieval woman, considering the alternatives. She actually managed to die of old age.

But there was still that moment of stepping through the door, then turning and watching while masons sealed it up. Maybe she concentrated on subduing the cat. For the animal would have struggled in her arms, sensing a trap. It would have fought to get free, to get out through the smaller and smaller opening before the final stone was in place.

How could she do it? How could she want to do it in the first place?

For those few seconds, in that empty room, I knew. It had nothing to do with wanting or not wanting.

'No,' I say now. 'I don't want to eat my meals alone. I don't want to sleep alone.' It's true enough. If not quite the truth.

Brian closes his eyes. Opens them. 'Okay,' he says. 'Okay. I don't want to live that way either. And the thought of losing you –' He starts to tear up again. Swallows. Swipes pugnaciously at his nose. 'I can't do it without you, Daisy. I mean, I feel as if I've been shot out into space all of a sudden. And you're like planet earth. I need you to be there. I need to be able to come home to you. So please let me help you. I can't just sit back and watch you disappear into yourself. I have to try to break through your depression.'

'I'm not depressed.'

'Oh, honey, you *are*. You've got all the earmarks. And it makes sense. Did you know that one form anger can take is depression?'

Did I say I was angry? I don't feel angry. In fact, ever since coming out of the anaesthetic, I haven't felt much of anything. Just very still and quiet. As if I'm all by myself. Funny phrase. *All by myself.* What does it mean, literally? *Completely self-made?*

'It's a common problem, sweetheart. But it won't just go away. You need to get help for it. And I'll help you find the help you need.'

*Help*. Helping hands. Breaking down the sealed-up door to the room where I sit. All by myself. Because I'm depressed. Because I'm angry. Because I had minor surgery.

'Brian —'

'I know what you're going to say. That it's such a cliché. *Get professional help*. But you wouldn't hesitate if it was something physical, would you?'

'No, but —'

'Or if it was me? I mean, if I started acting like somebody you didn't recognize, wouldn't you worry? Wouldn't you care?'

Everything he's saying is making perfect sense. And he did do a minor in psychology. 'Yes. Of course I'd worry. And of course I'd care. But —'

'Well, then you know how I feel.'

All I know is I don't like this diagnosis. I don't want to be depressed. It's too clinical. Too convenient.

Brian's eyes are bloodshot. 'Look,' he says. 'I'm in this for the long haul. Just know that much, Daisy. Even if you have to hate me for a while. Just know that I'm here. I can take it. And I will take it.'

'Oh for God's sake, Brian. I don't hate you.' And I don't. How could I? Up until three weeks ago, I loved him. Maybe I still do. And I just can't feel it. I did have surgery, after all. And that can do things to you. Or so I've heard. And maybe I do feel guilty, deep down. It would stand to reason. So maybe I could use a little help. At the very least, it couldn't hurt. 'Okay. I'll make an appointment with the campus shrink.'

Brian drops his head. When he raises it, he looks at once terribly tired and terribly relieved. Then he reaches into his pocket and pulls something out. I can't see what it is. It's so small he can hide it in the palm of his right hand. I keep looking at his right hand where it rests on the table, fingers curled around whatever he's holding.

'Look. Maybe this is crazy. Maybe the timing stinks. But you know me. The way I jump into things. So I have to tell you.' He stops and looks down at his right hand. A blush actually begins to rise from the line of his beard, up past his eyes to his forehead. 'I know we've always said we wouldn't legally marry, that we didn't need that kind of thing. Well, all of a sudden, I want the old-fashioned stuff. A wedding. Presents. Confetti. You in a dress. I want to take vows in a church. I want to make it official. So that if something happens to me, you'll be looked after. But it's more than that. I want to be your husband, and celebrate anniversaries with you, and get old with you and die with you. I want you to be my wife.'

He opens his hand. I see a ring box, hinged and covered with midnight blue velvet. He puts both hands in his lap and sits back, watching me.

I don't know what to do. Or what to say. Three weeks ago, I might have burst into tears, then blubbered on about how this was what I had always wanted, deep down, and I had only said I didn't want it for his sake, because I didn't want him to know what a bourgeois little goop he was living with.

He's still watching me, his eyes brave, trusting. I'm going to have to do something. Make a gesture. And there are so many gestures I could make. I could get up and walk away. No. Too harsh. Too hurtful. Or I could stay sitting but not reach for the ring box. No. Too ambiguous. Or I could reach for it and pick it up, in order to hand it back to him, unopened.

The ring is white gold. The diamond is small but brilliant.

'And there's something else,' Brian says. 'When you're ready, and only when you feel you can, I want to talk, just talk, about having a child. A planned child. A child we could be ready for and look forward to. Because believe it or not, that's what I learned from all of this. It threw me for a loop. It was the last thing I ever thought I'd want to do. But you know what? Brian Beagle wants to be a family man.'

I should have seen this coming. Maybe I did. Because I'm not surprised. It fits. I can practically hear it clicking into place. I can see Brian as a father. A good father. One of the best. And nobody can say he hasn't put his cards on the table. Nobody can say he doesn't play fair.

Would it be fair of me to take the ring out of the box? Just to see how it looks?

It's very light in my palm. *Brian Beagle wants to be a family man.* What does Daisy Chandler want? What did Dame Julian want? Except it has nothing to do with wanting or not wanting, does it? It has to do with being.

So what *is* Daisy Chandler? Is she all by herself? Or is she one half of Brian and Daisy?

*Brian and Daisy.* When our friends call us that, does the phrase run together like one word? One flesh, as people used to say? Does Brian's scent breathe out from the clothes in my closet? When I read a book, are his eyes on the page with mine? When I write, do I hear the words dropping one by one as often in his voice as in mine?

I slide the ring from my right palm to my left. A room of my own. A child of his. Could the door to the room be shut? Sometimes. Could the child be persuaded not to bang on it? Sometimes.

The hand holding the ring, my left hand, takes over. It rises and offers the ring to Brian. He picks it up from the palm. The hand could still pull away. He slips the ring onto the third finger. The hand could still make a fist.

The metal is cool at the base of my finger for just a second. After that, I can't feel it. And it's only when Brian reaches to wipe my face with the Kleenex I gave him that I realize I've started to cry after all. Maybe the tears are from all the feelings I used to feel. And all the ones I have yet to. But that I might still. With a little help.

'I guess this is the moment when the credits are supposed to roll,' I manage to say.

'Now you're talking like an actor's wife.' He leans across the table to kiss me. Then he snaps the ring box shut. For such a small object, it makes a very loud noise.

◆ ◆ ◆

215

*Daisy! Daisy, wake up!*

I had been sleeping for a hundred years. A century ago, somebody in a white mask, with eyes like Montgomery Clift, had looked at me upside down and said, 'Hello, Daisy. I'm going to put you to sleep.' Then he had started adding something to my IV bag.

I was lying on a padded table, wondering where Doctor Bernstrom was. Besides Montgomery Clift, there was a Chinese nurse who kept urging me softly to slide my 'buttum' farther down the table. 'You will feel an edge,' she said delicately. 'Like a hole. Yes. Thank you.'

My feet were in stirrups, my *buttum* perched on something very like the lip of a cliff, and Doctor Bernstrom presumably waiting in the wings when I felt myself losing consciousness. *Now I lay me down to sleep*, I thought absurdly. Because there was nothing voluntary about it. I could feel my consciousness being taken away. Removed, bit by inexorable bit.

The day before, Doctor Bernstrom had told me, from behind a sheet draped over my raised knees, that there was 'for sure something in there'. I had to bite my lip. His accent was dangerously close to Brian's all-purpose stage Scandinavian.

'And now I will insert the seaweed into the cervix.'

He had explained that a match-sized piece of compacted, dried seaweed would absorb my body fluids over night, thus dilating me slowly and painlessly. He had sounded oddly proud of the seaweed technique, as if he had invented it.

'Try to relax, please.'

I couldn't. I was trying not to laugh, trying not to imagine the routine Brian would work up.

*So, Doctor Bernstrom, what made you choose gynaecology?*

*Ja, vell, I vas missing the fiords . . .*

Just then the seaweed went in, and I had no trouble not laughing. 'Sorry it pinches,' Doctor Bernstrom said. 'In a minute you will stop feeling it.'

When I sat up I could still detect a tiny stabbing, as of a swallowed needle. Was the seaweed expanding already, drinking my fluids? Drinking *its* fluids? Could *it* register anything? Danger?

Something as simple as thirst?

'Now let's talk about the procedure,' Doctor Bernstrom said, once I had gotten dressed. I found myself studying his face, for some reason. It was a bony, homely face, the pale skin scrubbed pink. He reminded me a bit of Max Von Sydow.

'Tomorrow morning, I will first remove the seaweed, then insert the curette. I will scrape the inner lining of the uterus, then suction out its contents. It all takes about half an hour, and is practically painless.'

*scrape*

'Can't I have any anaesthetic?'

'Certainly. You can have a local anaesthetic, if you wish.'

*suction*

'No. I mean, can't I be completely unconscious?'

'We do not recommend a general anaesthetic for minor surgery. There is too high a risk.'

'What if I'm willing to take the risk?'

Doctor Bernstrom's nose pinkened. 'If you insist on a general anaesthetic,' he said crisply, 'we will require you to sign a form stating that you understand the dangers involved.'

*And absolving you*, I silently added, *if I should die before I wake.*

'Daisy! Wake up, Daisy!'

Somebody had put a sanitary belt and pad on me. Every few minutes the Chinese nurse asked me to please turn on my side so she could look at the pad. Each time, she thanked me and asked me if I was in pain.

I wasn't. Dr Bernstrom had told me I would probably have cramps afterward. I kept waiting for them, bracing myself. Nothing. I was hungry. Thirsty. But that was all.

No, there was something else. When the nurse told me I could sit up, I looked out the clinic window and tried to put a word to what it was. Empty? No. Some other word.

'Daisy?' the nurse said. 'Would you please read this pamphlet? It is very important that you follow the instructions. And your partner also.'

The pamphlet was titled, *After Your D and C*. It told me that for two full weeks, I could take showers but not baths. I could use pads but not tampons. Most important, I was to refrain from having sexual intercourse.

Two weeks. *Poor Brian*, I thought automatically. Then wondered why I hadn't thought, *Poor me*.

Brian would be here soon. He had promised to take a cab from the film site, and get me home. The clock on the wall said ten-fifteen. I had been admitted at nine, put to sleep at about nine-thirty. It really had only taken half an hour. Brian might even be here already. If I stood up and turned around, I might see him.

I stayed sitting, looking out the window. There were other beds in the room, but they were empty.

*alone*

There it was. The word I had been looking for. I was alone, truly alone, for the first time in weeks. No more constant presence I couldn't escape. No more feeling of being invaded. Occupied territory.

I was all by myself. For this little space of time. In this bare white room. On this narrow bed, with its taut sheets and plain grey blanket. When had I last slept in a bed this small, this simple? When had I last slept alone?

'Daisy? A gentleman is here to take you home.'

♦ ♦ ♦

Brian holds open the restaurant door for me, then takes my hand as we walk along to the print shop. It's going to be all right, I think. It's going to be just fine. I came close to cutting off my nose to spite my face, but the important thing is, I didn't actually do it. And now, things will work out. We'll come through this together and be better for it. Stronger. Closer.

Isn't that what everybody says? And everybody probably says it because it's true. Or maybe it's true because everybody says it. What do I know? I'm depressed.

While we walk, Brian swings my hand back and forth, grinning, excited, happy. People on the sidewalk look at us and smile. Some of them probably recognize him from TV. Mothers bending to children. Family men loading groceries into the trunks of cars.

This is good, I tell myself. I'm glad I said yes to it. Or at least, that I didn't say no. Not saying no is pretty good for a depressed person. It's a step in the right direction.

We pass a church. Catholic. Our Lady of Perpetual Help. I wonder out loud why people are going in on a Saturday. 'Wedding!' Brian says. 'Hey – let's have a big church wedding. Stained glass. Priest in robes. Organ music. The works.'

'They don't just marry you these days. That's what I've heard, anyway. They send you on encounter weekends first.'

'So encounter me, baby,' he growls, pulling me close and kissing me, a loud pop on the mouth. It's the first what-the-hell kiss he's given me in three weeks. I don't pull away from him. That's good. It's another step. We'll probably make love tonight. No. We will make love tonight. I'll see to it.

It's not a wedding going on in the church, I decide as we pass by. There are too few people going in, and they're too drably dressed. Confession, maybe.

I wasn't raised a Catholic, but the idea of confession has always appealed to me. Dame Julian confessed daily to a priest through her single window. What sins could she have accumulated, I wonder, in a twenty-four-hour period, in a whitewashed room? With a cat? And what penance could the priest in good conscience have imposed, day after day? The two of them must have racked their brains.

Or maybe not. Maybe they were old friends. Told each other about their encroaching arthritis. Memory lapses. Hemorrhoids. Loved each other, perhaps. Touched hands over the stone sill. Maybe the priest even confessed to her. She was the cloistered one, after all, and he the one out in the world, with all its occasion for sin.

*Sin* is a strange word. Secretive and shameful, like a stripe on your underwear. *Bless me, Father, for I have sinned. It is forever since my last confession, and this is my sin. Brace yourself.*

Would a priest forgive what I had done? He'd have to. It's his job, to absolve sin. Grant absolution. Absolution sounds like flushing water. Like cleansing. A thorough inner scouring, to empty me of the sin of having emptied myself. And then what? How heavy a penance? How many rounds of beads on my knees before Our Lady of Perpetual Help, her plaster face pitying but immobile?

But who knows – maybe it would help. Maybe I should attack this thing, this depression, from all sides. Talk to a shrink. Confess to a priest. Go on an encounter weekend. Become a vegetarian while I'm at it.

We're at the print shop. 'Sparrow colours!' Brian whispers in my ear, reminding me. I nod, smiling. I will decorate this man's home. I will be his immaculate, soft-spoken chatelaine. Who writes.

◆ ◆ ◆

Beastie neither hissed nor kissed me when I came home from the clinic. Instead, she went into earthquake mode and stayed in it for days, only emerging from under the couch to eat or use her litter pan. For once, we took her seriously. We kept examining the walls and shelves for signs of shocks or tremors, but couldn't find any. Brian finally came up with a theory. 'She knows we've found new digs,' he said. 'She senses a change coming. And cats hate change.'

I didn't think that was it. At least, I didn't think it had anything to do with moving. But I didn't tell Brian what I was thinking. I just started wrapping things in newspaper and putting them in boxes.

◆ ◆ ◆

Too red. Not beige. Too yellow. Not gray. Too blue. Not white. Too orange. Not charcoal.

The rack of prints is open like a big book in front of me. I've almost finished flipping through it when I find Van Gogh's *Wheatfield with Crows*. No sparrow colours here. The black of the crows is pitch black, not charcoal. The sky is acid blue, and the yellow wheat enough to make you squint. And then there's the road that stops in the middle of the field. Right at the spot where he shot himself.

This used to be my favourite painting. But it was almost ruined for me when I wrote a breathless undergraduate essay which prompted my art history professor to take me in hand.' Yeah, I know, I know,' he said, fingering the pages I had typed on the new portable my parents had given me when I started at Guelph. 'Everybody has this romantic notion of how Van Gogh died. They think he painted this marvellous symbol, a road ending in the middle of a field. Between the crows and the wheat. The eater and the eaten. They think he saw it all, in a big blinding flash. Saw that he was on the cusp between life and death. That he had done everything he could ever do. Had painted it all. Could only be a pale imitation of himself after that. And so, consummate artist that he was, he blew his brains out. He chose death over mediocrity.'

I remember sitting in this professor's office, trying to will the warm blood down out of my face. He was practically quoting from my essay.

'But do you know what really happened? Well, you do. I know you do. I can tell from your bibliography. He had the gun with him to scatter the crows when they got in the way. And it probably went off by accident. Because he shot himself in the *side*, Daisy. Missed all his vital organs. Walked home. Didn't even bleed to death. Went septic and died in bed a week later of a fever.'

I remember sitting there, my whole head on fire, desperately trying to think of something to say. Some retort. Some way to shout down what I was hearing.

'All I'm saying, Daisy, is don't deify the guy. Pay attention to what he did. Not what he was. Because he was a nutcase. Good painter. But a nutcase.'

I stand staring down at the painting in the print shop. Its uncompromising colours. The road ending. No. Not *ending*. Stopping. Deliberately, abruptly, ceasing to be.

'Hon?' It's Brian. 'What've you got there? Oh. Okay. But it's not exactly sparrow colours, is it?'

He glances up and catches me staring at him. 'I've picked something out. You want to come and see?'

I'm staring because he looks exactly the way he did that day outside the bus. When we held each other, laughing and kissing, and I felt the warmth of his skin through the cloth of his shirt. I remember a throb of wanting coming straight up through me, so strong it was almost pain. So strong I thought it might split me in two.

'Hello!' Brian says, waving his hand in front of my eyes. 'Are you in there?'

'Yeah. I am. Sorry. Let's go see what you've got.'

I follow him over to the rack he's been flipping through. My own stays open at *Wheatfield with Crows*. I'm aware of the painting as I walk away. I can almost feel it, as if it's throwing off heat.

What Brian has picked out is absolutely perfect. A pair of Japanese landscapes. Soaring mountains threaded with silver streams. Everything softened by grey mist. And in each, the requisite tiny human figure. A lesson in insignificance.

'We could hang them side by side over the bed,' he says. 'What do you think? And they've got some gorgeous frames. And mats. Come and see.' He goes over to the wall behind the framing table and starts looking at the V-shaped samples hung there.

I don't follow. I just stand watching him. He's taken his jacket off. The store is still heated for winter. Brian is one of those men who look marvellous with their shirtsleeves pushed up. I love the short strong line of his back. His neck is beautiful. So is the turning of his head. I take it all in, all the details. Memorizing them. I actually wish I had a camera.

*shiver*

Windows. As if something's hit them.

*rattle*

Now under my feet. Again. Tremor. Yes. Like the shuddering of some huge animal's hide.

I go quickly to Brian and touch his arm. 'Did you feel that?'

'What?'

'I think it's a quake.'

'No.'

'I think it is. I felt it. I felt a tremor. So come on. We have to stand in the doorway.'

That's what you do when there's an earthquake. You find a doorframe and stand in it. Brian taught me that. I run to the door of the print shop, which is propped open for air. I don't look back to see if he's following. When I get there I stand perfectly still, one foot in the store, one foot on the sidewalk. I strain my ears for the sound of glass shivering again in the window frames.

This is what Beastie has been predicting. Ever since I got home from the clinic. She was just a little premature, that's all. Because it's here. Or it's coming. It might even be the big one the experts have been predicting for years. Good thing we're on street level.

A hand on my shoulder. Brian's. 'Sweetheart. Come back inside.'

'No.'

'Honey. Listen. There's no earthquake. I've asked around the store. Nobody else has felt or heard anything.'

'I did.'

'It was probably just the wind rattling the windows.'

'No, it wasn't.'

'Or a bird hitting them. Look. Daisy. You've had nothing to eat. You're probably feeling faint. So come on.'

The hand tightens on my shoulder. I jerk away.

'Oh, baby, what *is* it? Will you please tell me what's *wrong?*'

I wrap my arms around myself and bend a little. I feel Brian's hand again. Tenderly, on the back of my head.

'Whatever it is, it's *ours*, Daisy. We'll work it out together. We can go for joint counselling. We can talk it through. We can do whatever we have to. You and me.'

I look down at the space between my feet. Where I expect a crack to open up.

'I killed my child.'

The hand on the back of my head becomes an arm. Around my shoulders. Trying to pull me close.

I brace my legs. Will not be pulled close. 'I killed my child, and I'm glad I did it. I don't mourn it. I don't miss it. I don't want it back. I don't want to replace it. And if I have to kill another one, I will.'

No crack opens at my feet. No windows rattle. The arm does not move from around my shoulders.

But its warmth becomes weight. Then its weight becomes heaviness. And we both know it is only a matter of time before it falls.

# Surface Tension

RUNNING DOWN A HILL. *Wobbly sideways baby steps. Heading for the big water. The whole world behind me, calling my name.*
*Then a wave. Lifting me like arms. Laying me tenderly face down.*
*no sky*
*no sand*
*no air*
*for ever and ever*
*amen*

'Do you remember pulling me out of the water at Port Maitland when I was three?'

'It was Port Dover. And you were two.'

Ted always remembers the details. We've had a week of me saying, *do you remember*, or, *I seem to remember*, or, *why do I remember*, and of him weighting the corners with fact. *That was in Uncle George and Aunt Ella's house, on Ash Street*, he'll say. Or, *No, it must have been Aunt Heather driving. Grandma McEwen never drove a car. Grandpa McEwen wouldn't let her.*

'You're sure I was only two, that time I almost drowned?'

'Yup.'

'So you were six. Not many six-year-olds can say they've saved a life.'

Ted shrugs, looking down over the gunwale. 'You were only a few feet from shore. And you floated like a cork.'

From our seats on the ferry's upper deck, we can see the captain greeting the last of the passengers. When everybody's on board he gives the signal for the gangplank to be drawn up. I hope he's older than he looks, which is about nineteen.

'But doesn't everybody? Float?'

'Not like you. Summers when I worked at the pool, the other lifeguards and I used to watch you. We couldn't believe how little water you drew. You were the most buoyant kid in the crowd.'

*Buoyant.* Such a cheerful-sounding word. Bouncy, bobbing along on top of the world. The sun must have been on my back the whole time. All that long minute before Ted yanked on the straps of my sunsuit.

A baby starts to wail. There is a young family near us on the upper deck. The mother is arranging a picnic basket, a stroller, a bag of diapers, all the amazing clutter infants generate. The father is rubbing sunblock onto the baby's bald head. The child is purple-faced, waving his fists in rage.

'Why doesn't that guy put a hat on his kid instead of smearing goo all over him?' I wonder out loud.

'Some babies won't keep a hat on. You never would.'

'I wouldn't?' Another revelation.

'Nope. You hated hats when you were a little kid.'

'Well, I still do. I only wear them now because of the sun.' Actually, as hats go, I don't mind the one I have on today. It's red with white polka-dots and shaped like a solar topee. Whenever I catch sight of myself, I look at once whimsical and wise, like something caught napping under a mushroom.

'I love hats,' Ted says almost reverently, adjusting his baseball cap. 'I've always worn hats.'

It's true. He has. A procession of Teds in hats marches through my memory. Ted in a ten-gallon Stetson, white with blue trim. Ted in a Davey Crockett coonskin cap. Ted in a Smokey-the-Bear Scout hat. Ted in a maroon and grey McMaster beanie.

Two old women are coming up the steps to the upper deck. They take each other by the arm and keep their eyes on their feet. When they make it onto the top step they pause and smile congratulations to each other before going and finding a bench. I think at first they must be sisters, but then I see it's only age making them look alike. They lift two orange life preservers down from the hooks on the gunwales and read the directions on the front. Then they help each other put them on. There is a feeling of connection between them. Couplehood. Old friends, probably. Maybe even lovers.

Everyone on deck, including the baby, is wearing a life preserver. Ted's first action when we came on board was to unhook two and hand me one. The bulky shape and the bright orange colour give us all a sexless, innocent look, like children in school uniforms.

I'm reminded of how friends of mine went wide-eyed and said, 'Oh, that's *nice*,' when I told them I was going to Maine with Ted. As if it was sweet, Hansel-and-Gretel-ish, the two of us toddling off together. The whole thing does embarrass me a little. But family relationships have always embarrassed me, with their obligatory, unchosen intimacy. When I think of the house I grew up in, what comes first to mind is not my bedroom, my own space filled with my own things, but the bathroom. The shared sounds and smells, the forced knowing and being known. I was always slightly constipated as a child. I never knew the joy of a fast, easy shit until I moved away to university and lived among strangers.

Still, I've enjoyed the trip so far. Ted's and my talk has been mostly bits and shards of memory, stirred up and surfacing as they will. No more or less revealing than old snapshots pulled randomly out of a shoebox. The comfortableness of it keeps surprising me, the way the weather has surprised me, day after day, by being perfect.

I wake up every morning to the smells of sea and coffee. I leave my ocean-view room in the cottage we've rented and go down into the kitchen to find Ted with a fan of brochures in front of him on the table. What do we want to do that day? We could tour the marine museum in Bath. We could visit Wiscasset, billed as the prettiest town in Maine. Or if we really wanted to hike, we could cross into Massachusetts and do Boston. The common. The market. The graveyard where Mother Goose is buried. The Oyster Bar with the plaque where John Kennedy used to sit.

The foghorn blows. The engine starts, making the boat lurch. All over the upper deck people raise their heads and smile. The man who was putting sunblock on his baby bends and whispers in a tiny ear. The child looks suddenly amazed, as if wondering where the voice is coming from.

'*Good afternoon, ladies and gentlemen, and welcome aboard the Sea Otter.*'

The captain's voice over the intercom is deep and mellow. He certainly sounds older than nineteen.

'*We'll be travelling a little more than ten nautical miles out of Booth-bay Harbour, and we'll dock in about ninety minutes at Monhegan*

*Island. Monhegan is the easternmost island off the New England coast,
west of Bermuda. It is a well-known artists' colony, and it has many
painters' studios and small galleries open to the public. There are also
nature trails to explore, though I will caution you that they can be rather
steep. The shores of Monhegan are extremely rocky, and the undertow
makes rescue almost impossible, so please be careful if you go near the cliff
edges. It's a beautiful day, and the sea is very smooth. Still, if you happen to feel a bit seasick, do tell one of the crew. We can let you know where
in the boat you'll be most comfortable. Thank you, and enjoy your day on
Monhegan.'*

'Looks like a place you might like to see,' Ted said at breakfast
this morning, handing me the brochure. I waited for him to add,
'what with your painting and all.' But he didn't, and I wasn't sure if I
was relieved or sad.

The only argument Ted and I have ever had as adults was about
my painting. When our mother died and we were going through her
things, I found a stack of my old canvases and wanted to throw them
out. Not because they were bad, in fact some of them were almost
good. But I wanted to throw out everything of mine I came across
that day. *This doesn't belong to me any more*, I kept thinking. My inner
voice was petulant, unreasonable even to my own ears. *I don't live
here any more.*

Ted kept trying to press things on me. He's a keeper by nature, a
saver. Even as a boy he was the one who organized family snapshots
into albums, who printed in silver pencil under each one the date,
the place and the name of everyone present. I could tell my incessant
'No' was baffling him that day as much as his repeated 'But don't
you *want* this?' was irritating me.

It was the stack of canvases that brought things to a head. 'If you
don't claim these,' he said, 'they could wind up in some garage sale!'
He said it the way he might say, *concentration camp*.

'Ted,' I said, and I still wish I hadn't, '*everything* of ours is going
to wind up in some garage sale.'

In the end, Ted salvaged the paintings. He's framed a few and
hung them here and there in our parents' house. *His* house. I should
think of it as his house. He's lived in it for years, after all. Now he
runs his business out of it. Pays the taxes. Cuts the grass.

I guess I just can't accept that he really wants to be there. Because he could move. He's gotten back on his feet. But he's content to fix his meals in the kitchen we ate in as children. Doesn't mind going up to bed in the room that once had cowboy wallpaper and model planes hanging from the ceiling.

As we chug out of harbour, a movement on my left makes me turn and look. The two old women who boarded and sat down together have just checked their watches. What caught my eye was the precision of the gesture, how practically synchronized it was. Now each is pulling a small book out of her purse. They open the books to a certain page, cross themselves and begin to read softly in unison.

'Look at that,' Ted says. I think at first that he means the women. But he's looking back at the mainland as we head for open sea. 'Is that New England, or what?'

Houses clustered trustingly on a rocky shore. The requisite prim white church spire. *Boothbay, Maine*. Even the name is somehow touching. *Oh please look after it*, I think, and then wonder who or what I'm petitioning.

*Click! Whizz!*

'Got it,' Ted says, adjusting his camera.

This morning when I was packing snacks and drinks into our knapsacks I saw him loading film and just stopped myself from saying, 'Do you have to bring that thing along?'

Of course he does. He's a photographer. Photography gave him something to do, something to be, after he was laid off. *Recycled by the Ministry of the Environment*, as he tells people who ask him how he got started.

But cameras irritate me. Maybe the fact that I've never been able to take a decent picture myself. 'Just point and click,' Ted will say, the few times he's gotten me to snap one of him. 'Believe me. That's all you have to do. It's a camera for the blind.' No matter. In my hands it will render Ted leaning at a forty-five-degree angle, or missing half his head.

It's the same frustration I used to feel when I was trying to paint. *This is not what I want*. Those words used to go round and round in my head like a mantra while I stood in front of my canvas, daubing, scraping, fighting tears. This is *not what I want.*

*Click! Whizz!* 'Just to make sure,' Ted says now, shooting the mainland again.

A month or so after we get home he'll present me with a booklet of photographs from our trip. He might even enlarge this one of the New England coast, then frame it as my Christmas present. Maybe he'll use the frame he found on Tuesday in that second-hand store in Brunswick. He's started setting his work into old wooden frames, the more stress-marked the better.

The store's proprietor had a high, liver-spotted forehead and hands that reminded me of our father's. He wrapped the frame in brown paper and tied it up with string from a huge ball hanging overhead. 'You folks from Canader?' he asked.

I can't get used to the New England accent. I keep thinking people are just affecting it for the tourists, and will start talking normally once they're on their coffee break.

We nodded. Ted said, 'Ontario.' We've stopped naming our respective cities. Toronto usually rings a bell, but Hamilton as often doesn't.

'You by any chance on your weddin' trip?'

I blinked twice. Then I said, 'He's my brother,' just as Ted said, 'She's my sister.'

'Ay-uh.' The proprietor nodded, completely unruffled. 'Now I see the resemblance. Well. That's a nice thing. Brother and sister travellin' together. An unusual thing.' He tied the string to leave a loop, then cut the end with a pen knife.

The captain's voice comes over the intercom again. *'Ladies and gentlemen, off to the left you'll see an osprey nesting on top of a buoy.'* He pronounces it BOO-ee. *'The osprey is a fish hawk, in fact fish are its only prey. You'll notice the white belly, the hooked beak and the black and white markings on the wings. This one's a female, and if you think she's a big girl, you should see her husband.'*

The osprey screams at us as we pass the swaying buoy. She spreads her wings for balance and a collective *Ohhh!* goes up from the boat.

*'That's a fifty-five-inch wingspan, ladies and gentlemen. The osprey is a hovering bird, like an eagle, and its wingbeats are slow and deep. It*

*can spot a fish from a hundred feet up, and when it dives it goes right under the water.'*

The bird spreads her wings again and gets another *Ohhh!* from the passengers. The two old women who were praying together are talking animatedly, as if sighting an osprey is the culmination of a lifelong dream. The young father is holding his baby up to see. The child stares fixedly at the hawk with a baby's look of mind-boggled wonder. The bird glares back with an expression straight from Olympus.

*Click! Whizz!* 'Got it.'

Ted, put that damned thing away. No, don't.

*'Ospreys were almost extinct a few years ago, but thanks to conservation efforts they are coming back. Over to the right, you'll see one of the nesting platforms that have been built to attract them. This one's decided to ignore it and take her chances on top of a buoy. If the birds are left alone and their food source isn't polluted or depleted, they can live as long as twenty-five or thirty years. And they mate for life.'*

'Nice that they're coming back,' I say carefully to Ted.

'Sure is.' He's doing something with his camera. Maybe he really is as contented as he sounds. I still walk on eggs around him when words like *conservation* come up. *Polluted. Extinct.*

'What does that mean, exactly, that they mate for life?'

'No divorce.'

'Yeah, I know. But if one of them dies, is the other one all alone forever, or does it find another mate?'

'Some do, some don't. Most of the time they pair up once and that's it. No second chance, no matter what happens.'

'That's kind of sad, isn't it?'

Ted shrugs. *Don't ask me,* the shrug says. *It's the way things are. I didn't make the world.*

This shrugging is a new thing, a middle-aged thing. Learned. A bit artificial. Maybe it's a technique a counsellor taught him. Maybe it saved his life. I don't know. I don't even know if he got any counselling when he was laid off.

But he never shrugged when we were children. It wasn't in his nature to say, *nothing to do with me.* As far as he was concerned, everything had to do with him. He owned the world. Collected bits of it. Leaves. Rocks. Shells. Feathers. Blown eggs. And everything was his business, including what went on in my head.

'What would you *drink?*' I had made the mistake of telling him about the Islands of Cadbury. 'And when you got near the Equator, the whole thing would melt. And even before that, it would dissolve. Chocolate's mostly sugar. Sugar dissolves in water.' I was actually flattered that he would take my daydream so seriously.

In my grade four classroom there was a large pull-down map of the world. It was sponsored by Cadbury's, and had paintings of chocolate bars in each corner. Those paintings were magnificent bits of *trompe l'oeil*, worthy of the Old Masters. They rendered the actual world flat and unreal by comparison. I named them the Islands of Cadbury, and, while the rest of the class was memorizing trade routes to Cathay, mentally floated round the world on them, peeling back the wrappers and eating chocolate whenever I got hungry.

'You can't *float* on an island. An island's part of the ocean floor.' Ted's exasperation at times like this was a thing to see. His every brush-cut hair would bristle with prophetic warning. I had better stop thinking the way *I* did, his hair said, and start thinking the way *he* did, and do it pretty darn quick, because *time was running out.*

Sometimes I miss the old Ted. Not that I want him back. I much prefer the tenderized fifty-five-year-old sitting in front of me. But I can never forget that something has changed. Something is gone.

I helped Ted move into his apartment years ago when he was hired, right out of school, by Queen's Park. That was thirty years ago, in the early seventies, when an environmentalist could write his own ticket. His apartment was in a brand-new luxury highrise at the foot of the Hamilton mountain. When we took a break from unpacking boxes, we stood looking through his living-room window out over the whole city, as far as the bay.

'Look at that,' he said.

'What?'

'What I'm pointing at.'

'The *sky?*'

'That stripe. Pink. See it? Right across the horizon. Been there for decades. Put there by Stelco and Dofasco. Pumping shit into the air. Day after day, year after year. Well. They're going to have to

clean up their act.' He sounded as if he was going to see to it personally that they did.

He worked for the Ministry of the Environment for twenty-five
years, commuting from Hamilton. In his first decade, he helped
draft new legislation. In his second, he helped enforce it. In his final
five years, he helped dismantle it.

Then one night I heard a knock, opened my apartment door and
there he was, smiling oddly and rubbing the back of his head. 'Forty
of us,' he said. No preamble. It was as if I had just asked him a question. As if we had been deep in conversation. 'Can you believe it?
They tell you at the end of the day, you know. Jesus, you should have
seen us. Forty of us. Just standing there. Nobody looking at anybody
else.'

I can't remember convincing him not to drive back to Hamilton
that night, or the next or the next. I can't remember now if we
decided he would stay with me for three days, or if the three days
just happened. I kept offering to sleep on the couch in the living
room, so he could have the bedroom. *I want to give him his own room*,
I kept thinking. *With a door he can shut.*

But he slept on the couch. Did chores. Replaced the washers in
all my taps. Tightened the legs on my dining room table. Caulked
the edges of my bathtub and kitchen sink. Took down all my framed
posters, yanked out the bent nails I had pounded into the plaster,
then rehung everything with proper hangers. I began to worry about
what would happen when he ran out of things to fix. He had always
fixed things.

*What did you go and do to it to bust it like that?* A roller skate missing a wheel. A music box that had stopped playing. There was no
point telling him I didn't do anything, that it just happened. As far
as Ted was concerned, nothing just happened.

He wouldn't really look at whatever it was until he was finished
tinkering with it. Then he would appear to see it for the first time, a
figurine or a bit of jewellery, and his mouth would twist in contempt.
*Some girl thing.* But as long as it was broken, its brokenness
demanded his attention. His respect. And the second I handed some
cracked or twisted thing to him, I believed it fixed, I *felt* it to be
whole again.

I slept more deeply, those three nights Ted was in the apartment, than I had ever slept as an adult. I woke up each morning feeling as if I hadn't moved all night, had just sunk down through the bed, through the floor, through all the floors in the building, through the street, down to the middle of the earth.

Had I slept that way as a child, I wondered, when Ted was in the room across the hall from mine, as near as he was to me now? I couldn't remember.

Family legend had it that he took me into his bed the night after I almost drowned. I could never remember that either, or even imagine it. Ted never let me touch him when we were children. If I brushed against him, he would pull away. If I tried to take his hand, he would make a fist.

But now I remembered having an earache from breathing in lake water. Waking up in the middle of the night with the ache finally gone and my pillow all wet. Did I go to Ted's bed to tell him about the lake coming out of me? Was he still half asleep when he pulled the sheets back and moved over to make room? All I knew was that our mother found us together in the morning, Ted's chin digging into the top of my head.

On the third day after he lost his job, I found him sitting on the couch, hunched over a column of figures he had written on a piece of paper. 'If I give up the apartment and the car,' he said, again as if we had been talking for hours, 'I can get by on the settlement until I find something else. And I phoned Mom. I told her. She said I can move back into the house. I can live with her. I can –'

He must have hated the texture of my sweater against his face. The slow circles my knuckles drew round and round between his shoulder blades. The wet, drowning sounds he kept trying not to make.

Ted's mouth is moving.

'Sorry?' I say. 'What?'

'How are you making out?'

'What do you mean?'

'Not seasick?'

'Not yet,' I say. 'But give me time.'

He smiles. He's remembering long drives to the cottage when we were kids. I used to get carsick, once memorably all over the canary in its cage.

'Seriously,' Ted says, 'if you think you're going to spew, just let it go over the side.'

'Well, what else would I do?'

'I was thinking you might try to hold it till you got to the can. But you don't want to go down there. I checked it out when we boarded. It's right by the engine, where the motion would be really bad. Boxed in. No windows. So you can't see the horizon. Two minutes of that and you'd be sicker than you were before.'

When I was packing for this trip, I wondered seriously if I would be able to stand two weeks of Ted's shepherding. Once we're on the island, he'll probably keep trying to orient me. At set intervals, he'll point back to the dock, explain that we're heading north and east or whatever, and ask, 'Do you know where you've been?'

I've lived alone for decades. I'd forgotten what it was like to have someone notice the small things of my existence. Comment on them. Worry about them. To my surprise, I don't mind it. It feels like a vacation from solitude.

As we leave the shore behind, I wonder if I will in fact get seasick. I have no idea, because I've never been to sea. I've never been to Monhegan Island, either. But in a few hours I will have. I'll be someone who has been to a place she cannot now imagine.

Do other people play this game of *what will I be like a few hours, days, years from now, once whatever it is has happened?* A birthday party. An exam. High school. My forties.

I'm fifty-one, my name is Daisy Chandler, I'm a writer and I'm on a day trip to an artists' colony. Maybe I'll meet somebody with paint in his hair. A look in his eye. A whiff of varsol masking his B.O. Maybe I'll stay on the island. Spend the rest of my life sharing his bunk and hot plate. Watching him paint.

Right. And in half an hour, I'd be pining for Toronto. Worrying about Ted chugging home on the ferry by himself.

I don't often have fantasies about men any more. And it's years since I slept with a real one. 'You know, you're sending out a message that you're not interested,' a friend told me not long ago. 'It's coming across loud and clear.' She meant it as a warning. But I really am not interested any more. I do feel the odd stab of desire, but the thought of acting on it is as fanciful now as the thought of digging down to China.

Maybe menopause did something to me. Strange word. Meno*pause*. As if things have just stopped for a while, and might actually start up again. I don't want them to. Not just the monthly blood, but the whole exhausting dance.

I've had six lovers. I almost married the third. I think about those six men sometimes. Run their names in order through my mind. For years, number three was like a mountain peak in the middle. But, as we sing at Christmastime, the valleys shall be exalted and the mountains made low. Together, my old lovers have become an episode of my past in which I no longer quite believe. Like a scene in a movie I saw, or something I read in a book.

Lovers. Love. Loving. The words sound and feel like the friction of sex. Maybe that's all sexual love is. Friction. The rubbing together of surfaces. In the middle of some howling aria of an orgasm, I was always quite contained within my own skin. And when each affair ended, though I howled again, in time the separation came to feel more natural than the brief connection ever had. In fact, my singleness and celibacy are starting to feel more and more like investments. Garnering interest. Though at what rate and in what currency I can't imagine.

So if the artist-on-the-island fantasy wasn't about sex, what was it about? Could *I* by any chance be the one with paint-stiffened hair? Do I nurse a secret regret that I chose to believe the art professor who told me I didn't have an eye? Who said, 'Daisy, why don't you stop telling stories through your paintings, and just *tell stories?*'

All right then, maybe *Ted* will meet someone today on Monhegan Island. A potter with grey braids and eyes two different colours. She will greet him as if she's known him for years. He will look at her, and that certain grin, the one I haven't seen since he got his first car, will slice across his face. *Dais*, she will call me. Not Daisy. Dais, just like days. *The Book of Dais*, she will call my latest publication. *Dais of our lives!* she will greet me when I visit them once or twice a year. And peeking out of her embrace of mohair and herbal tea, I will see Ted, happy at last, his two women tied together in a knot.

*Ted.*

*Happy at last.*

I think I've always felt Ted's loneliness. Heard it, rather, like a low sound coming from his room across the hall, humming through the phone lines between Hamilton and Toronto, wafting on the sea breeze now from where he sits, inches away. It's a loneliness that has nothing to do with solitude.

I first became conscious of it when I was twelve or so and Ted about sixteen. I went looking for something in his bedroom closet. Whatever it was, I didn't find it. But I did find something else. Hidden behind some boxes in a far corner, there were three of my nylon stockings. I had only been wearing nylons for a year or so, but I had at least a dozen pairs, because they were my favourite thing in the world and I kept spending my allowance on them. One of the legs I found in Ted's closet was still fresh and soft. The other two were strangely stiff, as if some kind of glue had dried in them.

I had no idea what Ted could be doing with my nylons. I thought of scooping them up, showing them to our mother and demanding justice. But I didn't. Something warned me not to.

I put the stockings back where I'd found them and closed the closet door.

Over the years, from time to time, I've thought about that discovery. At first, once I was old enough to realize what the gluey substance was, I tried hard to be shocked. Disgusted. I couldn't manage either reaction, because I simply couldn't think of my brother *that way*. Later, when I could think of him that way, I dismissed the whole thing as harmless, typical of what teenaged boys got up to. And later still, I began to wonder if there was something sadly ironic about the stockings being in the closet.

I still don't know about Ted. He and I have never sat down to one of those conversations siblings have in low-budget, critically-acclaimed films. The kind that are laden with silence and dotted with epiphany. For all I know, he could have a parade of women or men marching through that house. He never married, but then, neither did I.

*Never married.* I smile, remembering how our mother used to say those words. A person might be rich, successful, even deliriously happy. But if they *never married*, her tone of sad wonder made it a failing, bordering on a wrongdoing, that outweighed all the good.

'*Ladies and gentlemen, the snack bar is now open on the lower deck. Please place empty pop cans in the recycling bins provided. If you do take drinks or packaged food onto Monhegan Island, please bag any garbage and bring it back with you. Thank you.*'

The two old women start unwrapping some sandwiches they have brought with them. Salmon, it looks like, in waxed paper. My God, somebody still uses waxed paper. There is a carefulness in the way one hands a sandwich to the other. Passing the thermos of what looks like tea back and forth is a ritual. *Sister?* I can read their lips. *Thank you, Sister.*

They're nuns.

Are they on vacation? Do nuns get vacations? Do they ever retire? I read somewhere that a lot of convents were closing, and older nuns were being put into homes or stuck in apartments by themselves after decades of communal living. Maybe that's happened to these two. Maybe the other is all either of them has.

*Sister?*

*Thank you, Sister.*

I wonder how old they are. How many years they've called each other and themselves by that title. Looked at their watches. Opened their books. Recited their prayers. Brides of Christ. Are they merely waiting for death? Even looking forward to it? Consummation at last?

Or are they in a way already dead, their final vows a kind of drowning, a willing surrender to a God that now washes through every second of their existence, sluicing its remotest corners? Does anything remain of their air-breathing selves?

I realize I'm staring, and look toward the horizon. Horizon is all there is. We're completely out of sight of land.

'Hey, what've we got to eat?' Ted says.

I unzip my knapsack. 'Juice boxes. Apples. Trail mix. Cookies. I just packed bits of things, because the brochure said there was a restaurant on the island.'

We each have some trail mix and juice. All around us, people have started to eat. The baby is struggling and grunting in his father's arms, watching his mother peel and mash a banana for him in a plastic bowl.

'Here,' I say to Ted, holding out a plastic bag for his juice box. Bags are appearing all over the upper deck. The couple with the baby have several. The two nuns have one, which they examine and carefully fold. I wonder if people will now obligingly produce garbage with which to fill the bags, just so they can do the right thing by bringing it back to the mainland.

And with that thought comes one of those sudden, inexplicable hits of joy. That sense of well-being that can consume me all at once, for no apparent reason. It could be just a rise in my blood sugar level, from the trail mix and juice. Or maybe it's cumulative. A week-long buildup of peace and contentment.

Because it really is as if Ted and I are under a spell. Even our cottage keeps turning up everything we could possibly need. Lobster pot? Up there on that shelf. Something to read? Choose from the jumble people have left behind through the years. Everything from *Reader's Digest* to Nietsche. Jigsaw puzzle for the long evenings? Here, in this blanket box. No spiders when I lift the lid, either. And probably, when we've clicked the last piece into place, we'll find none missing, no extras that don't belong.

*Thank you*, I think, and again I have no idea whom I'm addressing.

I don't know when I started mentally sending up these little votive offerings and petitions. I wouldn't call it praying, exactly. But I've been doing it a lot during this trip. This place strikes a chord in me I've never been able to name. Even the words *New England*, signifying as they do both memory and hope, can move me to tears if I let them. The people who named these parts never forgot for a minute that death was a breath away. Never once said *Till the morrow* to each other without adding, *God willing*, or, *if we're spared*.

'*Ladies and gentlemen, a harbour seal has been following us for some time now. He's smaller than his deep-water cousins, and can be recognized by his brown speckles.*'

'Look,' Ted says, pointing at a slick button floating to the right of us. 'There's his head.' The seal lifts his nose out of the water and watches us quizzically. He looks like an old man with a moustache. His nostril slits open and close like elevator doors. Then he dives, showing his splayed back flippers.

*'This one's out pretty deep for a harbour seal,'* the captain goes on. *'But he's obviously curious about the boat. He appears small, so maybe he's too young to know what's good for him. Could I ask you please not to throw him any food. And that applies to wildlife you encounter on Monhegan Island, too. Thank you.'*

'He's good, isn't he?' Ted says.

'Who?'

'The captain. I mean, this could be just the equivalent of driving a taxi. And for a lot of guys, that's all it would be. But this one's studied up. Made the job into something.'

*So have you, Ted,* I think. I'm not sure what I mean, or what keeps me from saying it out loud. But I envy the captain Ted's approval. I still want it, after all these years.

Ted started school, the way he did everything else, four years ahead of me. I have a strange, out-of-body memory of my own face, stretched and wailing at a window, watching Ted go up the street with his books and pencil box.

Everything I did after that, every day until I started school myself, I did for Ted, to run and show Ted the second he was home. Drawings. Finger paintings. Plasticine sculptures.

School had taught Ted to put a check mark beside things that were right and an X beside things that were wrong. School had moved him to ask, one Christmas, for a stamp pad and a star-shaped stamp. These he held while he examined my artwork. I held my breath, waiting for him to stamp a star. Or not stamp a star.

One day he looked for a much longer time at a drawing I had done of the willow tree in our back yard. '*You* do this?' he asked. He sounded mad. I nodded. 'By *yourself?*' I nodded again, my eyes on the stamp and ink pad he held. 'Mom didn't help you?' I shook my head. Would the stamp never move?

It did. Once. It pressed a perfect star in the upper right corner of my drawing. And then it moved again. Pressed again into the pad of dark red ink. Rose again to hover for one breathless second over my drawing. Then came down. Left a second perfect star beside the first.

Now I look at Ted again and feel a sudden, shattering tenderness for him. A few years from now, I know, he will call or write to me with a business proposition. That's how he'll put it. A business proposition. That I stop wasting my money on rent, when he has a house big enough for the two of us. *Because we're not getting any younger*, he'll say, *and neither of us has kids to look in on us.*

He will not say, *Because our friends are dying off.* Or, *Because the other morning I went into the kitchen and saw that I'd left a stove burner on all night.* Or, *Because we grew up together, for God's sake. For years, we ate all our meals at the same table. Where does all that go? Why are we living in different cities?*

It's not going to happen next week, or next year. But it is going to happen. And when it does it will be my decision.

I do sometimes get lonely. Especially in the summer, when things slow down or shut down and everybody goes to their damned cottages. And then at the end of the summer, they do a kind of double-take and say, Oh, we should have had *you* up to the cottage, Daisy.

I forgive them. What's the alternative? I know they see me as completely self-sufficient, and for the most part I am. As for those occasional bouts of loneliness, I regard them the way I do a hangover. My fault and well worth it.

Moving in with Ted would be more than just an end to my solitude. It would be like moving back into my past. And I'm not sure that's where I want to be.

If I catch sight of an old acquaintance on the street or the subway, someone I haven't seen in decades, most often I look the other way or lower my face into a book. It has nothing to do with whether or not we liked each other. It's just that absence does not make the heart grow fonder. Not my heart, anyway. If anything, it makes it grow smaller. The few times I have gone up to someone and said, *Could you be* – I've found that I just don't have room for them any more, for the complicated, cluttered person they've become, with their marriage and divorce and kids and career.

But maybe, in time, I'll become frail and frightened. Maybe, when it comes, I'll be glad of Ted's offer. Right now, at fifty, I'm not accepting any offers of any kind. *Fifty.* God, I like the sound of that. What a hefty, kick-ass sound. *Fifty.*

*Don't decide this minute,* Ted will say, on the phone or in a letter. *Sit on it for a while and get back to me.*

In the last year or so, I've started doing something. Every now and then I wake up in the middle of the night and can't get back to sleep. So I get up and walk the rooms of my apartment in the dark. There's enough light from the windows for me to make out the shape of all my things. They're both familiar and strange, the way things are in a dream.

Once I've walked around, I stand still in the dark and the quiet. I feel the rough carpet or the cool floor under my feet. The air on my skin. I listen to my own breathing, my own heartbeat. And I feel *full.* That's the only way I can put it. As if I have everything I could possibly have. As if I am everything I could possibly be.

It's a kind of love. The kind nobody tells you about.

When Ted makes his pitch, it will all be up to me. If I say yes, there will be no going back. If I say no, he will never ask again.

I'm looking out over the water while all this is going through my mind. I'm looking at a certain spot far out on the surface. There is no reason for me to be looking at that particular spot. It is no different from any other. Except that, seconds later, from that exact spot near the horizon, a mountain comes up out of the sea.

*'Ladies and gentlemen, a whale has just risen off to the right. Judging from the distance, he's a big boy, about a hundred feet long. To put that in perspective, this vessel is sixty feet in length. His shape would indicate that he's a blue whale. Blues usually travel in pods, but this one seems to be a rogue. They are endangered, so we're lucky to see even one. Blue whales are the largest whales in existence, making them the biggest creatures that have ever walked the earth. And they did walk the earth at one time, in the form of animals related to the modern deer. But about sixty million years ago, for reasons we'll never know, they returned to the sea.*

*Keep watching. This one will come up three or four times, just to show himself to us. Then when he's ready to say goodbye, he'll do the deep dive, tail up. You'll see his flukes.'*

As if to indulge the captain, the whale submerges. When he comes up again, he is bigger than he was before.

*'That's about one hundred and forty tons of whale, ladies and gentle-men. And he could be as old as seventy. He's one of just five thousand blue whales left worldwide. Hunting, collisions with ships and pollution have reduced his population to ten percent of what it once was.'*

Once more the whale submerges and once more he rises, bigger still. We have all crowded to one side to see. The ferry lists to the right with our weight. We point and laugh and yell, *Look! There! Look! There he is!*

The next time the whale goes under, there is a sudden silence. Nothing but the breathing, kissing sound of the sea.

*'I've shut the engine off.'* The captain's voice is perfectly calm. *'The noise has been known to disorient whales and sometimes provoke them into uncharacteristic behaviour. I assure you, there is no cause for alarm. But it would help if you went back to your seats and were as quiet as possible. And let me take this opportunity to remind you, if you haven't already done so, to put on life preservers.'*

We obey. Slowly and quietly, for the sake of the whale, we return to our seats. The baby utters one sharp, questioning cry and is hushed by his mother. We sit smiling at each other, waiting.

*Awaiting the whale's pleasure*, I think suddenly. And what is the whale's pleasure? Probably, most likely, almost certainly in fact, to swim away and leave us alone.

Or come up right beside us, all one hundred feet to our sixty, and suck us down in the churning whirl of his deep dive.

Or ram us broadside, splintering and shattering our ridiculous boat.

Or come up underneath us and topple us screaming into the sea.

I picture all that might happen with an amazing clarity. My thoughts are bright, glinting, like the sun on the waves.

We sit. We wait. We stay still and calm and smile at each other. I look at Ted's face and see our mother's face in it, and our father's. Grandparents. Aunts and uncles. Cousins. I wonder, very calmly, if Ted's face is the last thing I will ever think about.

The whale has still not surfaced. I wait for a nudge from beneath, a huge caress such as he might give a lover. I wait for him to roll with us, tenderly, playfully, hushing our cries in the thrashing foam.

The two nuns sit as quiet and as still as everyone else. *Why don't you cross yourselves?* I think. *Wouldn't this be a good time?* And as if reading my mind, they do, in slow, perfect unison.

'*Ladies and gentlemen, the whale has surfaced on the other side of the boat. He appears to have gone underneath us and is now swimming away. And yes, look, there is the deep dive. He's saying goodbye.*'

The flukes are like the spread wings of an immense bird. Their solidity is shocking in all that moving water. They are a thing sculpted. Formed. Made. There is wildness in their curved configuration. They are so definite. So indisputably there.

As they sink beneath the surface, I mouth the words, *Oh please. Oh please.* Do I want the whale to show himself again? Do I want him to disappear from my sight forever? All I know is that I want.

I follow the flukes down as they slip beneath the surface. I bend at the waist. The life preserver constricts my breath.

I follow the flukes deeper into the loud green silence. I see and do not see them ahead of me, undulating, waving hail or farewell.

*Open, open, let the water in,* they sing to me.

*open, open, go to sleep*

*open, open, let the water in*

*open, open, go to –*

'Down! Keep your head down! Right between your knees!'

Ted. Ted's voice. I try to straighten up. Can't. Something is holding me down. A hand. Ted's hand.

'Ted,' I gulp, sounding as if I'm swallowing my tongue. 'Ted.' The pressure lifts. I straighten, and the whole world flip-flops right side up.

'You fainted,' Ted says. He is standing over me. 'First time I've ever seen anybody faint from a sit.'

I look up at him. The sun is right behind his head. His face is dark, featureless. 'They were mine,' I say.

'What?'

'They belonged to me.' I speak as if I've just wakened. Words from a dream. I don't understand them, but I must, *must* remember them. 'They were mine.'

'Never mind,' Ted says, smiling, humouring me. 'You're all right. Your colour's coming back.'

I keep looking up at him. He's so much bigger. So much older.

Always has been. Always will be.

And then I remember. The nylons. My nylons. That was the thing about them. They were *mine*.

'How are you doing? Want some water?'

The sudden, breakable hope in Ted's eyes when he asked me if I would like to go with him to Maine. All the years when I would have done anything for him. When he could have gotten me to do anything for him.

But he didn't.

Not ever.

Not once.

'Oh, hey,' he says now, embarrassed. 'Hey, come on. Don't do that.' He bends and unzips a knapsack. 'Did you say there were cookies in here?'

I nod and sniff, running my sleeve across my eyes. 'Chocolate chip.'

'President's Choice, matter of fact,' he says, pulling the bag out of the knapsack and opening it. 'Not bad. Not bad. Here. You have one of these. Because I think your blood sugar's taken a dip. That can happen when you faint.'

I take a cookie out of the bag. I'm just raising it to my mouth when the baby sets up a wail. He is sobbing and pointing at what I have in my hand. 'Don't mind him,' the mother calls. 'We do feed him now and then. Honest.' She turns the baby to face her, but he squirms around to look back at me, his face a twist of anguish.

'Couldn't he have just one?' Ted says. 'He's more than welcome.'

'Thanks,' the mother says. 'That's very kind of you. He's not hungry. He just always wants what anybody else has.'

Ted takes the bag of cookies over to the family. The mother chooses one and offers it to the baby, who grabs it with both hands. Then, as I knew he would, Ted offers the bag to the father, then to the two nuns, then to the rest of the people on the upper deck. He's grinning, enjoying himself.

*'Ladies and gentlemen, Monhegan Island is now visible.'*

And it is, just barely. It is no more than a thickening of the horizon, halfway in colour between the pale of the sky and the dark of the sea.

Everyone on the upper deck smiles and applauds. For the captain. The safe voyage. The beautiful day. The cookies. The whale.

I break a piece off my cookie and eat it. As my mouth contracts around the sudden sweetness, a movement catches my eye. The baby has half of his cookie in each hand. He is waving the halves about as if conducting a choir only he can see, and only he can hear.

# Acknowledgements

Several of the stories in this collection have appeared in print, in slightly different forms: 'Sunrise Till Dark' in the *Capilano Review* no. 50, 1989, and in the second *Journey Prize Anthology*, 1990; 'To Hell and Back' in the *New Quarterly*, vol. XVI, no. 3, 1996; 'Missing Person' in the *Capilano Review*, Series 2, no. 22, 1997; 'Egypt Land' in *Writ*, no. 27, 1995, and in the eighth *Journey Prize Anthology*, 1996; 'Give Me Your Answer' in the *New Quarterly*, vol. XVIII, no. 2, Summer 1998; 'Sparrow Colours' in the *Capilano Review*, Series 2:28, Spring 1999; 'Surface Tension' in the *New Quarterly*, vol. XX no. 2, Summer 1999; and 'Brébeuf and Lalemant' in PRiSM *international* 37.4, Summer 1999.

K.D. Miller was born in Hamilton, Ontario. She graduated in 1973 with an Honours Bachelor of Arts degree in Drama and English from the University of Guelph. In 1978, she graduated from the University of British Columbia with a Master of Fine Arts degree in theatre.

Her stories and essays have appeared in *The Capilano Review*, *Canadian Forum*, *Writ*, *The New Quarterly*, *McGill Street Magazine* and *The Lazy Writer*.

K.D. Miller's first collection of short stories, *A Litany in Time of Plague*, was published in 1994. In this, her new book, two stories – 'Sunrise Till Dark' and 'Egypt Land' – have been nominated for the Journey Prize, 'Missing Person' was nominated for the National Magazine Award in 1998, and 'Brébeuf and Lalemant' was a runner-up in the 1999 PRISM *international* Short Fiction Contest.